Annie Sanders is, in fact, two people: Annie Ashworth and Meg Sanders. Together they make a successful writing team with seven bestselling novels and ten non-fiction titles to their name. They specialise in razor sharp social observation that's sassy, witty and irreverent. Both have families and live in Stratford-Upon-Avon. Visit their website at www.anniesanders.co.uk

By Annie Sanders

Famous Last Words

Annie Sanders

An Orion paperback

First published in Great Britain in 2010
by Orion
This paperback edition published in 2011
by Orion Books Ltd,
Orion House, 5 Upper Saint Martin's Lane
London, WC2H 9EA

An Hachette UK company

1 3 5 7 9 10 8 6 4 2

A CIP catalogue record for this book
is available from the British Library.

ISBN 978-1-4091-1718-6

Typeset by Deltatype Ltd, Birkenhead, Merseyside

Printed and bound in Great Britain by Clays Ltd, St Ives plc

The Orion Publishing Group's policy is to use papers
that are natural, renewable and recyclable products and
made from wood grown in sustainable forests. The logging
and manufacturing processes are expected to conform to
the environmental regulations of the country of origin.

www.orionbooks.co.uk

'Do not take life too seriously.
You will never get out of it alive.'

Elbert Hubbard

R

How it all began

The moon must have woken me, slanting in through the window onto my face, but once I woke, my brain started ticking over and I just couldn't get back to sleep. So here I am curled up in my favourite chair. I left my watch on the dressing table next door, so I'm not sure what time it is now – but the moon is throwing light across the small patch of grass I grandly call my lawn and it must be two or three a.m.

I pull the blanket more closely round my shoulders and stand up to look out of the window. I love these windows – they must be twice as tall as me and then a bit. They're what sold the flat to me all those years ago. Whilst the estate agent was wittering on about how convenient it was for town, I'd fallen in love with the high ceilings and panelled doors of this old Victorian house; had already made the flat mine in my head. I could imagine us both in it, could see the Christmases we'd spend, with the tree set up here in this bay and Nat's presents piled up underneath.

Buying this flat was probably the last spontaneous thing I did for years. Until recently, that is, when I tried to fit a lifetime's postponed spontaneity into a few short days.

Something catches my eye and I watch as a fox creeps gingerly out onto the grass, sniffs about and then scuttles away out of sight. A vixen, I think, on her own and off to raid a dustbin somewhere to feed her young. I can relate to the loneliness. At times in the past I even came pretty close to scavenging, if you count charity shop trawls and the 'marked down' section at the supermarket.

But here I am. I can see my smile reflected in the glass. These last few weeks have turned everything upside down, and I don't think I'd recognise the woman who lived here before it all happened. Before the most extraordinary few days of my life when I thought it was all over. The woman I was before I met Micah.

It's so late now it's hardly worth going back to bed. I'm not sure I could sleep anyway. Come on. I'll tell you all about it.

Chapter One

My name is Lucy Streeter. It's always been Streeter. Of course, like we all did at school, I've tried to imagine what it would be like to be married and have someone else's name. I assumed by the time I was about twenty-eight I'd be proudly saying, 'I'm Mrs Bloggs', but it didn't happen that way.

So the name Lucy Streeter is me, and I am Lucy Streeter. Not that I regret keeping my name, you understand. And anyway, sticking with it makes things much more straightforward and uncomplicated.

And uncomplicated is how I've liked things. In fact, the pattern of my life was pretty much without change or variety for years, once Nat was at school, and even more so when he headed off to university in Leicester – once I'd stopped crying and going into his room to smell the air. But until he was five, life was far from uncomplicated. It was more like a balancing act of single motherhood and scratching a living, whilst pretending that I was young and fancy-free to anyone around me. You don't realise how wonderfully irresponsible your teens and twenties can be, until you have to be responsible.

What my father termed my 'downfall' was the fault of a trait my grandmother would have called 'being headstrong'. Teenage bloody-mindedness, combined with the desire to challenge my father's iron will and snobbery, made me determined to

3

do everything I could to defy him. And that included going out with the most unsuitable boy I could find. We lived near Warwick then, in a sprawling development of what they now call 'executive homes', each with slight differences but basically the same. With their usual habit of being sensible, my parents had bought it because it was convenient: my brother, Chris, and I would be able to walk to school – for him the nice private boys' school, for me the nice private girls' school, up the hill.

My route took me across the park and in the early days, when Mum walked with me, it wasn't a problem. In fact, sometimes we'd stop on the way home and I'd play on the swings. Even better, if she was in an especially good mood, I'd be allowed an ice cream from the thatched café by the pond. Mum would sit on the bench and watch as I swung upside down on the playground equipment, pushing my luck and secretly hoping I'd fall off and have a spectacular bruise to show off at school for my daring.

The downside was that the path sent me into headlong collision with the kids heading home from the comp in the other direction. By the time I was fourteen or fifteen, I was going to school on my own. I avoided the other kids in the morning because school started earlier for us – a fact that only exacerbated our sense of intellectual superiority – but at home time, if I timed it wrong and if I didn't have a music lesson or late games, I'd see them coming over the bridge and along the path through the park. Noisy and showing off, self-consciously smoking cigarettes, pretending to push each other into the river; then they'd be there in front of me: Neil Bartlett and his coterie.

'He's got a wicked face,' my mate Kate would giggle when she was with me – and she was right. Dark scruffy hair and eyebrows that met in the middle, Neil oozed attitude. His shirt hung out, his tie was never tight, his school bag was written on in Tippex. I was into Tiffany, 'I Think We're Alone Now' and 'Having the Time of My Life' (can't remember who that song was by at the moment). He was into the Beastie Boys, all baseball cap and the ubiquitous VW badges hanging round his neck.

I saw *Dirty Dancing* four times. He was into *Full Metal Jacket* and the gratuitous violence of *Robo Cop*. But to me then, stupid and naïve and romantic, he was my Heathcliff. I knew he was all wrong but when he pulled me close in the park and kissed me hard and inexpertly, his mouth too wet and his clutch clammy, I shook with excitement and sexual awakening.

I can't even remember now how the relationship came about. I suppose we must have started to chat when we collided, like Montagues and Capulets, by the rowing-club boathouse. Kate, who would have flirted with a lamp-post if it had shown the slightest sign of responding, probably set it going somehow, but in only a matter of days I was lying to Mum that I had a late rehearsal and was hanging around longer and longer. Neil's mates eventually peeled off, I shook off Kate (who was tactful enough to know when she was surplus to requirements), and the two of us would kick about.

I cannot imagine for one second what we found to talk about, the only thing we had in common being the fact that we lived in the same town, but I do know that I spent a long time being polite, listening to him trying to be impressive – the big I Am – and struggling with how much I liked him touching me and how much I knew he shouldn't.

'You're posh,' he'd tell me over and over again, making it sound like a criticism.

'He's common,' my father spluttered, when he found out, thanks to my brother Chris's sanctimonious hints over Sunday lunch, and that was *definitely* a criticism.

For my father it was the ultimate crime. He'd paid through

the nose for my schooling to make sure I didn't fall in with the likes of Neil. My plan had worked.

We continued our odd, secretive relationship throughout that summer term. I flunked my end-of-year exams, too busy dreaming about Neil and what we were going to do when we met next, and my parents were hauled in front of the head, who was at a loss to understand what had gone wrong with my performance and my attitude.

'It's that bloody boy,' my father fumed on the way home. 'You're far too young to get involved – especially with the likes of him – and you'll mess up your education. You only get one crack at it, you know!'

The nadir of my downfall happened when my parents went to Darlington overnight to see Auntie Jayne. Chris and I refused to go. It was boring and the prospect of us sulking in the car was enough to persuade my dad to agree to us staying behind. I know that Mum wasn't happy leaving us and she was no fool. Chris scarpered to a friend's no sooner had the tail lights left the drive, and I was on my own and due to meet Neil at five.

'Go on, they'll never know,' I can still remember him saying, his lips so close to my ear that it made my legs shiver and go weak, and the sense of exhilaration was mixed with terror as I bundled him into the house, hoping the Goughs next door hadn't noticed.

It doesn't take much to imagine what happened. No interruptions; the novelty of a soft bed as opposed to a grope in the bushes by the river; add to that the heady and dangerous cocktail of teenage hormones and curiosity.

Happy that my teenage rebellion was spent, I gently shook off Neil – making excuses why I couldn't see him – before I realised I was pregnant. I'm telling you this because it will explain things. Why I'm who I am, why I'm still Lucy Streeter, and despite all I've done in between, why I'm still the girl who threw away her future on Neil Bartlett one sweaty Saturday afternoon in the July that I was seventeen.

It also explains why every morning for the last ten years, ever since I moved up the road to Leamington Spa, the town that blends seamlessly into Warwick, I would shut the front door and head up Warwick Road, make my way round the bin bags that someone always left annoyingly on the corner, and eventually on to Paradise Street, pick up a paper from Deepak at the newsagent and open up my shop. That's how the days would go. Straightforward and uncomplicated, because I had a son to care for and perhaps, too, because everyone was waiting for me to mess up again. Better to be boring than give them the satisfaction.

That week – *that* week – was no different. In fact, it amazes me now how we can go on with the same routine for years. Perhaps there's some reassurance in it – too much change and we get nervous – and I have to say that hearing Deepak's 'whatcha' every morning when I picked up the *Guardian* was a sort of marker buoy in the very familiar sea that was my life.

I tried not to look at the front of Sandy's shop as I passed that Monday. I say Sandy's shop, but the windows had been whited-out for a few days now and a big To Let sign had been erected over the weekend. 'Custard' – absurdly named after her childhood cat – was Sandy's shoe venture. It had kept the holistic element of Leamington in oddly-shaped and deeply un-sexy footwear from Scandinavia for years. She seemed to have been doing okay to me, but perhaps Custard had too small a fan base to make it viable (even though this town has its share of yogurt-eating knitters). Its closure, virtually overnight, was too raw a reminder of how all of us on Paradise Street are holding on to our livelihoods by our fingernails. And our landlord wasn't making it any easier, but more about that later.

The last stop before my shop was, as usual, the Deli. The warm smell of coffee wrapped round me as I opened the door. There were a couple of people in there reading the paper and sipping from tall glasses of steaming latte.

'Hi, Luce, good weekend? What can I get you? One of these?' Sally's smile was broad and welcoming. Her hair, as always, was scrunched up on the top of her head and her hooped silver earrings waved as she bustled over a wicker tray of muffins, all of which would be sold to hungry shoppers by eleven.

'You are an evil temptress and I will be strong in the face of your malevolence,' I said, or something stupid like that, and ordered a skinny latte to go, as I always did and as she knew full-well I would. But more often than not a muffin would find its way into the paper bag with the coffee. I think I must have peered through the door behind the counter to see if Richard was there.

'Where's your brother, then? Nursing a hangover or recovering from another bonkfest?'

Sally laughed as she blasted steam into the milk. 'Both. He's pretending he has a really important meeting first thing with the accountant, but I know damned well he hasn't. He was last seen in the Pig and Whistle on Friday night with some gorgeous slip of a thing.'

I handed over the money for the coffee. 'Pathetic in a grown man, but you have to admire his ability to still pull the chicks.'

''Bout time he grew up, I reckon,' she laughed and I waved goodbye.

Looking through the shop door, I could see a couple of bills on the mat as I balanced my bag, the coffee and the keys to reach the Yale lock. Monday post tends to be bills or strange blanket mailings trying to sell you stretchy chair covers or hearing aids. Today's haul looked no different. I was tempted to put the bills in the bin with the mailings but instead slipped them into a drawer to fester until I could juggle the cash flow sufficiently to pay them. As I pulled up the blinds, the shop flooded with light reflected off the white buildings opposite, casting bright slashes across the stripped wooden floor. By twelve, the sun would have come round and would be pouring in through the glass, something I had mixed feelings about. It would catch the gold in the embroidery on the coat standing on the mannequin in the window, and lift the emerald-green silk lining, but if it stayed there for too long, it would fade the fabric.

I suppose the shop always smelt the same, but you can't really smell a place you are familiar with, can you? My friends say it has a fragrance of hyacinths, but that's only because I fill the place with them the minute they are in season, cramming them into odd-shaped pots, along with tiny narcissi, because I adore them. There were always flowers of some kind, though, and on that particular day it smelt of lilies that had opened with obscene speed in the summer heat. Their heady scent didn't quite mask the smell of damp that had filled the place for weeks since the roof had leaked and rainwater had come through the ceiling of the empty room above and down into the shop onto a rail of jackets. My business manager at the bank at the end of the road would probably say buying lilies was an extravagance I should have resisted, and I should have settled for an air freshener, but what the hell? It lent something to the shop, and life's too short to be entirely sensible.

Ain't it just?

I probably went through the rails and displays of shoes and bags and accessories because I always do, making sure the stock looked good, spreading it out to make it appear as if there was more than there really was. These days, more and more of the pieces are my own designs, but it wasn't always that way. It had taken all my cash (and my energy) to transform the place from the chemist it had been into something close to my dreams. It still had the wonderful drawers for potions and pills, but I'd had to take out the awful striplights and the vinyl flooring, replacing them with chandeliers my mum and I had found at an auction and polishing the floor until I had no fingernails left.

Because of that, I'd played it very safe and stocked tried-and-tested designers (or at least those who were prepared to supply a tiny, little-known shop in Leamington Spa), slowly sneaking in a few of my own pieces as I grew more confident. There were still the safe items – stylish but wearable tops and flowing skirts that were close enough to high-street designs to attract passers-by who didn't know about me. It was the steady flow of their purchases that had paid the rent, but little more, for years.

Rarely did those sort of shoppers part with their cash for *my* coats and dresses, though I'd watch with irritation as they fingered the silk and the velvet – in raptures over the fabrics, the colours, the embroidery.

'You've got such a talent,' they'd coo and my hopes would be raised, until they knocked me back with a sigh. 'But I've got nowhere to wear it.' So they played it safe for their parties and holidays, and the clothes I'd made stayed on the hanger.

One woman in particular – Mrs No-Buy, I'd christened her – seemed to have made a habit of coming in, getting just to the point of buying before she bottled out and complained about the price or the cut. No. My flights of fancy were more often wrapped in tissue and slipped into the stupidly expensive carrier bags I'd ordered, for my regular customers – usually friends – who'd whip out their debit cards with an 'I know I shouldn't' and 'I don't really *need* it'. And thank God they did, because their largesse (and their husbands' bank accounts) kept me and Nat out of the workhouse. And kept me motivated enough to keep designing.

How can I describe the clothes I make? You'll have to imagine something as far from my personality as you can, and if I tell you that I am the sort of person who would rather lock myself in a darkened room than stand up in front of people and speak, then you'll have some idea of just how shy I am.

At school, I used to be amazed how girls would get up on stage in plays and *love* it, lapping up the applause and the attention. I'd be the one hiding in the shadows, happiest behind the scenes, building sets or making costumes. It is probably deeply unfashionable to enjoy sewing – it certainly was then and I kept my fascination quiet, as if it were some shameful habit – but the school drama wardrobe was my haven. With its labelled shelves crammed with hats and shoes, scarves and fabric, it was my escape: an irresistible treasure house for the imagination.

I'd sign myself up to help in all the school productions and while the cast were rehearsing upstairs, I would stay on late to create frock coats or Victorian bustled dresses from cheap bolts of lining fabric for dress rehearsals looming fast on the horizon.

Of course, my tryst with Neil Bartlett brought an end to all that. It brought an end to school completely, in fact. But that short time in the theatre does explain my designs. 'Dandyish' my mate Tamasin calls my frock-coats. Their three-quarter length and embroidered lapels do have a slight Louis-Quatorze quality about them, I suppose. Extravagant fabric – the more lush and jewel-like the better – has always been my weakness. Nat will vouch for that. Any holidays we went on – and there weren't many – usually ended up with him standing waiting while I rifled through vintage clothes stalls at markets. I must have spent a fortune pacifying him with ice cream to make up for it. I remember one trip to France when we camped in a very cheap campsite miles from any attractions that were suitable for an eight-year-old boy and I led him from one flea market to another in search of bits of braid and buttons. That cost me a hideously expensive day at the newly-opened Disneyland Paris on the way home.

Poor lamb. No wonder his favourite artist is Lichtenstein and he's decorated his room at university in wall-to-wall IKEA.

So that is the shop. My pride and joy, where I holed myself up, sewing like some latter-day clogged Hans Christian Andersen character, waiting for the door to ping as someone walked in, and my heart to race in the hope that another purchase would be made. *That* week, I remember, I was creating a dress and coat for Tamasin. Her willowy daughter, Harriet, who'd been saved from a tedious future making canapés for directors' lunches when she met her rich banker, was due to waft up the aisle in a couple of weeks' time, and Tamasin had given me the commission to transform her into the most stunning mother of the bride anywhere north of the M4. For once I was grateful that the shop was quiet – anyone with any sense would have been sunning themselves in Victoria Park – because I could concentrate. It was so bloody fiddly and I kept jabbing my finger.

By six each evening I was stiff and sore from concentrating so hard and, by Wednesday night, I was growing more and more irritated with the stitching, which in turn became irritation at the fact that the coat was for a wedding, and why was I never the bridesmaid, let alone the ruddy bride? I didn't usually resort to self-pity on the relationships front – or only when I reminded myself how long it had been since I'd last had sex – but the summer heat and the fiddly work had got to me. The prospect of stopping by at the Deli for a well-earned glass of wine was a delicious one. Well, there was sod all to go home for.

Chapter Two

The rest of the Paradise Street crew were at the Deli already; in fact, I think our custom of meeting every week or so helped keep Richard and Sally afloat – a sort of local business community self-help consortium. Retail communism! Someone had flipped the 'closed' sign on the door, and the group were gathered around a table at the back, close to a wide-open window overlooking a tiny terrace. A couple of bottles of chilled wine were already open on the table.

We're a motley crew. Over the years some faces have come and gone as business have closed or moved, but the core suspects have been the same throughout. We've become a tight-knit little group, helping each other out when necessary (which made it all the more shocking that Sandy had left without a word). In fact, that's how I'd met Richard and Sally in the first place. I'd just taken over the shop and was trying to smarten it up before my big launch – a few friends, a warm bottle of white wine and a rail of samples I'd bought on my business loan. I'd managed to pull out the canopy, easing its rusting brackets, and had been attempting to scrub the dirty, striped fabric with an old yard brush soaked in soapy water. I hadn't been able to reach and the water had been pouring off the canopy onto my head, until my hair was in rats' tails and my dignity in tatters.

'Can I help?' There Richard had been beside me – tall and dark, his eyes crinkling in amusement. He looked me up and down and I remember pushing the hair off my face, which probably didn't help my look at all. I checked he wasn't too smartly dressed – though I know now Richard never is – and gratefully handed him the brush.

'You might be able to reach. I think there's about a hundred years of accumulated muck up there.'

'Victorian bird poo, I expect,' he laughed as he stretched the brush to the back of the canopy.

'Perhaps we ought to alert the British Museum,' I think I replied, liking this friendly man straightaway, and he gave me a broad smile back, a smile that's become wonderfully familiar over the years.

When he'd finished the job, he introduced himself and invited me into the Deli they'd opened twelve months before for a restorative coffee and to meet his sister, Sally. From then on the three of us had become firm friends and I'd been included in weekends on Richard's boat, where he taught me to sail via barked instructions. Sally would look on sympathetically, calling Richard 'Captain Bligh' and telling me to threaten mutiny. Richard isn't only a brilliant sailor, he's an adventurous one, too, and though I've crewed the odd overnight trip, he never managed to persuade me to go with him on jaunts to the Mediterranean, too worried was I about my safety and my teenage son at home – until it was Nat who was nagging to crew instead of me. And he often had.

Gaby was there in the Deli that Wednesday evening, her ample bosom resting on the table, the scale of it emphasised by the panel of sequins on the bodice of her blue batik dress. Gaby has owned Pets' Corner, which is, unsurprisingly, on the corner of Paradise Street, since I can remember. In fact, I used to stand in there for hours as a little girl, touching the glass of the guinea pig cage, knowing it was pointless to hope for one because my mother would never relent. Gaby's voice and temperament are as big as her size-twenty frame and she used to scare me a bit – still does – but her survival is testament to the British obsession with spoiling their pets.

To her left sat the greying, bearded, bespectacled Martin, who runs the secretly quite successful tile shop two down from me. In these days of DIY superstores, it is remarkable that he has stayed afloat. But the secret of his success lies in the fact that he is 'top end', knowing just what his moneyed customers are looking for to decorate round their Agas or their state-of-the-art bathrooms in the handsome Regency houses that fill this quirky Midlands town. Every year he 'does' Europe and North Africa, sourcing the most beautiful handmade tiles, and comes back triumphant, like some ancient traveller returning from the Far East. He also brings great wines back with him, too, and we, as The Paradise Street Crew, feel it our duty to test them out. Martin is fatherly and caring and, I fear, enjoys our local business pow-wows because they are a good reason not to have to go home to his overbearing wife.

Next to Martin sat Fen. Small, chubby and a bit pompous, Fen is the expert on everything and is teased relentlessly by all, not least Richard who makes a point of asking Fen for advice on subjects he probably knows more about himself, then sitting back to watch as Fen earnestly explains the answer. Fen runs one of those hardware stores that smells of oil and wood and sells simply everything. How he has managed to survive with the big chains as competition is a miracle, but he seems to have a steady stream of customers coming to him for universal bath plugs and nails, and he exploits the father-and-son heritage of the business as his USP. His dad, a rather intimidating man with glasses and a thin little moustache, died a few years ago now but, like the characters in *Open All Hours*, Fen keeps values as they have always been.

Sally was sitting next to Deepak, from the newsagent. Sal's boyfriend, the lovely Karl, works in London so she never hurries home and she was enjoying unwinding from the day. She'd taken off her Deli apron and her floral-print dress hung loosely over her figure, lean and wiry like Richard's. Richard was hovering, placing little dishes of nuts, olives and artichoke hearts on the table for everyone to dip into. He turned and enveloped me in a bear hug as he always did.

'Oh, don't squeeze too hard. I'm aching!'

'Haven't the little elves been helping you out today?' He laughed deeply. I think it amused him to see me as some poor Victorian seamstress earning nothing for her labours – like a little match girl. But I'd forgive him, because often he'd just appear in the shop at lunchtime, still in his long green apron, and hand over a thick, delicious sandwich without a word before hurrying back to serve the lunchtime customers.

'How are you after your ... er, vigorous weekend?' I asked cheekily and he wiggled his eyebrows comically.

'I'm a babe magnet. What can I say?'

I snorted and sat down, took a long slug of the ice-cold white wine Martin had poured out for me, and relaxed back in my chair. These were my friends. Life was good.

Usually on these occasions, the chat is a mixture of congratulation for anyone who'd had a good week sales-wise and grumbles about the cost of keeping our heads above water. But tonight things were a little more tense. Martin coughed to quieten us down.

'Right,' he began, shaking a handful of nuts and throwing them back into his mouth. 'We've had a reply from Sayers.' The group groaned as one. 'He says, and I quote, "You are, of course, fully entitled to go to arbitration but I would remind you that a new and higher basis of rental value has now been established following upon agreement in relation to another of my properties in your street, and that agreement will constitute irrefutable evidence for the purposes of any such proceedings."'

'Pompous arse,' muttered Gaby.

'Listen to this bit,' Martin continued. '"I will be serving rent-review notices upon all remaining tenants in order to seek increased rents in line with the newly-established rate."'

My stomach clenched. This was confirmation of what we had feared. Just to fill you in – when we all opened our shops over a space of about twenty years, our landlord was Fitch and Wakeling, a couple of local men who'd been in Leamington since Noah commissioned the ark. Old man Fitch had died a few years back and when Wakeling followed him shortly after, their property company was sold to the elusive Mr Sayers. We'd all been informed, of course, in curt little missives telling us that nothing would change and reminding us that our rents were up for review shortly. As if we needed reminding. We'd all waited anxiously, certain that rents would rise, but none of us had en-visaged the figures Sayers was demanding. The rents were high enough already, as we'd all signed up for Internal Repair Leases at the beginning, meaning the landlord was obliged to maintain the rest of the building, something Fitch and Wakeling had done faultlessly but which Sayers was very slow to do.

'What does he mean "agreement in relation to another of my properties in the street"?' asked Deepak, his forehead creased with confusion. 'He can't mean Sandy. She folded a while ago.'

Gaby leaned forward earnestly. 'I miss her. I didn't think things were that bad for her, actually. She seemed quite upbeat and then all of a sudden she was gone. Perhaps the bank fore-closed, but she had scuttled off with her Cornish pasty-shaped shoes before I could ask.'

'No bad thing in my opinion,' I heard Martin mutter. He was the type of dresser who seemed to polish even the soles of his shoes. Not Sandy's target market at all.

'What does he mean, then?' Deepak pressed.

'He means, my dear Deepak, that some snake in the grass

has agreed to a higher rent.' Gaby sat back heavily in her chair, taking a large swig of wine. With a new pet store popping up near Sainsbury's, she was feeling acutely the pain of a drop in business.

'Henry?' Fen suggested. Henry, a curmudgeonly Irishman, ran the noisy and permanently busy bar at the end of the road, half on Paradise Street and half on Regent's Street, so he wasn't part of our clan. 'It's bound to be him. You know what he's like: selfish; and he can afford to be.'

Martin sighed. 'He swears it isn't him. I asked him outright, but I don't trust him.'

Richard had been listening from the counter as he cleaned up. Now he sat down in the empty chair beside me and poured himself a large glass of wine. 'It's all very well going to arbitration, but it'll cost us,' he said. 'I spoke to my solicitor this morning. If we lose, then we'll each have to pay out a couple of grand at least.'

We all slumped back in our chairs then.

'Sayers hasn't mended that sodding gutter yet either.' Sally rubbed her tired eyes.

Martin threw the letter down on to the table. 'He has added at the bottom that "for reasons of security" he will be gating off the access road at the back – so that puts paid to parking my car and vans being able to get in and deliver.'

'All tried-and-tested techniques to get us all to move out,' Richard shrugged. 'Another glass anyone? Has he mended that roof, Luce, after the leak? Did you call again?'

'Um.' I knew I should have phoned and hassled but Sayers' receptionist was like Cerberus at the gates of Hades, and she had fobbed me off so often with 'the builder has been informed and there's nothing more I can do, Miss Streeter' that I'd buckled under.

'I'll take that as a no?' Richard teased.

'Yes. I mean no. I will get round to it,' I bluffed. The thought of the future was suddenly very worrying. 'I can't believe we'd all have to move out. I mean, I suppose I could find somewhere else if I had to, but what about you two?' I looked at Sal and Richard. 'You've got such a great place here and people know you. You'd never find a location this good anywhere else in town.'

'What do you think, Sal?' Richard smiled at his sister. 'Shall we just give it all up? You go and marry Karl and I'll take to the high seas. That's been my dream all along anyway: me, a yacht, a Caribbean harbour and a beautiful woman.' It made a lovely image in my mind. How heavenly would that be? I wondered briefly if one of his glamorous girlfriends would cope with scrubbing the decks.

Fen leaned forward urgently. 'Richard's right, Sally. Though you could maybe move the business to the other side of town. There are cheaper places. Or Warwick, maybe? I've heard there are some premises there that are to let.'

'What, after all the bloody time we've spent building this place up and fending off certain chain coffee shops I could mention who've tried to queer our pitch? No thanks, mate. Karl or no Karl.' Sally's expression was sheer dejection. She rubbed her eyes quickly to stop any tears falling and looked out of the window until she had control of herself again. Richard leaned over and patted her knee.

'I'm joking,' he said gently. 'I'll fight Sayers as hard as you will. My solicitor is looking into whether we have enough protection and my mate Rob is a chartered surveyor in Birmingham. I'll give him a call and see what he says.'

Martin knocked back his drink. 'Well, I've got to run.'

'Wifey tugging on the rope?' Richard muttered under his breathe so only I could hear.

Martin stood up. 'Don't forget my launch party, will you?'

Gaby shifted her wide girth in the chair. 'What is it this time, Martin? More tiles from Tuscany that you've marked up two hundred per cent?'

Martin's eye twinkled. 'And some! Morocco this time, actually. I need all the moral support I can get to persuade the buggers to buy them. At least then I'll be able to afford to survive if Sayers does force us out.'

I left soon after Martin and wended my way back home. There was a message from Mum on the machine, nothing much on TV and even less in the fridge so, feeling a little bit squiffy from the wine, I got into my PJs and into bed with Dan Brown. Well, a girl needs some company, doesn't she?

Chapter Three

Everything seemed perfectly normal the next day. The day it all kicked off. Same old routine – up and showered, dressed – I can remember this exactly because of what happened later. Black jeans and a pale green T-shirt with a black fleece over the top to keep out the early-morning chill, sneakers on my feet, latte and – yes, I admit it – a cranberry muffin clutched in one hand. I opened up the shop as usual, a couple of minutes late if anything because I'd had to wait in the Deli while two college kids ordered croissants, but it's not like anyone's ever banging at the shop door. No one champing at the bit to get in and spend or anything. No, to all intents it was just the same as the day before, and the day before that.

I needed to get on with Tamasin's coat because she'd said she was coming in after lunch so, as soon as I'd finished the coffee (well away from the dove-grey dupion silk) I set to work. I was particularly keen to get the coat in a state where she could try it on and it was going pretty well. From my work bench, I could see through the display window of the shop and anyone outside could see in. I like to be visible from the street – and visibly busy, not standing around looking as if I'm waiting for someone to come in. Which I am, of course. But I just don't want to give that impression. So while I was sewing, I thought about Tam and everything that was going on with her at the time.

She's a great mate, Tam, and, though she started out as a customer, she soon became a friend. I think I first met her when she came into the shop after school one day, must be getting on for ten years ago now. I know Nat had just started high school and was smart in his new blazer, with the knot in his tie still somewhere close to his neck. He was lurking around at the back of the shop pretending to do his homework but really just gazing into space, waiting for me to finish for the day so we could go home. It was dark outside, and close to Christmas. In an attempt to attract festive trade, I had hung a silk party dress in the window, where it matched the baubles hanging from the spray-painted twigs around it. Christmas decorating on a budget, as always. There was a sort of flurry, as there usually is around Tam, as she entered, and I thought she was alone until a dark-haired girl about Nat's age trailed in sulkily behind her.

'Hello!' She greeted me as if she'd known me for ever, but it wasn't irritating. You can't be irritated by Tam. She has no guile and her face is too open to distrust. The thing that struck me first was how pretty she was – swathed theatrically in necklaces and knitted layers of green and blue, and with a lively, friendly face, framed by wavy fair hair kept back with combs jabbed in haphazardly. It was the party dress that had caught her eye as she'd walked past on the way back from school with Harriet, and as she slipped into my makeshift changing room to try it on, I remember we exchanged a glance of complicit amusement at our children, who were self-consciously pretending the other didn't exist. Oh the glorious days before hormones kick in!

The dress suited her beautifully – the green wild silk perfect against her pale freckly skin. It needed taking in at the waist a bit so I pinned her, and we arranged for her to collect it the following week. That was when we really cemented our friendship and, since she bought that first dress so spontaneously, I've never had the worry that she's just buying my stuff as a way of supporting me – although I'm sure she buys more from me than she strictly needs to. At least I know she really loves the clothes I design. If anything, she's encouraged me to go further than I perhaps would have done otherwise, gushing with praise at the silly indulgences and extravagant pieces I've knocked up over the years without any hope of ever selling them.

'Let's have a coffee,' she blurted as I wrapped the altered dress together with a scarf she'd bought at the last minute. 'Can you get away? Just close up for an hour?' She had all the innocence of the non-working woman who assumes that other women work only to fill in the time or for pin money, but why not? I buried my scruples and did just lock the door and we wandered up to the Deli, its windows steamy against the cold day outside. Richard and Sally knew Tam already, of course. Even the traffic wardens in Leamington know her by name – she's that kind of woman – and I remember on that first day Richard accommodated her weird coffee order (soy caramel latte with hazelnut syrup, or some shit like that) without a murmur. He, like everyone else, fell under her irresistible spell.

'Now tell me all about *you*?' she'd asked without preamble and despite my usual reluctance, she had the whole story out of me before I could see the bottom of my coffee cup.

'Oh how brave you are!' she gushed. But in some way I felt she really meant it. My experience was so far removed from hers with her big house on Beauchamp Avenue and her rich husband Giles who keeps her in frocks and lattes, and her arduous regime of light lunches. 'And I think you are a genius,' she went on. 'I simply *love* that dress and I'm going to be back for more, you know.'

And she was. That's the thing about Tam. Her enthusiasm is universal, but insincere it isn't. What you see is what you get. We chatted on about teenagers and spots, and that was when it all came out about Harriet. The same age as Nat, she went to the posh school, of course. Tam and Giles had only married recently and Harriet had been used to having her mum all to herself.

'We'd planned the wedding for ages, and had those painful conversations across the dinner table with Harriet to make her understand, but she's been an absolute bugger. Giles has been a saint and Harriet acted like a martyr, rolling her eyes every time the W word was mentioned.'

'That's cos she's had to share you,' I ventured, realising that was one problem I hadn't had to deal with yet. 'How long had you been on your own?'

That set her off and she regaled me with a hilarious and exaggerated story about young love in London where she had been pretending to study drama at some second-rate theatre school in Ealing, only to fall for some rake who fancied himself as a playwright. They'd married against her and her parents' better judgement. He'd left her for the lead actress in a Pinter play, and Tam had come home to her parents in Kenilworth with her baby under one arm and her tattered thespian dreams under the other.

'The thing is, Lucy,' she confided, 'Giles is my dream man, and sooo rich!' She giggled. 'But money can't buy everything, it seems, and I've had expensive doctors from Birmingham to London with their speculums up my fanny for the last few years trying to work out why I can't get pregnant again.' For a moment her breezy act faltered, and there was real pain on her face. 'We know it's not him – nothing wrong with his swimmers – and they are scratching their heads because Harriet came along after one cap-less bonk. They can't find anything wrong but still … Anyway,' she pulled herself together and carried on over-brightly, 'tell me more about your delicious dressmaking plans. Are you going to be the next Christian Lacroix?'

That was the beginning of a firm friendship, but my business hadn't moved on and neither had Tam's hopes of becoming pregnant. She tried IVF for several years, and I'd even gone to the clinic with her sometimes, with her pee samples, and held her hand when they told her the disappointing results of her blood tests. It was heartbreaking to see. It was like a hunger for her – something that could never be satisfied. And despite the fact that Giles adored her and would do anything to make her happy, for her there was something mammoth missing in her life.

She'd recently given up on the IVF route and I knew reaching this decision had been terribly painful for her. I'd sat for many hours with her as she sobbed out her agony and disappointment. But, being Tam, she rallied, put a brave face on things and now she'd thrown herself – and her money – into organising Harriet's wedding, but also into a kaleidoscope of new interests. She'd got a rescue dog – a very endearing but fairly mad terrier cross called Martha – she'd joined the local amateur theatre, she was fund-raising for a variety of charities, she'd done a course on Japanese cooking. She was a blur of activity. Giles, phlegmatic as ever, let her get on with it but declined to get involved himself so, when the need arose, she would drag me along as her companion. I never minded – we went to places I probably wouldn't have dared try on my own and she was always good company.

So that's how it happened that day. I'd got the sleeves tacked on by the time Tam came in on a waft of expensive cologne – Serge Lutens or Annick Goutal, probably – and hugged me tightly. Then she caught sight of the coat over my shoulder.

'God, Luce! It's heavenly,' she breathed. 'Even without the decoration. Can I try it on?'

She shrugged off her linen jacket, dropping it casually onto the floor, and slipped her arms carefully into the figure-hugging silk I held out for her. We were both silent for a moment while she twisted this way and that, looking at herself in the long mirror. 'Oh!' she sighed eventually. 'It fits like a dream.'

I was more critical, tugging at the shoulder seam and comparing the set of the sleeves, but even I had to admit, it was a pretty good piece of work. And on Tam, it looked fantastic. 'You're going to wear your hair up, aren't you?' I asked, lifting her plait to check the stand-up collar.

'Oh yeah!' She pulled the edges of the coat together and turned sideways on to examine the effect. 'Look at that!' she exclaimed. 'You're a genius, there's no other word for it.'

We discussed the details of what she wanted for a while then, once I'd made some notes and taken a few pics with my digi-cam – oh yes, ever so high-tech – she slipped off the coat and handed it back to me, then sat down on the painted boudoir chair. This was a cue for me to put the kettle on so I slipped into the back of the shop – not far enough to interrupt the conversation, which started in the usual way.

'So, how's business?'

'Oh fine – you know. Nothing startling. Sold one of those skirts on the sale rail yesterday and that friend of yours – Miranda, is it? – stopped by to have a look for a prom dress for her daughter. Not sure it was quite what she was after, though.'

Tam laughed. 'Probably not what her daughter wants anyway – doubt if any of your designs show enough flesh.'

'Oi! You make it sound as if I were designing habits for nuns.'

'Touchy! That was supposed to be a compliment. After all, I am your muse – aren't I?'

I handed her a short strong coffee and laughed at the idea. 'Well, you're a-musing but I'm not sure you're a muse. That sounds a touch too Yves Saint Laurent to me.'

'Huh! And there was me thinking I was your inspiration. Ah well! I'll just have to find another role in life. Speaking of which ...' She left a significant pause and I looked up suspiciously.

'I went for that audition for Mrs Burling in *An Inspector Calls* and guess what?'

'You got it?'

She tutted. 'How did you guess?'

'Easy. You wouldn't have asked me if you hadn't.'

'Fair enough, but the competition was pretty stiff. The thing is, they're having a bit of a do there tonight – a sort of fund-raiser for the members – and you can bring a friend. What do you reckon?'

'Doesn't Giles want to go?'

'He'd rather have his toenails pulled out one by one. Come on, it'll be fun. They've got some people doing cabaret acts. Nothing formal, just some singers. Oh, and I want you to meet this bloke who was at Carrie's the other night. He's new on the scene – well, I've not met him before, so he can't be important! – but he's quite entertaining. A bit intriguing. Does some sort of fortune-telling thing.'

'Oh, is he a tall dark handsome stranger?' I asked cynically.

'He's tall but a bit theatrical, I'm afraid. Not your type at all.'

'Does that mean he's as camp as a row of tents?'

'Not exactly, but there's something a bit unworldly about him. Not the rufty-tufty type, but he's heavenly. And Carrie thinks he's brilliant. Apparently he told her she was going to come into some money and she won the lottery the very next day.'

I took a pin out of my mouth. 'Really? How much did she win?'

'Well, only a tenner – it was a scratch card – but still! They say he's really good. Come on, I'll treat you to a ticket and you can buy me a glass of wine. What do you say?'

What was there to say? It sounded like something a bit different so, of course, I agreed. It wasn't like I had anything else planned, after all.

And that was how it all started.

I was due to meet Tam outside the theatre. It had recently re-
located to a disused church near the bottom of the Parade and
the fund-raising drive was to help pay for all the refurbishments.
There were posters up outside advertising the new season of
plays and plenty of people were stopping to look. The place had
an energy that was infectious and I started to feel quite buzzy
myself – no small feat at the end of a day spent on French
seams. People were streaming in. A few of them I recognised by
sight but no one well enough to talk to. I've always envied Tam
that confidence to walk into a new situation and just be herself,
yet fit in at the same time. If it had been her waiting for me
(by the way, that's never happened), she'd have been chatting
away to all kinds of people by now. I just tried not to look
conspicuous and kept scanning the roads around for a glimpse
of her rushing towards me, bracelets rattling.

'Boo!' Her voice behind me made me jump almost comically. She'd been inside all the time and we were still laughing
about it when we got upstairs to the bar, which was housed
in the old organ loft. As promised, I got us both a large glass
of chilled white wine. The place felt new and fresh, even the
stained-glass windows sparkled, and everyone was a bit giddy
and loud. When I got back to the table, Tam had met up with a
few other people who were obviously co-actors. They were a bit
luvvy-ish to be perfectly honest, and quickly lost interest in me
once they knew I wasn't keen on acting, so I looked round at
the other tables and groups of people standing around and – of
course, because I really can't help myself – I had a look at what
they were wearing. There was quite a spread, age-wise. A few
studenty types who were, unsurprisingly, the most eccentrically
dressed, the boys wearing charity shop old-man hats and the
girls looking vampish in that black-and-white film-star kind of

a way – red lippy and heels. The older women went more for pashminas and big earrings with a safer boho look. The men just wore … well, what men wear. Except … except in the corner near the piano there was a man who looked different. Quite a crowd had gathered around him and they all seemed to be focused on what he was saying; he was definitely the one who stood out.

It wasn't just that he was so tall – although he must have been going on for six foot four – he was also very, very thin and his face was so pale he looked almost unhealthy, as if he was about to faint. His jet-black hair against his skin didn't exactly dispel the gentle air of 'something of the night'. Also – and this was what really caught my attention – he was wearing a deep-red smoking jacket and, even from across the room, I could see that it was the most exquisite cut and quality. The group around him seemed to be talking at him, and he had his hand raised in that one-question-at-a-time manner teachers use.

'Oh,' someone tapped my arm and brought back my attention to the group, 'Tam says you're a whizz with the needle. Don't suppose you'd like to join our little troupe? We're always on the look-out for a wardrobe mistress.'

I felt my heart sink. Theatrical design was one thing, but this would be more a question of silk purses and sows' ears – sourcing outfits for rather intense am-dram productions from the British Heart Foundation shop on no budget, and that wasn't quite where I saw my career going. I gave Tam, who was blatantly smirking, one of my looks and I was just about to say thank you very much and explain what a terribly busy life I had when someone played a rippling chord on the piano.

'Good evening and thank you all for coming …'

It was the artistic director, so Tam whispered in my ear, an overly vivacious, middle-aged woman who clearly thought the National Theatre had missed a trick with her. 'Friends, comrades, fellow battlers at the coal face of *theatrical* endeavour,' she projected breathily, prolonging the 'th' of theatrical theatrically, 'thank you sooo much for coming here tonight to celebrate our little achievement.' She waved her arm at the vast expanse of space above her head. 'We're nearly there,' she sighed modestly, 'but we just need to dots those 't's and cross those 'i's.' There was a polite titter at her wit around the room. 'And we need your help once again. But I know you're going to love this evening's offering and dig deep in your pockets as a result, as we meet friends old and new.' She glanced over at the tall, pale man in the corner, obviously expecting a response but he was looking the other way. 'So,' she turned back to her audience, 'let me introduce our first act ...'

A young but surprisingly good singer then proceeded to rattle through a few Chet Baker classics and finished with 'Me and Mrs Jones' – to rapturous applause. More introductions from the increasingly loquacious director preceded more acts – including a cringe-worthy rendition of Robbie Williams' 'Angels' in the pub style with plenty of bass vibrato. Only a couple more bottles of warm house white on our table made it bearable.

I was just wondering how soon I could slip away when she started again. 'And now, ladies and gentlemen, I'd like to introduce a *very* special young man whom some of you have already had the good fortune to meet. He's new to these parts but he's already made quite an impact. I predict – although that's his forte, not mine...' pause for more polite laughter '...he's going to go very far. I am going to give him the floor – but be warned, you'll have no secrets from him! Let me hear you welcome the mysterious *Micah*.'

The pale bloke in the smoking jacket stepped forward. He looked a bit surprised by the applause, and glanced round as if to check it was aimed at him. We all laughed and he grinned back warmly, obviously enjoying this in a boyish way. I don't know why but it made me feel oddly protective of him and I was inwardly rooting for him as he walked into the spotlight. Then he raised his head and spoke.

'Actually, could we have the house lights up a bit?' he asked. 'I need to see who I'm talking to. Is that all right?' Nicely spoken, with no discernable accent, but his voice was older than he looked, if that makes sense. He sounded more confident than before and I began to relax.

As the lights came up and the spotlight faded, he strolled between the tables, the mic balanced between his fingers, but he didn't say anything. The silence stretched out and I heard someone giggle nervously. Some people were trying to get his attention, some trying to avoid it by looking down or away, but that didn't seem to influence him. He stopped next to a table of teenagers and looked down at one of the girls. 'You're going to get an offer from both of them,' he said.

'What?' She looked startled. 'Me? Both of who?'

He smiled. 'Both the ones you're applying to. But ...' He closed his eyes for a moment. 'The one further south would be better.'

She gasped. 'How did you know?'

He shook his head gently and walked on, leaving the girl and her friends in a whispering huddle. He repeated a similar act two or three times more: telling Fiona – a particularly air-headed mate of Tam's whom I met at the occasional party – that her dog needed to see the vet urgently; a man that he should be ready to raise the offer he'd put in on a house; a couple that they should make sure they wrote down their passport numbers before they went on holiday. It was getting pretty banal, to be honest, although the people he'd chosen to speak to were all a-twitter over what he'd said. I turned to Tam to say as much but she was staring past me, her eyes wide. Micah had come up to our table without making a sound. Not a footfall. When

I turned, he was standing right next to me. I cringed – please God he wasn't going to talk to me in front of all these people – but he was staring down at Tam.

'It's going to happen, y'know. It is.'

'What is?' Her voice was hardly audible and I looked between them, puzzled at this sudden approach. Had they been speaking before? It looked for all the world as though he was continuing a conversation they'd been having earlier.

'You've waited so long and I know you think you've given up. But you haven't really. Not in your heart, have you?'

I looked back at Tam. Her eyes were huge and she shook her head slowly. 'No,' she whispered. 'I haven't. When?'

Micah smiled. 'Soon. Already maybe. I see a double celebration. Something planned and something not planned but wanted.'

I heard a shuddering sob and turned to see Tam's eyes fill with tears. 'Thank you. Thank you so much.'

I couldn't believe it! Just when she was finally coming round to accept things the way they were, this great goon had come along with his big staring eyes and his ridiculous smoking jacket and given her false hope again. He couldn't have known how she'd take his ambiguous comments, but he should have been more responsible. I was torn between trying to limit the damage as far as Tam was concerned and giving him a good ticking-off, but by the time I'd turned to give him a piece of my mind, he'd drifted off to speak to someone else. I sat there seething, not wanting to burst Tam's bubble but wanting to find a way of sparing her any more pain. If eight attempts at the best IVF clinic in the land hadn't managed even a hint of a pregnancy, it was hardly going to happen on its own. I didn't know what else to do, so I just held her hand, tightly, under the table where no one could see while she gradually subdued her tears. But then she turned to look at me, her eyes full of joy.

'I'm so happy, Lucy,' she sighed breathily. 'Just think, by the time Harriet gets married, I'll be pregnant. That's what he meant, isn't it? That must be it. I just know it. When he looked at me, it was as if he was seeing right into my heart. I've never known anything like it. I'm absolutely certain he's right!'

I couldn't trust myself to speak. It was as if the last few years hadn't happened and she was back to that initial state of blissed-out optimism that had gradually shrunk, with each disappointment, to resignation – until a few minutes ago. Giving her hand a final squeeze, I got up and pretended I had to go to the loo, diverting through the crowd to find Micah. I didn't know what I was going to say but I had to get him to take back what he'd said so carelessly.

I peered over everyone's head but couldn't make out his dark hair above the others.

Carrie, the one responsible for finding this charlatan, was beside me, wide-eyed, a glass of wine in her hand and her cheeks flushed. 'Wasn't he marvellous?'

'Mmm,' I said noncommittally. 'Where's he gone?' I could hear the people in the group beside me still twittering about him.

Carrie looked around. 'Oh, he's disappeared again,' she said airily. 'He has a habit of doing that. Perhaps he's gone home.'

'So where did you meet this … performer?' I asked, gritting my teeth.

'Oh, he stopped me in the street to ask the way. He was looking for one of those old people's homes on Kenilworth Road. He must have a relative there or something, I expect. I told him but we got chatting. I'd just come out of the newsagent and I had one of those scratch cards in my hand – yes I know but it's a bit of harmless fun, isn't it? Anyway he told me to try the card straight away, cos he was sure it was a winner – and it only bloody was!'

I peered over her shoulder to see if I could see Micah again. 'A tenner? That's hardly spectacular.'

'Yeah, but!' She shrugged. 'Anyway I asked him how he knew and he told me he does a bit of a line in fortune-telling so, well, I sort of invited him along to a party. He was new in town but I could just tell he had an aura – it was so strong I could practically feel his energy. He's the real thing, you know.' She wiped her brow theatrically. 'It must be exhausting all this clairvoyance. It drains him. He gives so much.'

'Not as much as I'm going to give him,' I muttered under my breath, and fought my way back to the elated and tearful Tam.

Chapter Four

The funny thing is I'm not a confrontational person at all. Not much gets me fired up, a trait thankfully inherited by my son. There are parts of him I don't understand, those characteristics that must come from his father's gene pool, but his ability to avoid (or bury) confrontation is definitely a Streeter characteristic. So the anger that was still boiling away when I woke up the next morning surprised me. I positively stomped about the flat getting ready, slamming drawers and yanking the handle down on the irritating toaster that always pops up too soon. Serves me right for buying a cheap one.

It was Friday and I should have headed for the shop, of course, but, after a moment's hesitation, I picked up the phone and called Carrie.

I knew I'd wake her. Like a badger, Carrie rarely shows herself in daytime and, like a bat, she usually crawls out of her flat, wrapped in a long velvet coat, as night falls, to go to work. At forty-five Carrie is a career waitress, great at her job but without an ambitious bone in her body, surrounding herself with a security blanket of alternative therapies, healing oils and chants, absurd doctrines and ridiculous people like Micah.

''Lo?' she croaked after my second attempt to call.

'Carrie, it's Lucy.' I remember I sounded uncharacteristically brisk and businesslike. 'How do I get hold of this Micah character? Do you have a number?'

'Luce?' She yawned. 'Oh God, darling, I was asleep. What time is it, for heaven's sake?'

'Early. Sorry. Where does he live?'

'I knew you'd be fascinated by him. Hang on.' I could hear her moving about and muttering to her cat, then, just as I thought she'd forgotten I was holding on, she came back to the phone. 'It's down by the station somewhere. I've only got an address. Wait a mo, I wrote it on my board.' Eventually she gave me the details and hung up.

I don't usually move my car during the week. It sits patiently – or 'depreciates patiently' as Richard puts it – outside the flat, awaiting some attention. Richard thinks it's mad that I even have a car, until he wants to borrow it, that is, because his Alfa is up on the ramps at Mike's being mended – again. Italian it may be but like an Italian woman it's high maintenance. I run a little Japanese model – efficient, safe and boring. Much like its owner.

But it would have taken me ages to walk to that end of town, and I couldn't leave the shop closed up for too long, so I hit the morning traffic to find the address Carrie has given me.

Leamington is small enough that everyone tends to know each other – or at least those that orbit in the same galaxy, like the theatre or shops – so as I manoeuvred through the streets, I was wondering why I'd never come across this curious man before. Carrie had said he was new on the scene and, as I'm not exactly the epicentre of the town's social life, perhaps I'd just missed his debut. Finally I found his road in an area that was pretty grubby and not one I knew well. I squinted at the doors to find number 66. Most of the buildings were businesses: betting shops or late-night grocers, takeaways, electrical goods and another shop promising to unlock mobiles. Tucked in between, though, there were doors to the flats above, and 66 had light blue peeling paint and a cheap tarnished knocker.

I found a space a bit further along, put an hour's ticket on the windscreen – I certainly wasn't going to be longer than that – and randomly pushed each bell until I got an answer.

Judging by his appearance when I finally got Micah, I'd clearly woken him too. Fortune-telling was obviously not a first-thing sort of occupation.

'Hello,' he said, opening the door wider. He didn't question why a woman he'd barely acknowledged the night before was on his doorstep at nine o'clock the following morning. In fact, his nonchalance took the edge off my anger and, as I went up the stairs behind him, I had to remind myself why I was there: I would not apologise for the early-morning interruption, I would flex my assertiveness muscles again.

The flat was as grubby as the door suggested it would be. There was one largish lounge with a window over the street and what was probably a bedroom and a kitchen off the landing the other way. Micah indicated I should go through to the lounge and asked if I wanted coffee.

'No thanks,' I said, trying not to wrinkle my nose at the squalor. Judging by the clothes spilling out of the backpack on the floor by the sofa, he really was new on the scene.

I turned to face him. He looked paler than he had yesterday, if that were possible, and his eyes were wide with dark shadows beneath. He was even thinner than I'd realised, and the T-shirt and skinny jeans he wore now made him look like an emaciated teenager. Perhaps he was. His age was hard to determine.

'I'm sorry to come by so early,' I began, wanting to take control of the situation, 'but I have to get to work and I couldn't let this wait.' Micah looked hard at me and shrugged.

'That's okay. It's nice to see you.' He stopped, waiting.

'You won't remember me, but it's about last night at the

theatre and what you said to my friend Tamasin,' I stumbled on, feeling the anger coming back nicely. 'You have no idea how devastating what you said to her is,' I carried on, ungrammatically. 'You might fancy yourself as a bit of a clairvoyant but that woman has been through so much trying to have another baby, and you have completely and unfairly raised her hopes that she will actually get pregnant.'

He didn't say anything for a while, and I was beginning to feel a little uneasy.

'I can see that you're not a fan of people like me,' he said eventually.

'Er, no actually I'm not.' I could hear the scorn in my voice. I couldn't remember the last time – if ever – I'd spoken to anyone like this, but wading in on Tam's behalf made it so much easier. I felt justified. 'Playing around with people's emotions. It's so irresponsible.'

Micah shrugged and sat down on the edge of the sofa, his elbows resting on his knees. 'Sometimes these things need to be said,' he answered quietly.

'Oh, for God's sake.' I moved my weight onto the other leg, aware I was towering over him now. 'I don't really know what your game is. In fact, what you said to Tam was horribly ambiguous.' I remember it striking me then that what Micah had told Tamasin hadn't been exactly specific – just a coincidental choice of prediction he happened to have plucked from the air perhaps – but stupid and irresponsible nonetheless. 'You weren't to know that she has been trying for a baby for years, and now she'll be all excited about things and it will all come to nothing.' I threw my hands up in exasperation, and let them fall. This was pointless. He wasn't really listening, just looking down at his hands, so I hooked my bag onto my shoulder and started to make for the door.

'She should be excited,' he said just as I moved away.

I looked back and his eyes were penetrating me. I remember being a bit unnerved, suddenly acutely aware that I was alone in a flat with this stranger and I knew nothing about him at all.

'So you maintain she's pregnant, then?'

'Yes, I do. Sure you wouldn't like a coffee? You haven't even told me your name.' He put out his hand in greeting.

I ignored it. 'Lucy. Lucy Streeter.'

Something flashed across his face that I couldn't read. I know now exactly what it was, but at that moment it was a bit unsettling. He seemed very alert but confused for a moment and stared at me, frowning.

'And no coffee, thank you very much. We'll prove Tam's not pregnant with a test, won't we? Then you'll look stupid. And how do you propose to make it up to her when she's crushed with disappointment?'

'I won't have to.' He sounded almost dismissive. 'She *is* pregnant.'

There was a pause. I wasn't expecting him to be so confident.

'All right,' I said, clearing my throat, 'if you're so clever, what's in store for me, then? Untold riches? A tall, dark handsome stranger?'

He wrinkled his brow and then looked away. 'Er, no.'

'What then?'

He was silent for a moment, then muttered, 'I don't know.' He coughed nervously and flicked another look at me. 'I don't know.'

'Now you're scaring me,' I remember saying quietly. It occurred to me again that I was alone in this flat with a man I knew nothing about. What if he was a psycho? I glanced at the door, wondering if I would have enough time to get away if he lunged at me, but his expression wasn't frightening or threatening. He just looked sad.

'Come on, tell me.'

'I'm afraid I don't see anything for you, Lucy.'

I laughed shrilly. 'Perhaps I'm not giving off the right vibes. The gullible vibes, I mean. No sick dogs or longed-for pregnancies for me then!'

'No,' Micah stood up. 'Nothing. I can't see anything for Lucy Streeter. Not a future at all, I mean.' He put his hand gently on my arm and I pulled away roughly.

'Oh, for God's sake,' I snorted, burying the ridiculous tide of panic that had welled up. Anyone would have reacted like that, wouldn't they, to such a hideous suggestion? 'There's no need to get nasty just because I've seen through you and your nonsense. I'm not as gullible as the others, you know.'

He shook his head. 'This must be a shock to you, I know, but it's just a matter of days, Lucy. Next Friday, I'm afraid. It's a shock to me too.' His face was a picture of puzzlement and concern, but I wasn't having any of it.

'Don't be so ridiculous!' Angry now that he was being so dramatic, I made for the stairs, not even looking back, and slammed the peeling blue front door behind me. Back at the car, I threw my bag onto the passenger seat and pulled out into the traffic, keen to get away from this wretched little street as soon as I could. Micah's manner reminded me of a girl at school – Jeanette somebody or other – who'd played on being a witch, pretending her mother was the seventh daughter or something, and she'd put the willies up everyone with her pronouncements. It was stupid rubbish and I couldn't bear the thought of Tam being hurt by it.

I dropped off the car at home, steam slowly beginning to recede from my ears, and hurried towards the shop. I needed some normal people around me.

'You're late this morning,' Richard appeared from the back of the Deli as I came through the door, his dark hair dishevelled, and began to make my coffee. 'Gone part time, have you?' He smiled that full smile of his and for the first time that morning I smiled back.

'Yeah. I've met a millionaire and don't need to work again. Ever.'

'Sounds great. Hope he's got a big—'

'Thank you. That will do!'

'I was going to say *car*.'

'Of course you were.' I looked at the cake display defiantly. 'And this morning I'm going to have one of your croissants!'

He put the stream spout into the milk and, as it blasted, put a crisp, shiny brown croissant into a bag. 'Good girl. Go wild, for tomorrow you die.' He put on a wicked cackle.

I laughed in response. 'Mm, you're not the first person today to say that.' I wanted to change the subject. 'Seeing that floozy tonight then or is she doing her nails?'

'Now, now. Actually, I was going to go to the flicks to see that new French film and, Miss Sarcastic, I was going to ask you if you wanted to come with me.'

I took the piping-hot coffee from him. 'Why? Subtitles a bit of a challenge for her?'

He smiled sheepishly. 'Okay, so it's not really up her street, and I want to see it. Wanna join me?'

I thought about the prospect of another night in. Richard and I both shared a love of those obscure films that get reviewed in the *Guardian* and never hit the mainstream. We'd been to see quite a few together over the years, sharing a box of popcorn in the dark. 'Why not? What time?'

We agreed to meet outside the Deli at about seven – I would be the designated driver, naturally – and I headed for the shop, tiptoeing around the rubbish on the corner as always. Croissant consumed and coffee drunk, I set to work on Tam's coat, tucking in the darts even closer in some sort of defiance against

Micah and his voodoo nonsense, confident that Tam's figure wouldn't be getting any fuller any time soon.

The highlight of the morning was Mrs No-Buy, who hadn't been in for a week or two. At one point, after the third outfit she squeezed into and paraded around in, I almost thought we'd broken the jinx and secured a sale. But at the last moment she saw the error of her ways, and I politely and weakly said 'never mind, hey' and hung it all back up again as she and her large bottom waddled out of the shop. There must have been a couple of other calls, too – there was certainly a very hurried one from Nat asking for a sub to tide him over until next month – until the phone rang again.

'Luce?' At first I wasn't sure who it was. She sounded breathy, barely able to get her words out.

'Tam?'

'Yes, darling. It's me. You are just not *ever* going to believe it.' Her voice convulsed into a sob.

'Whatever's the matter? Has something awful happened?'

'Oh God, no. Something so truly, truly wonderful. I've done a test. I mean after what Micah said,' she was gabbling now. 'I just had to and I am.'

'What? I asked stupidly.

'I'm pregnant.'

I processed the information hurriedly. 'Are you sure?'

This time the sobs wouldn't stop. 'Oh Luce, I've done six tests. It cost me a fortune, and the lady at the chemist says that a yes is almost definitely a yes. Isn't it so wonderfully wonderful?'

For a moment I couldn't speak. 'Yes, darling, it is wonderfully wonderful.' I glanced over at the velvet and silk coat on the mannequin, my needle still in the fabric.

'Micah was right all along! How amazing is that?' she went on breathily. 'I can't wait to tell him.'

My arms went cold with fear, and my voice sounded tight.

'Oh Tam, don't be so superstitious. It's probably just a happy coincidence.'

'Oh no,' she urged. 'I don't think that at all. I think he really has a gift. Why else would this come out of the blue? He doesn't know me – or any of us – so how could he have got it all so right?'

I consciously tried to get a grip on my usual rational self. I swallowed, 'Oh come on, Tam, he was being very vague and you're just interpreting what he said—'

'No, no,' Tam interrupted urgently. 'You're wrong. Fiona called me earlier. You're not going to believe it. You remember what he said about her dog? Well, it's got a twisted gut. She only just got him to the vet in time.'

Chapter Five

I can't remember now what else I said. Something. Nothing. Platitudes. I don't expect it mattered because Tam was way beyond hearing anything. She was in ecstasy and marvelling at the culmination of so many years of trying and failing and trying again. It *was* wonderful news. The very best, and she really deserved it. And how astounding that, finally, it should happen on its own, without any intervention or medication or latex-gloved doctors. I think she said something about it being a miracle, and I agreed, and we made plans to celebrate as soon as we could. Eventually, I put down the phone and just stood there in the quiet of the shop, thinking.

At first, I was just thinking about Tam and how happy she was going to be all through her pregnancy and how it would be when the baby came, and what she'd do about a nursery. Then, prodding their way into my thoughts, came other, less welcome images. So, Fiona's dog. Another bullseye for Micah, it seemed. Boy, his record was beginning to look good. Suddenly my hands felt sweaty and I wiped them on my trousers.

Oh, it was all nonsense, of course. It had to be, although it was natural enough that Tam would connect her pregnancy with Micah's very vague comments at the theatre. The dog business – that had to be a coincidence, too. Statistically half the nation have dogs, and half get ill. Perhaps Fiona had dog hair on her jacket and he'd made an educated guess. Hardly rocket science.

And yet.

I shook myself. Get a grip, Lucy, I chided myself. I pulled my hair back into a punishingly tight ponytail and started crashing around the shop, moving bolts of cloth that didn't really need moving and clanking coat hangers together as I rearranged the displays. It was displacement activity, of course, and I knew it, but I needed to be surrounded by noise and bustle – even if I had to create it myself. I'm not remotely superstitious – never have been. I'm the sort that quite happily walks under a ladder – but it was almost as if I had to chase Micah's words away with actions, driving them from my mind like chasing spiders out with a broom. But still they lurked. And even though the sun had moved round and was shining straight in through the shop windows, I felt chilly and eventually put my fleece back on. If I ever needed customers to distract me, it was now. Even the most indecisive would have been a welcome diversion, but the afternoon stretched out unbroken.

Eventually, I ran out of things to move and sat down with my stock book. I phoned the factory in Derby about the autumn stock of jersey pieces – comfortable and drapey in pinks and mauves – to check the delivery dates were still on track for early next week. While I was listening to the ringing tone, I started to plan a window display that would show them off. Maybe some wood and colour, to make it look autumnal, or was that too clichéd? Forward planning was suddenly very important.

After a short wait, Abby answered the phone, sounding slightly harassed. I'd been dealing with her and her family's factory for years and I recognised the signs straight away. There was going to be a delay. 'I was just about to call you, actually. You must be psychic.' I winced at that one. 'We've had some people off sick and you can't just get anyone to do the making up. It's set us horribly behind. Will delivery next Friday be okay?'

Next Friday. D-day, according to Micah. Bloody Micah!

45

I didn't even know his surname. A spark of defiance ignited inside me. Suddenly it was very important to make plans for Friday.

'Yes, fine. Friday will be fine. I'll be here.' And I wrote down the details in my diary, pressing hard with the pen on the paper and underlining it firmly.

And I damned well would be here on Friday.

Curiously, business picked up as the afternoon wore on. Maybe I was giving off vibes of decisiveness because one woman, who couldn't make her mind up between two belts, bought them both and then I took an order for an evening dress with a nice long completion date. Feeling skittish and positive, I even shut up a little early and made my way home through the warm afternoon, the thought of a cool drink and a shower seeming very appealing. I had an evening ahead of me with an old mate, and I'd wear that pink floral top that always made me feel good. Maybe I'd even tell Richard about this whole Micah thing and we'd have a laugh about it.

It was just before seven when I pulled up in front of the Deli. I sat there for a bit, watching Richard and Sally through the windows as they cleared up for the night, their movements efficient and graceful. From here it could almost have been a dance: Richard swinging chairs up onto tables while Sal swept the floor in long, practised movements. I could see they were chatting, their quick smiles echoing each other as they went through a routine that had probably become unconscious over the years. From here, too, I saw similarities between them that weren't obvious closer to. Richard is far taller, of course, but they both have square shoulders and a way of tilting their heads to the side when they are listening to someone that makes them look slightly quizzical. Sal's hair is darker – I think Richard's is bleached by the sun and salt from his regular sailing trips – but the way it grows straight back from the forehead is similar on both of them, although Sally manages to tame hers by tying it back. They worked on in companionable silence, Richard wiping over the surfaces and Sally polishing the glass door. I didn't feel like disturbing them just yet.

The last hour or so hadn't quite panned out as I had planned. When I got home, I'd thrown open the French doors to let in some air and poured myself cold juice from the fridge. I even sat on a garden chair for a moment, but that was where it started to go wrong. Last night, Micah, Tam's call, Fiona's fucking dog – the thoughts started to crash in on me as I sat in the early-evening sunshine. Determined not to let it get to me, I jumped up. It was too hot out there anyway, and I was sure there were things I needed to do. The recycling, for example. It was beginning to overflow into the hall – and sorting that out would occupy my head, wouldn't it? So I set to on the piles. I'm terrible at throwing things away, but an urge to get things in order came over me and I pulled down a stack of dusty rubbish from on top of a wardrobe. Most of it was wrapping paper and old magazines but in amongst, I unearthed an old portfolio from way back – one of those black ones with a zip – and the dust made me sneeze. It took me a moment to remember where the folder had come from in the first place, then I recalled Mum and Dad had given it to me as a way of encouraging (or ordering) the drawings I seemed to churn out so prolifically in those days. It was a remnant from another lifetime, a time when anything was possible, but also a time before the arrival of the most important thing in my life. It was impossible to imagine my existence without Nat.

I knelt on the floor, opened the folder carefully and peeped inside. The sketches – I wouldn't go as far as calling them designs – were spread over sheets and sheets of different-sized paper. I always seemed to have a crayon in my hand in those days but some of these I couldn't even remember drawing! The heads and features of the models were vague, of course (I'd never been interested in that part), but their clothes were in varying states of detail. I could see now that some of the ideas were unworkable but I could feel a smile on my face as I looked through them. Had I really created these? I must have seen *Doctor Zhivago*, because there was a series of long coats with fur trim and braid. I'd even done a leather jacket with intricate stitching on the back. Some sheets had small swatches of fabric stapled to them like a mood board – dark silks and embroidery threads, even a bit of blue leather (where on earth had I cut that from?). I'd been such a squirrel, stealing bits of fabric here and there and begging off-cuts from the old fabric shop – now long gone – in Smith Street.

Some of the sketches were fanciful – mermaids swathed in pearls and jewels – and others more practical, including designs for the masks for a school production of *The Tempest*. These had even come to fruition – though in a more prosaic form, thanks to the intervention of the ever-practical wardrobe mistress – but I'd been so proud to see them come to life on stage.

What did the contents of this folder say about me? That in those days I'd been spontaneous; there had been a joyful, risk-taking quality to my style. Since then anything I'd worked on had to be more sensible and marketable. It was as if my ideas had been like a hot air balloon that had strained at its guy rope. What I did these days seemed so cautious by comparison; it needed some air pumped into it. I picked out a small doodle-like sketch that had been tucked beneath the others – the beginnings of an intricate, intertwined pattern of flowers and feathers and an idea grew in my head. Perhaps I could adapt this for the embroidered panel on Tam's coat.

I stood up stiffly, my feet beginning to go numb, slipped the drawings back into the folder and put it back where I'd found it. As I showered, the cool water cascading over me, soothing me, I felt a pang of self-doubt. Had I compromised too much? Of course I had to be sensible and make a living – I had a child to raise, for heaven's sake, and so much to prove – but had I not done enough of the ground-breaking designs? Had I lost the sense of fun, of daring, that was so irrepressible in those drawings? And – I scrubbed my skin harder than was necessary – what if I *did* go under a bus (Micah or no Micah), what then would be my legacy? Lucy Streeter, who'd been mediocre, playing it safe because she'd got out of the habit of pushing the boundaries.

'You're very sensible for one so young,' the head teacher at Nat's primary school had told me, and at the time I'd taken it as a compliment. Nat was always well turned out, on time for school, nothing missing from his bag. It struck me now that perhaps he hadn't, in fact, meant it as praise but, from the viewpoint of a man with daughters my age, he'd been cautioning me against not growing up too soon and missing out on the fun.

And now here I was hovering outside the Deli, watching two people I knew getting on with their lives while I sat getting more and more irritated with mine. I saw Richard glance at his watch and say something to his sister. She laughed and replied, shaking her head in amusement and he turned and looked out into the street. That was my cue. I got out of the car and normal life, or at least an appearance of it, continued.

Things felt a bit better by the time we got to the Arts Centre cinema. Richard's usual teasing had gradually got me out of my self-pitying mood and, once we'd parked in one of the multi-storeys scattered around the university campus, we strolled across to the Arts Centre arm in arm.

'Whoa – crowded in here,' he said. 'I'll get the drinks in. Grab a table, if you can. The usual?'

I was about to nod without thinking when something stopped

me. The usual? How lame! 'No,' I called. 'Actually, I'll have a …' For a moment I couldn't think of another drink other than white wine spritzer. 'I'll have a Martini on the rocks.'

He turned and looked at me curiously. 'Shaken or stirred?' he smiled.

'Very shaken, thanks!' And he pressed into the throng around the bar. I moved back where it was quieter and looked around. It was a fairly mixed crowd – some were students, most obviously not. There was a chamber music concert on in one of the halls, starting earlier than the film, and I amused myself trying to guess who was going to which, although it was cheating a bit because the concert goers (certain age, comfortable separates in various shades of dung) were rushing to finish their drinks in time to take their seats. The film crowd (younger, dressed in black, self-consciously Retro specs) were taking their time. I sat down at a recently vacated table and moved the discarded glasses to one side. I wondered what others would make of me, if they noticed me at all. After a little while, Richard emerged triumphant with a short glass for me, a lager and a bag of pistachios held awkwardly between his fourth and fifth fingers.

I took a sip and the unfamiliar liquid felt strange and exciting on my tongue. 'Hey, big spender,' I smiled as he tore open the bag of nuts and offered it to me.

'Well, you only live once. Might as well have the best, eh?'

I tried to laugh and held out my hand, hoping he'd be distracted enough by the task of shaking some nuts into my palm not to notice anything strange in my manner. It was like that weird phenomenon that occurs when you learn a new word – suddenly you seem to hear it everywhere you go. Now everything seemed to be about life – and death.

Richard leaned close to me and I could smell his familiar scent. 'Don't look over your shoulder but there's a bloke at three o'clock that looks like a boiled egg in fancy dress!'

I stiffened. How could I *not* look round after that description, and which way was three o'clock anyway? 'Okay to look yet?' I muttered.

'If you're quick.'

I shot a furtive look and spluttered with laughter. Sure enough, over on the benches was a man without a hair on his head dressed in some kind of Peruvian knitted jacket with a long pointed hood.

'Christ! He looks like an extra from *Lord of the Rings*!' I giggled.

'My preciousssss!' Richard whispered, and we had to busy ourselves quickly with the nuts as the man looked over our way. 'Perhaps you should consider that look for next season's range at the shop. He could be your muse.'

'I'll get right on to it, if you'll agree to model it.'

'I think it would look lovely with a leopard-skin loin cloth. What do you reckon?'

'Not with legs as hairy as yours!' I lobbed back, and he laughed wryly.

'No worse than yours, I'm sure.'

I reached over and pinched him through the sleeve of his linen shirt. 'Cheeky bugger. I would remind you that I'm a laydeeee and therefore have legs as smooth as silk.'

He raised his eyebrow sceptically. 'Don't tell me you're one of these high-maintenance types who spends hours in the bathroom. You're shattering all my illusions. I always thought you were the wash'n'go type.'

I smiled at his teasing, comfortable with his easy manner. 'Hmm – I'm not entirely sure that's a compliment. Anyway, I thought you men liked that earthy French look.'

He screwed up his face comically. 'There's earthy and earthy. I mean – armpits. There's no excuse for that! Oh – that reminds me. There's a Godard retrospective during October. Just the New Wave ones. Three films a week for five weeks and talks from one of the Film Studies lecturers. Fancy getting a season ticket?'

October. Such a long time. And who knew what might happen between now and then? My fists clenched, unbidden. 'I don't know. I'll have to see. No, I don't think so. I might be busy or something.'

He tutted. 'I knew you'd say that. Why not? You can't have anything booked *that* far in advance.'

I looked across at him. He drained his glass of lager and placed it back on the table, suddenly brisk, then glanced at his watch. 'Come on. Finish that drink, if you're going to. We should get in there.'

I hesitated. 'No. You're right. Let's do it. Let's get a season ticket. It'll be great.'

His face lit up. 'No shit? Great. We'll buy them after the film. C'mon.'

I followed him into the auditorium. We settled down in our seats and the credits started to roll. Sod Micah. Sod his stupid predictions. Sod being sensible. Roll on October and Godard. Bring it on! I'd be here. Then I turned to look at Richard's familiar profile, his gaze intent on the screen. So solid and real and certain. I smiled to myself and knew one other thing was certain – Richard was the last person on earth I could talk to about Micah and his fortune-telling. I wasn't going to make that much of an idiot of myself.

Chapter Six

Saturday

I couldn't exactly ignore Tam's invite to go over and see her, now could I? She'd texted twice while we were in the cinema to check I'd be there in the morning, and as I dutifully chomped my way through a worthy bowl of muesli, she called.

'Darling, can't you just open up late this morning? It is Saturday, after all. We're cracking a bottle of bubbly. Terribly naughty in the morning and I shouldn't be on the stuff, of course, but a little glass can't hurt, can it? And I *need* you to be here!' Good old Tam – still completely oblivious to market forces. But of course, her pregnancy was far more important than anything else I had to do and I quickly agreed.

I grabbed my cardy, ditched the muesli and stuffed a Bourbon biscuit in instead, left my coffee cup unwashed on the side, and headed out of the door. The morning was already warm and as I passed the bags of rubbish on the corner, a putrid stench hit my nose and I felt a wave of anger that I suspect had been building since halfway through yesterday. Suddenly enraged by the rubbish, by Micah, by the nonsense Micah had spouted and, most of all, by myself for being affected by his ridiculous pronouncement, I kicked the nearest bag with my plimsoll-shod size sixes.

It was pathetic; it achieved nothing except a bemused look from a passer-by and it didn't even make me feel any better. I could only snarl impotently and head off up the road to Tam's.

I hurried past the Deli, keeping my head down in case Sally saw me and queried what I was up to not opening up the shop. I'd tell her all about Tam later.

I walked so briskly up to Beauchamp Avenue that by the time I was outside her immaculate front door, framed by perfectly clipped box trees, I was perspiring and a little out of breath. Tam's tall Georgian house – the kind of architecture you usually find in Belgravia but can get your hands on in Leamington for a tenth of the price – is as immaculate on the outside as it is on the inside. The joy of being rich must be that you can simply invest in a look, regardless of the price. Her planters always look better than mine because they are better quality. End of story. Her sofas are more comfortable for the same reason and, whilst I could usually ignore the little green-eyed monster that pops up every now and then, this morning I couldn't suppress a silly little smile at the thought of what a mess a baby would make of such moneyed order.

The expression on Tam's face when she opened the door and threw her arms around me demonstrated that she wouldn't care what sort of vile and sticky substances were smeared on her Osborne & Little. Her eyes glittered with tears, her skin was flushed and she exuded sheer joy.

'Oh Luce, isn't it wonderful?'

I rubbed her back as she squeezed me tighter than was entirely comfortable. 'Yes, it is truly wonderful. How are you feeling?'

She threw her arms out. 'Well, exactly the same as normal. That's why I never guessed. I must admit, filter coffee has been making me feel a bit queasy but I didn't think anything of it. I suppose you don't really think about these things if you aren't looking for them. Come on in – we've cracked a bottle.'

I assumed she'd meant Giles until I saw Micah's lanky frame leaning up against the handmade units in Tam's capacious kitchen. I felt a shudder of unease.

'Let me introduce you to the brilliantly clever Micah! I don't think you met him properly the other night,' she gushed, and kissed him on the cheek. He didn't seem remotely surprised by this and I suspected that Tam had barely drawn breath in her praise and gratitude to him since his happy prediction had come true.

Oddly enough, he wasn't going to get the same reaction from me.

'Hello, Micah.'

'Hello, how are you?' His arms were folded and his expression was vaguely smug.

'Fine, considering, thanks,' I answered coolly.

I took the elegantly tall glass of champagne that Tam handed me and I didn't miss the look of puzzlement she shot the two of us.

'Well,' she breathed, raising her glass, 'here's to you, Micah, and to me and to junior.' She put her hand protectively on her stomach in wonderment.

'Giles have anything to do with it?' I smiled. 'How is the lucky daddy, by the way?'

Tam giggled, skittishly. 'Gobsmacked but rather pleased with himself. He went off to play golf this morning like the cock of the walk.'

'Appropriate choice of words,' I muttered.

'He was terribly cynical about Micah, of course,' Tam went on.

'Of course.'

'But when I told him about Fiona and—' She broke off, nearly chocking on her champagne. 'You'll never guess – he also told Debby Lyons that Gary was playing away and do you know what—'

'I didn't quite say that, to be fair,' Micah cut in quickly, holding his hand up.

'Well, no, but you said there was trouble or something.' Tam waved her hand airily. 'And lo and behold it turns out he's shagging some woman from the office in Maidenhead.' She raised her eyebrows and shrugged her shoulders as if to demonstrate the level of QED this implied. 'His advice to Sally Barnum about keeping in touch with relatives was spot on. Turns out her dad has had a bad turn. *And,*' now she was unstoppable, 'this is actually spooky, isn't it, Micah? He only told Penny Swaver to avoid driving for a while. She didn't and she's written off the car!'

This was not what I wanted to hear but, knowing Tam, she'd probably edited the stories heavily to fit. 'Is she okay?' I barely knew the woman but it seemed uncaring not to ask.

'Yes, fine, bit shaken but that's not the point.'

'I expect it is very much the point for Penny.'

The doorbell went again and Tam put down her glass on the marble worktop and fluttered into the hall to answer it.

There was silence in the kitchen and I took a minute sip of champagne, which I didn't want. I'd been glib about Tam's reports but the unease in my stomach had increased as she had reeled off every success story. I brushed my foot across the floor idly, avoiding Micah's eyes.

'So it sounds as though you are uncannily on the button,' I managed eventually. I could hear the almost sulky tone in my voice. He had predicted the end to my life and I was damned well going to be petulant.

Micah shrugged. 'I'm sorry, Lucy. You did ask me.'

I could hear Tam coming back across the hall, talking to someone.

'How's it going to happen?' I asked sarcastically. 'Will it be sudden and painless?' I realised I needed to know, and I can remember now thinking it had to be the oddest question I had ever asked anyone.

Micah shook his head. 'I can't see that, I'm afraid. But, Lucy, some people don't even get a week to prepare,' he added quietly as Tam came in followed by Sylvie Green-Irwin.

As I've said, I'm not one to have strong feelings either way about anyone or anything – except for hip hop music and fennel, of course – but Sylvie Green-Irwin is as close as I come to loathing. Petite and pretty, she has, after years of believing herself to be infinitely superior in every way, managed to acquire a facial expression, and permanently raised eyebrows, that is so unutterably self-satisfied she deserves a damned good slapping. Simply by smiling beatifically, and taking in my clothes or my haircut, she manages to make me feel clumsy and useless. Naturally, Sylvie orbits on a higher plain to mine and her very existence seems to be for our universal benefit. Her small son, Pascal, brilliant and accomplished, of course, has just turned one and his exhilarating first twelve months, including his natural and perfectly orchestrated birth, have been celebrated on a website built and dedicated to him alone. Okay so I didn't have to look it up, but could you resist a ghoulish fascination?

Sylvie had always discounted me from being a normal reproductive woman because I'd had Nat so young – therefore, by her reckoning, it didn't count because it couldn't have been the nurturing, planned, wholesome experience it should have been. But instead of seeing her as ridiculous, the sense of self-congratulation she oozed in her little T-shirt and white linen trousers made me feel as much of a failure today as ever.

'Luuucy,' she cooed. 'How are you?'

'Fine thanks, Sylvie. No Pascal with you today?'

'He's with Colette. I can't bear to be away from him, but I've dropped them both at baby yoga. Such a relaxing experience for him.' Tam poured a glass of champagne and held it up to Sylvie, who refused the offering smugly. 'No thank you, darling. I'm still breast-feeding.'

'Of course – you've such will power, Sylvie,' Tam giggled. 'Is this Colette an au pair?' I couldn't detect the slightest hint of irony in Tam's tone.

'No, no.' Sylvie was quick to put her straight. 'She's an inter-cultural influence. Colette talks to him in French, so he will absorb the language unconsciously. *So* important in his development.'

I'd had enough. I glanced at my watch ostentatiously and put down my glass. 'Tam, darling, I've got to go and open the shop.' I gave her a warm hug. 'Make sure you start looking for an inter-cultural influence for junior as soon as you can, won't you?' I whispered as she embraced me.

Her eyes danced with laughter and, waving at Sylvie and Micah, who was still standing motionless, arms folded, against the kitchen units, I gave her another big hug and scuttled away from the weird tableau as fast as I could.

Everything else about the day was normal – or at least I made it so, pushing the thoughts that came into my head to the back of my mind. Without the normality I would have gone insane and, as a gesture of defiance, I even bought an extra long-life eco light bulb for the shop. Pathetic but it made some sort of statement.

I felt jumpy, and every time the phone rang I leapt. The calls were business-related and I dealt with them briskly and efficiently, and at half four shut up shop for the weekend and headed for Jephson Gardens. The afternoon was warm, with a light breeze moving the flowers and small clouds skitting across the denim-blue sky. I strolled past the municipal planting of the flowerbeds and smiled at the toddlers as they played, their parents sitting on benches watching them. I observed the teenagers flirting with each other, and the band of grubby winos who were always there, colonised on a park bench swigging from cans.

Everything was normal, like any other day: noisy, busy and normal. Why on earth would it be any different? But somewhere in my head was the 'what if?' – the possibility that Micah *had* actually got it right. That he had a track record of getting these things right – well, you do hear such things, don't you? – and his recent record was quite impressive. As I finished my circuit round the garden and headed back towards home, my head was full – rationality arguing in equal measure with irrationality – and by the time I put my key in the door the 'what ifs' were winning out.

Perhaps it was these nagging doubts that made me unusually effusive with Nat when he called that night.

'Mum, you're being a bit weird,' he said after a barrage of questions from me about what he was doing, eating, watching. 'Are you okay?'

'Yes, yes fine, darling,' I sniffed, my eyes stinging. 'Probably a bit hormonal, that's all.'

'O-kay,' he replied slowly, as disinterested in his mother's hormone patterns as any man. When you raise a son alone, you have to play the father and mother roles. I've never worried about discussing masturbation – much to his acute embarrassment – or the need to check for testicular cancer. We've talked about sex – I even broached the subject of the female orgasm halfway up the M1 (the car's a great place to bring up these tricky little topics with teenagers – they can't escape). But periods and hormones are a chat too far for Nat and it's become a sort of joke between us that I mention them just to make him squirm.

He was clearly keen to go – his girlfriend Gemma a far more enticing prospect than a cosy chat with his unusually inquisitive mother – so I wound up the conversation.

'See ya,' and he rang off smartly.

I let the phone drop onto the seat beside me and lay staring at the ceiling. I don't know if it was Micah that had stirred it up, or the thought of Tam bringing a vulnerable new life into the world, but everything inside me seemed suddenly very unsettled. I always imagined I would end my days in some old people's home, gaga and dribbling, with Nat all grown up and settled into the world with a family of his own. Like everyone else, I thought death was something that happened to other people but, whether it was going to be Friday or in two years' time, I found myself with that very unwelcome thought – the thought every parent pushes away – what would happen to Nat if I popped my clogs now?

The sense of responsibility overwhelmed me and I felt dizzy and sick. I took a ragged breath and then let it out, and with it came my grief. I howled unattractively, my nose running and my mouth distorted. I was gushing like a tap and, in between reaching for more kitchen roll (I was out of tissues), I wallowed in self-pity, pulling out the albums from the big chest of drawers in my bedroom and touching Nat's little face in the pictures as I sniffed revoltingly: Nat in my parents' garden; Nat on my mother's knee; Nat on his first day at school; Nat playing football; blowing out birthday candles; making sandcastles. Nat with his arm around me, all lanky and awkward and towering above me. A sudden sense of my own mortality flooded through me, and I was struck with the terror of leaving him alone without a parent. I grieved for my parents, who'd be without me, and for my friends. And then I wept again at the thought that they might not miss me at all – as if I'd never existed. Eventually I fell asleep, surrounded by photographs, and snored so loud, with my nose bunged up after the crying, that I woke myself up several times.

I'm quite sure you must think me mad that I ever believed Micah and, sitting here now in the dark, I do too, but the next morning something happened that convinced me he was the real deal.

I woke very late with a crashing headache – not helped by clanging church bells – as if I'd seen off a couple of bottles of cheap plonk. I turned my back on the housework – the weather was too sticky anyway – and, needing a walk, I headed out of the door. My eyes were so puffy I kept my sunglasses on and, hoping I wouldn't bump into anyone I knew – I'd blame hay fever – I almost masochistically followed the sound of a fair that had set up on the park for the day and was blaring out a cacophony of thudding music. Already it was in full swing and the air was saturated with the heady stench of diesel and frying onions.

Swallowing down my feeling of nausea, I headed into the mêlée of activity and lights. Teenagers were giggling in clumps, eyeing each other up self-consciously. Blank-faced, chain-smoking booth operators were trying to drum up business, delivering their sales pitch devoid of any emotion. The cynicism radiated off them as they pushed notes into their already bulging money-pouches. I didn't intend to take part in anything – who needs a badly made replica of a Disney character as reward for hooking up three plastic ducks in a row? – and I certainly wasn't in the right frame of mind for a pair of flashing bunny ears, but there was some comfort in being amongst the company and noise.

I saw Sandy before she saw me. Perhaps she didn't recognise me behind my cool shades, but I would have recognised that wide beam anywhere. For years I'd watched her waddle in and out of her shoe shop, Custard, across the road from mine, but since she'd shut up so abruptly none of us had seen or heard from her and I agreed with what Gaby at said at the Paradise Street Crew meeting last week: I missed her quick smile and that dirty laugh. At least I *thought* it was Sandy, but she looked rather different – her shoulder-length hair was blonder than ever, platinum even, and instead of the shapeless kaftans she disguised her curvy figure with, she was wearing unflatteringly tight white trousers and a gold belt. A gold belt, for goodness sake! And this was the woman who shunned every fabric that wasn't Fair Trade hemp.

But then she turned and it was unmistakably her, a tight white T-shirt with a gold-threaded tiger motif appliquéd across her heaving bosom. In place of the little cloth bag with those odd mirrors embroidered onto it, which she usually sported over her shoulder, was a seriously expensive-looking leather number with an ostentatious clasp.

She was with her tweenage daughter, whose name I couldn't remember, a pretty little thing in shorts and a very petite T-shirt. As they stopped to buy a hot dog, I drew alongside them.

'Sandy?'

She twirled round and, after a moment's blank look, she recognised me.

'Lucy! How are you?' she roared, balancing her food precariously at arm's length so as not to risk getting ketchup on her top. She leaned forward and we kissed the air, the smell from her hot dog wafting up my nose.

'Fine, fine,' I replied. 'But what about you? We were worried – you just did a night flit.' I lowered my voice. 'Is everything okay? I mean, you look wonderful,' I lied, 'but the bank didn't foreclose or something awful like that, did it?'

For a moment I could have sworn she blushed, and her glance flicked over my shoulder – something Nat used to do when he was lying, and which had me instantly on the alert.

'No, no, thank God.' She laughed, then nudged me conspiratorially. 'Although it came bloody close at times! Nooo, I just had enough, you know.' She wrinkled her nose and shook her head and with a heavily ringed forefinger wiped up a bit of ketchup that had escaped from under the sausage.

'Oh, I see,' I said, not quite sure I understood. 'What did you do with the stock?'

'Well ...' Sandy seemed to stall a bit, concentrating hard on her fried onions.

'That bloke came and took it away, didn't he?' the daughter chipped in and her mother shot her a glance I couldn't read. Perhaps Sandy had been in more trouble than she wanted her daughter to know, so I thought I'd better change the subject quickly.

'You certainly look ... er, different. What are you doing now? Are you working?'

Sandy waved her hand airily. 'Just taking a bit of a break, you know. See what comes along. Er ... have you been on any rides?' As a group we started to wander down the avenue of stalls and attractions. The hum of generators thumped out from the lorries parked behind each ride, like some drum'n'bass beat and it was like an assault on my senses. It had been a stupid idea to come here and now all I wanted was to shake off Sandy and go and lie down in a darkened room. We passed some horrendous-looking contraption called Oblivion, which seemed to throw people into the air in a way that the human body was never designed to withstand, and the avenue opened out onto the grass area in front of the bandstand, around which was a small crowd. Sandy and I followed aimlessly as her daughter made for the group, and Sandy wittered on to me, through mouthfuls of greasy bun, about their new puppy that had attacked her new leather sofa. I was just beginning to compute the revelation that Sandy, with her vegan principles and hideous Scandinavian shoes, had a leather sofa and was eating a sausage, when the girl came back and tugged at her mother's arm.

'Come and look, Mum. It's some bloke telling fortunes. He

looks like a right Goth. Maybe he's a vampire like Edward in *Twilight*!'

I knew who she meant before I even looked up and was about to turn on my heel when Micah's voice boomed over towards us and, curiosity getting the better of me, I edged closer, hiding behind Sandy in case he spotted me. He was in full flow, even more theatrical than he had been the other night at the theatre, his fingers pressed to his temples as he 'focused' presumably – or whatever it is these sort of people do – and he was encouraging people to come forward.

'Wait, wait,' he intoned. 'I sense there is someone here who has a decision to make.' I tutted loudly. Well, that whittled it down to about a hundred per cent of the sample. 'It's about a car?' He shook his head quizzically, as though he wasn't sure he was on the right track.

'I'm thinking of buying a car!' a small woman at the front piped up.

'Are you? he asked meaningfully. I remember now that I yawned expansively at this point, and even started to move away a little bit as Sandy pushed forward towards the bandstand. 'You've looked at … ' he continued slowly, 'the Nissan.'

The small woman's mouth practically dropped open. 'How did you know that?'

'Lucky guess,' someone else muttered and I felt myself nod.

'A green one. But I think that the Ford is a better idea. The Nissan needs a new clutch.' The small woman clasped her hand to her mouth and her friend put her arm around her. Everyone muttered their amazement and Micah smiled, knowing that he'd convinced them. I'd never been very good at probability at school, but seeing as how those are two of the biggest selling makes in the country, it seemed to me he had a pretty good chance of guessing right. I pushed my way back through the gathering crowd.

'You!' Micah boomed and I turned sharply to see him pointing straight at Sandy, who blushed, nudging her daughter beside her and smiling broadly. The sparkly tiger T-shirt had obviously caught his eye. 'You're feeling guilty, aren't you?' Sandy blushed even deeper as everyone turned to look at her. 'It wasn't like you to do a thing like that, was it?' Sandy sort of shrugged, and looked uncomfortable as her daughter muttered something. 'Don't feel too bad about the others,' he went on, his hand out to her. 'They'll be all right. And by the way, you're not the only one who's succumbed, but think about where your loyalties lie.' Sandy stopped smiling at this but I could only see the side of her face from where I was. I couldn't imagine what Micah was talking about, but something in Sandy's expression suggested she knew exactly. But then, we've all got a guilty secret somewhere. I still wasn't convinced at this point and was about to move away again when he turned violently towards the rides on the other side of the grass and shouted so loud we all jumped.

'Stop it! Get them off!'

For a moment no one reacted. The noise from the fair was too loud – and if he was going for a spectacular effect then it had fallen flat – but in one leap he was over the metal railings of the bandstand and running, his long coat flowing out behind him, towards the operator of the Oblivion ride who was tucked inside his booth. The whirling mechanical arms of the ride slashed through the air to the accompaniment of the excited screams of the teenagers on it. Micah reached in and grabbed the man's arm and shouted something we couldn't hear. Everyone at the bandstand was transfixed as the man tried to shake him off, angry, mouthing something abusive, but Micah was undeterred and we could make out his arm trying to reach further into the booth towards the controls before he was forcibly pushed away. He staggered back just as a sudden bang followed by a gut-wrenching screech rang out from the mechanism. I'm not quite sure what happened next – people were rushing towards the ride and blocked my view – but the ride seemed to falter then slow and stop in mid-air, and the screams of enjoyment turned to screams of fear.

The operator, who must have pushed some sort of emergency stop, rushed out, his face a picture of panic, and looked up, as we all did. One of the arms of the ride was suspended at an angle thirty feet up, like a hideously broken limb, the metal sheered and broken as if a joint had snapped, and from a seat-pod hung a young girl in a yellow T-shirt held in place only by her companion who was clutching on to her desperately.

Pandemonium broke out, Micah's warning now forgotten as emergency services were called on mobile phones, and people rushed forward trying to help. Forgotten by everyone but me. My movements are a bit hazy now, but I practically walked backwards out of the park, my heart thudding and not out of fear for the girl hanging on for dear life to the broken ride.

As I wandered up the road, back towards safety and home, I was muttering to myself out loud. I couldn't dismiss all this any longer, couldn't put it down to coincidence, or luck or fluke, or educated guess. Micah, somehow, had known that accident was about to happen. He'd known with utter certainty. 'How could he?' I almost gasped. 'How could he, unless he really can see the future?'

Chapter Seven

Looking back now, I'm not even sure there was any pattern to my thoughts for the rest of that day. For a good hour after I got home I could hear the sound of emergency vehicles bombing towards the park, and it even made the local news on the radio, which I'd turned on, unable to bear the silence in the flat any longer. The girl was all right, which of course I should have been relieved about, but all I could focus on was the newsreader's comment about 'the remarkable quick-thinking of a member of the public' who'd been asked to come forward. Clearly Micah had scarpered as soon as the ride was stopped.

I played mental ping-pong with myself, but what's strange is that the panic receded and my thinking had a curious clarity about it, as if some sort of defence mechanism had taken over. As I saw it, I had two choices. Either I could curl up in misery and climb in a hole until next Friday or I could make something of the time. *Carpet Deum*, as our old cleaner used to say so innocently. Seize the day. Perhaps I should do something wonderful and worthy – devote my last remaining days to good works and the betterment of mankind.

But it took something as straightforward as a song to focus my head in the end. As I shuffled into the kitchen, knowing I had to eat something even though I wasn't faintly hungry, the upbeat sound of Van Halen's *Jump* came out of the radio. I'd always loved the track – it reminded me of being young, a carefree teenager with my mates, when all we had to think about was ourselves and the fun we were going to have. Turning up the volume, a sensation bubbled up in me – a delicious realisation that once I was six feet under a headstone in the cemetery, it wouldn't matter what I'd done in my last few days. And what could I really achieve that would better the world? What I needed to do was settle my own scores and put my own house in order – and looking at the mess in the flat, that wasn't just a metaphor.

Lucy Streeter needed to be brave enough to face the world on her own terms – even if it was only for a week.

So, I thought, as I mechanically unloaded the laundry from the washing machine and draped my knickers over the drying rack, what are you supposed to do on the first day of the rest of your life? My mum always says that the best thing to do if you don't know where to start is to make a list. So, after carrying the drying rack out into the sunshine, I seated myself at the small garden table on the tiny lawn, got out my notebook and wrote, slowly, in big loopy letters:

Lucy's List

A blank page – how symbolic! How uncomfortably close to the truth. Just to fill up some of the space, I doodled around the title – rainbows, monkey faces, little houses with smoke rising from crooked chimneys, seagulls. Then stopped, embarrassed. It looked like an adolescent girl's scribble on a textbook – and I'd done more than my share of that in that last summer at school, when I was mooning over Neil and trying my name out with his: Lucy Bartlett, over and over again, swathed in hearts and flowers. I stopped and tutted.

Where to start? Given how short time was, there was plenty I wouldn't manage – those 1,000 things-to-do-before-you-die dreams: snorkelling off a Pacific island; seeing the Northern

Lights; ever getting the zip done up on those heavenly chocolate-suede trousers I'd fallen for in the January sales – none of those would happen now. I split the page in two and headed one column, 'Things to Achieve'; the other, 'Things to Put Right', then nibbled on the end of my pencil. And it hit me powerfully – what was the point of trying to live a healthy, puritan life when it seemed I wouldn't have an old age ahead of me?

Throw out muesli and all worthy foods

This was more like it. I almost smiled. No more low-fat yogurt. I was going out on clotted cream and high cholesterol. Next up:

Buy loads of cherries

I'd never allowed myself to buy them, so appalled by the price, but why not blow some cash now on a couple of punnets' worth?

Eat enough chocolate buttons to make myself sick

I wrote that with a flourish. Not very sensible but wasn't that the idea? I sat back in my seat. So far I was going to end my days fat and sick. What else could I do that was depraved?

Be more spontaneous

Even as I added it, I was quite sure that wasn't a very spontaneous thing to write but I put it anyway, just to remind myself. After all, everything was emphatically now or never.

Rent 9½ Weeks on DVD

A bit tame, I know, but I'd always wanted to see it and had

been too embarrassed in the video store, in case they thought I was some sex-starved, middle-aged woman. Didn't really matter any more. Then I scratched that out and wrote *Porn Flick*. Might as well go for the whole shag-fest. Which reminded me of knickers.

Buy outrageous underwear

I'd been too embarrassed to ever buy myself one of those frothy sets. It had always seemed a little keen, if not desperate, and nothing in my drawer matched. I'd wear my new lingerie on Friday so that whatever happened I'd be in my best bra and knicks. I then added *Killer Heels* to the list. The higher the better.

HAVE SOME SEX

I wrote that in big letters. It was perfectly true: I hadn't had sex – not even a fumble or a snog – for absolutely ages. And I wasn't sure a vibrator counted. I tried to think back. The last time it had been the real thing was with Owen. But how long ago was that? I winced as I realised it had been over eighteen months since we parted – not dramatically, just slightly bored with each other. And it hadn't been all that great even when we were together. A relationship we'd fallen into without a reason not to – two lonely people paired up at a supper party. The sex had been functional and workaday – and about as mutually satisfying as our relationship. He gamely talked dirty – I always suspected he thought he ought to – but couldn't stop himself from clearing his throat self-consciously before every carefully worded phrase.

Sex. Now, how was I going to set about getting some of that? There were no likely candidates, except perhaps Richard!

I smiled to myself – not such a horrific prospect, come to think of it. But how would his girlfriend take it? Then I vaguely toyed with the idea of paying for it; how I'd go about finding an escort agency that provided such things. If I could do that, I could certainly rent a porn flick.

I stretched and thought about what else to add. I looked back at the list. There was nothing earth-shattering there and, except for the sex, I could probably manage all of it. Had I been too tame, too restrained? But there was no time left to climb Kilimanjaro. Perhaps I'd be better off with the 'Things to Put Right' column instead; I knew exactly what would go at the top of that one.

Rubbish in street – find out who's dumping it and get them to stop
Mrs No-Buy in the shop – remind her I'm not there for her entertainment but to make a living
Make the old bag in the chip shop smile

Now that would be a tough one. We'd been going in there for years on nights when I couldn't be bothered to cook or had caved in to Nat's pleas, and I must have spent hundreds of pounds on her soggy offerings, but the woman had never even feigned recognition of me or been nice to Nat, even when he was at his cutest. Over the years we'd set a running joke between us as to who could make her face crack. I was determined not to die before I'd won that one.

I was liking this. I could be like Zorro or Batman, only without the masks. Righting wrongs and seeking out injustice. Is it a bird? Is it a plane? No, it's Lucy Streeter.

Then I added some sensible stuff about putting my affairs in order and sorting thing out so Nat wouldn't have to – that would mean disposing of my huge stockpile of paperbacks and my collection of gorgeous shoes that were too uncomfortable to wear. I drove away a creeping image of Nat's desolation at my death by writing as quickly as I could. Then I added the two items of unfinished business. The issues that I'd been avoiding for years but that had been trying to push their way to the forefront of my mind:

Make peace with Dad

I put a line under that. I didn't want to leave without trying to put things right between us so he didn't remember me as his big disappointment. Then I added the other one:

Make contact with Neil

Chapter Eight

I wasn't sure where that conviction had come from, but I knew as I wrote it that I wanted Nat to know the parent he'd been missing all this time. If he was going to lose me, then the least he deserved was his father and the truth.

What I also wasn't sure of was where to begin with my search. The last time I had seen Neil had been an excruciating moment on Regent Street in town, so long ago that Nat had been a toddler in a pushchair. It must have been late summer, and I was with my mother, who was distracted by something in a shop window. I'd stopped, blocking the pavement, and had looked up to see Neil standing there in front of me. We were suspended for a moment looking at each other, then he looked down at Nat and back up at me. He hadn't changed. The hair was longer and wilder, but he still looked scruffy in greasy over-alls, his grimy hands ingrained with oil. And he still looked like trouble, but he felt like a stranger, not the father of the precious child in the pushchair. In fact, he didn't look old enough to be a father at all. Thinking about it later, it was very odd that we didn't utter a word and our son just gazed up at the two of us, but I do remember the astonished expression on Neil's face, as if he had forgotten we existed. After a while, he sidestepped us and walked on and the awkward moment passed. My mother didn't see him and I didn't even mention it.

That had been twenty-one years ago.

I had heard the odd thing about him since through school-friends I bumped into in town – that he'd been in a band, that he'd flunked out of college, that he was working as a car mechanic in Whitnash – but that was all years ago. The phone book wasn't very helpful. I even tried Facebook but wasn't convinced that it was Neil's scene, so, for want of anything else to do and not knowing where else to start, I got into the car and headed for Warwick.

The roads are so familiar to me, but each time I head down them I see the houses and buildings I have known all my life being shrouded by more and more new housing and develop-ment. These familiar old places – houses where schoolfriends like Kate had grown up – now peep out from beside new executive developments, their gardens more mature and their brickwork mellower. As I drove, I could see myself walking home from school or cycling into town to the cinema, past the postbox that had been there for ever and over the canal bridge. Of course, the cycling and the walk home from school had stopped as soon as I was pregnant.

I hadn't even realised that I was, too stupid to clock the implication of missed periods and nausea, and was about eight weeks' gone before I finally bought a test. Kate had sat with me and held my hand as I shook with panic at the result and the thought of the future and, as we walked round and round the park in an unseeing terror, it had been Kate who had encour-aged me to talk to my mum.

'You're not going to be able to hide it for long and if you ...' We were both too frightened to mention the elephant in the corner – the prospect of an abortion. That was something that 'loose' girls had done, girls we read about in magazines or heard about on the grapevine, and I hadn't thought of myself like that. I was a private-school girl and private-school girls didn't get into trouble.

'Oh, bloody hell, Luce,' Mum had said and, predictably, she had taken me in her arms. 'What do you want to do?'

I didn't know, but I did know that I couldn't face Dad. A daughter up the duff at seventeen was not in his game plan, it wasn't why he'd struggled to educate us at the 'right' school and it wasn't going to go down well at the golf club. My mother, as always, knew how best to handle him. How he would survive without her as his filter, his moderating influence, doesn't bear thinking about. Calm and serene, she has always known how to handle his snobbery and his social climbing, and it was she who knew that taking him for a walk by the river with Fred, our unimaginatively named basset-hound, was the best scenario in which to drop the bombshell.

I pulled up outside our house. It belonged to someone else now – my parents had downsized to Archery Fields some years ago – and the new owners had improved it considerably with UPVC windows and flash gates, but my bedroom window just to the right above the front door would always be my bedroom window whoever lived there. I could feel tears pricking behind my eyes. It was in there that I had cowered on my bed waiting for them to return from the walk and, as I heard their footsteps on the gravel and the front door opening, I had thought I was going to vomit from fear.

By the time his footsteps had come to the top of the stairs I was beside myself, even pathetically contemplating hiding in the wardrobe, but he gently opened the door and stood there in the doorway, his expression unreadable.

'You silly, silly girl,' he said and I held my breath. Then he did the last thing I imagined he would, he put out his arms and I ran into them and cried until I was exhausted.

I was his little girl and I'd gone and got myself pregnant.

I suppose knowing your daughter is sexually active must be agony for any father – I tend to push that side of Nat's life into some box in my head marked 'don't go there' – and I guess now I can sympathise with Dad to some extent, but it wasn't as straightforward as that then. Despite the touching scene in my bedroom he couldn't let it go and, throughout the pregnancy, throughout the time when the school was told and, in a terrifying interview in the head's study when it was decided I should leave, he would wait until we were alone and make little snide comments about my downfall. About why I'd let 'that boy' do that to me, perhaps out of some hope that I hadn't been a willing party to the conception.

He'd even insisted on checking over the letter he urged me to write to Neil. Thinking back, he virtually dictated it, using words I never would and which Neil probably never understood, but which conveyed in no uncertain terms that Neil would not be expected to be involved in the baby's upbringing or to provide any child support – which must have come as a relief. When Nat finally arrived in the world after a long, excruciating labour, during which I nearly broke my mother's hand at each contraction, I only just managed to beat my father to registering his birth because I knew he would leave Neil's name off the certificate. Up and about sooner than I should have been, still hobbling from the sting of the stitches, I made it my business to get down to the registrar's office and put Neil's name firmly in the right box.

I sighed now. Dad had been so dominating, particularly in those early years, and I could see now that I'd been a coward, caving in to him, cowed under the weight of his disapproval. Did he have any idea how he had made me feel? That was a conversation I might never have now. Not with the little time I had left. But it still felt like unfinished business. In the meantime, I had to find Neil.

I pulled away from the house and headed up towards town, past Warwick Castle – the view from the bridge as breathtaking as ever. We'd 'done' the castle on numerous school trips – I knew the place backwards and spent many happy hours with Nat in the grounds when he was little. Friends had been supportive at first – especially when he was born. Okay, okay, I know we are all biased, but truly he was a beautiful baby, as dark as his father but with my mother's cornflower-blue eyes, and girlfriends like Kate had cooed, playing dollies with him until they got bored. Then, as he got bigger and more demanding, I was no fun because I couldn't come out to play. I was set up in a little one-bed flat down the road from my parents – my father wouldn't have us in the house any more, though he helped me with the rent, and Mum would babysit, of course, positively encouraging me to go out with mates. But as the evenings spent in dreary pubs or bars wore on, with everyone giggling and on the pull, I'd find less and less to talk to them about. I was out of the loop on school gossip anyway, and I'd miss Nat so much that I'd escape off home early.

How ironic that after a degree and a short career as a lawyer, Kate is now the Chelsea-tractor-driving mother of three, living in the Home Counties and sitting on the sidelines at swimming galas with her stopwatch, being the all-round über mummy. We don't see each other any more but chat occasionally on the phone, always promising to meet up and never actually making a plan, but I still tease her about it. About how she has made a career out of her children, and she teases me back saying at least she didn't have a baby instead of A levels. She's right, of course, and the barb hurts a bit – but I would not have swapped Nat for anything. Not even a social life, discos and snogging. And besides, the richer she has become – her husband being something important in industrial design – the more delighted I am that I made her Nat's godmother! She blissfully provided the treats that I couldn't and I have to admit that I accepted her largesse gratefully over the years.

I knew I was making my way to Morrison Road before I really admitted it to myself. I hadn't been there very often – a couple of times with Neil during our short relationship when he went home to change and come out again, slamming the front door behind him. So my contact with his parents had been brief, but I'd liked his mum. Not so much his dad, who couldn't contain his disdain for me, the posh girl. How well he would have got on with my father; how ironic that they should have so much in common – intolerance of anyone from another class or background. The only difference – his father thought Arthur Scargill should be canonised and my dad thought Thatcher was a gift from God.

But Neil's mother had a kind face and tried to make conversation with me on the two or three occasions I had stood in the hall during that short summer in my silly pink boots and leg warmers, awkwardly clutching my cardigan, waiting for Neil to get his uniform off so we could go to the park. I'd not seen her since the day of the awful tea party – I use the term loosely – when my mother, showing uncharacteristic insistence that we go, had driven me round to their house with newborn Nat. I'd been dead against it, and my father would have been apoplectic had he known, but very gently she'd reminded me how she would feel if my brother Chris had fathered a child, and she hadn't had the opportunity to meet it.

'He may not have been planned, darling,' she said, as we drove towards Morrison Road, 'but he is still their grandchild and Neil's son. It's only fair.'

And so we'd sat in their small front room with Nat gurgling in his car seat aged just a few weeks. Neil's father had barely looked at him; Neil had sat on the sofa staring down at the floor and not speaking. His mother had rocked the car seat, gently muttering kind words to Nat who had gazed at her in fascination as we sipped our milky tea and failed to find anything to say. His mother asked quietly if she could hold him, and the palaver of getting him out of his car seat and her rocking him had occupied a few moments until we could think of an excuse to leave.

My mother and I had driven away, letting out the breath we hadn't realised we had been holding, and that was the end of it, except for the tiny matinée jacket crocheted with exquisite care and wrapped in tissue that Neil's mother had almost furtively pressed into my hand as we left and which is still packed away in a drawer here in the flat. The visit was never mentioned – our little secret – but my father had been right on one thing: there was little point in chasing for maintenance. Neil had been at college on an apprenticeship and earning nothing, so there was no need to make contact after that, and I never went back to Morrison Road. Until now.

I pulled into a parking space behind a Ford Fiesta that was being washed by a man in a vest and sports shorts. The Bartletts' house was on the other side of the road, but I had no idea if they still lived there. It didn't seem to have changed much – a small post-war semi with the same cherry tree, only considerably bigger now, in the small front garden. But of course the car on the drive was different, as it would be. Plucking up courage, I got out of my car and locked it, then just stood there not really knowing what to do.

'Can I help, love?' The car washer stopped and let the sponge in his hand drip into the bucket as he looked me up and down.

'I was wondering,' I swallowed, 'do the Bartletts still live there?' I nodded towards the house opposite.

'Sure do. Been there for ages, I think – though I've only had my place for five years.'

I looked back at the house, but I couldn't see any movement behind the windows.

'At least *she* does. He passed on a couple of years back. The fags caught up with him, I think. Difficult old bugger he was. Yes, she lives there on her own now.'

I felt a wave of relief that I wouldn't have to confront him, then chided myself: he'd been Nat's grandfather, for what it was worth. At that moment I almost chickened out and got back into the car, but I wouldn't get another chance to come back. Time was something I might not have so, steeling myself, I thanked the Fiesta man and crossed the road.

Someone was mowing the small patch of grass in the garden next door and cars were noisily passing up the road so when I rang the bell, I couldn't hear any footsteps approaching until the door opened and there she stood. Greyer, plumper, more wrinkled but unchanged really – like one of those 'how you'll look in twenty years' computer mock-ups you see on TV.

She looked hard at me.

'Hello. I don't suppose you remember me. I'm—'

'I know exactly who you are,' she said suspiciously but not unkindly, and leaned against the door frame, crossing her arms, a small smile on her lips. 'What brings you here after all this time?'

'I was wondering ... I wondered if ...'

She opened the door wider. 'Come on in. There's no point in standing there.' I followed her short, wide frame down the hall. Even after twenty years the smell was still the same. A bit musty but disguised with air fresheners. The same picture of a horse was on the wall at the bottom of the stairs. Only the flowery carpet had been replaced with a plain one.

She led me through to the front room, which hadn't changed much either, and bustled off to make tea. As she clinked cups in the kitchen next door, I took in the furniture, the old TV, and a half-read thriller from the library left open on the table beside her chair.

'You're looking well, dear,' she said wheezily, putting down the tray and pouring me a cup. 'S'pose you're married now with a brood?'

'Er, no, I'm not actually. Just me and Nat.'

She looked up in surprise. 'A pretty girl like you?'

'I'm more than happy with my boy.'

She sat down heavily and sighed, before taking a sip from her cup. There was an awkward silence.

Eventually, she asked quietly, 'Will you tell me how he is?'

We talked for half an hour or so; or rather I spoke and she, with her head on one side, listened. She was polite, greedy for information about Nat; and the more I talked the more I enjoyed it. Apart from my parents and my brother, this family were the closest blood relatives Nat had, and I was surprised by how much I wanted to tell her about her grandson, about how well he'd done at school, how he'd broken his leg in year seven, won the drama prize in year nine, decided to go to university – something none of us had managed. Luckily I had a photo of him in my handbag taken on the beach at Newquay a couple of years before. She almost stroked it.

'He's got your smile,' she said, tactfully perhaps not making any reference to any likeness he might have to Neil. 'He's a fine boy.' She handed the photo back and didn't say anything for a moment, twisting her wedding ring round and round on her plump fingers. 'I *have* seen you a few times, actually,' she said eventually, sheepish at the admission. 'I saw you in the park quite often. I'd watch you playing with Nat. I went there sometimes, hoping you'd be there in the afternoons.'

I was amazed. 'Really? You should have come to say hello.'

'I couldn't do that, dear. With Neil not being involved and that. It wouldn't be right.'

I supposed she was referring to the letter and let it pass.

'Mrs Bartlett,' I blurted eventually, 'I need to see Neil. It's not about money or anything,' I added quickly. 'I just need to talk to him. Could you give me his phone number?'

'Is everything all right?' She looked alarmed.

'Um, yes,' I said slowly. 'I just need a brief chat with him.' How long would it take to explain to him that, after twenty-two years, I suddenly wanted him to know about his son? 'I mean, does he live close by?' It suddenly struck me that he might have emigrated for all I knew.

'Of course, yes.' She stood up slowly, a bit wobbly in her pins, and picked up a business card from the ugly sideboard. 'He lives in Leamington. Here's his number.'

Grange Motors, it said in a bold typeface. The premises were in a part of Leamington I didn't know at all, but from the card it looked respectable.

'He's done quite well for himself in the end.' She chuckled and I looked at her curiously. 'You might want to rethink that money thing!'

I smiled too and stood up to give her a warm hug. She smelt of cheap talc.

'Come back and see me again, won't you, dear?' she said gently and I could only nod, not trusting myself to speak.

I drove as far as the car park at the station and sat flicking the card between my fingers for an age, before I eventually pulled out my phone and tapped in the numbers, my fingers shaking.

It rang for a while and I almost pressed cancel when a woman answered brightly. 'Grange Motors. Can I help you?'

I swallowed. 'Is Mr Bartlett there, please?'

'I'll just see. Who's calling?'

'It's a customer. He, er … doesn't know me.' Or not any more.

'Okay,' she didn't sound sure and I could hear muffled talk

as she put her hand over the receiver, then a click as the phone was transferred.

My heart pounded as he answered. 'Neil Bartlett. Can I help you?' His voice was deeper, the accent if anything a bit stronger.

'Neil. It's Lucy. Lucy Streeter.'

Chapter Nine

I didn't sleep well that night. I had trouble dropping off in the first place and I kept waking up gasping for breath as though I'd been running. It was incredibly unpleasant. At one point, I even wondered if I should call a doctor or go to A&E, but then I remembered that Micah had said Friday and, for the first time, it was strangely reassuring. It never seemed to cool down during the night and when I woke, hot, cross and early, it felt as if a giant tea cosy had been dropped over the town. Even though I'd left the windows wide open during the night, I still felt stifled. There didn't seem to be a hint of wind and the sky, when I peered out, was a flawless blue. A cool shower and a quick hair-wash perked me up, but I still felt on edge. I hated to admit it to myself, but I think the conversation with Neil, brief though it was, had affected me.

He'd seemed surprisingly unsurprised to hear from me, almost as though it was a call he'd been expecting. But, then, he always was a cool customer. Almost always. I remembered a few unguarded moments and the look in his eyes when we lay side by side after the very few occasions we'd had inexpert teenage sex. It was all so long ago, and I was a completely different person now. Our relationship had been so immature and inadequate – two teenagers exploring sex amateurishly – and neither of us saying anything faintly romantic to each other. In that department he certainly wasn't Heathcliff. I can still remember his fingers fumbling in my knickers rather painfully. He must have learnt the basics from a magazine and we certainly didn't have the time or the tenderness to refine our techniques.

We'd arranged to meet up on Wednesday – tomorrow – and I could tell by his voice he was understandably curious about why I was in such a hurry to see him after all this time, but he hadn't asked why.

'I'll move a couple of appointments to fit round you,' he said, making himself sound important, and we'd ended the call abruptly and awkwardly. But I couldn't help wondering how things would go when we finally saw each other. I'd spent quite a lot of time, over the years, wondering about him and wondering if he was wondering about me. And I was going to find out soon.

Wearing only my bra and knickers, I opened my wardrobe and glared at the contents. It was stuffed with my usual anonymous uniform of yoga pants or crops, T-shirts, V-necked jumpers, fleeces baggy and dark. Newer items were all mixed in with the old, faded stuff that had seen better days. At that moment my only priority was to be cool, so I reached in more or less at random and pulled out a pair of long black linen shorts and a loose button-through shirt in a soft green. With my hair pulled back in a scrunchy, I was comfortable but not even my best friends would have described me as smart. In fact, one of them – a certain Richard – would probably tell me I looked like a dodgy Scout master. The thought of his likely reaction almost made me laugh, despite my hot and cranky mood. As if I'd ever dress to impress him! But, as I closed the wardrobe door, it did occur to me that maybe I should get rid of some of the excess so that when someone – Tam? Mum? – came to empty the flat they wouldn't have armfuls to take to the charity shop. How odd that would be. I shuddered at the thought. That felt too final.

I laced espadrilles onto my feet, and checked myself very quickly in the cheval mirror in the corner which I used more for hanging clothes on than for self-scrutiny. The person who looked back at me seemed younger than my thirty-nine years and perhaps a little edgier than usual – some of my anxiety seemed to be spilling over into my face – and I turned away quickly. I started to make myself a cup of tea but when I checked the milk in the fridge, it had gone off so I switched off the kettle and tipped the coagulating curds down the drain and rinsed out the bottle for recycling. Why was I bothering saving the planet now?

It was still early but I didn't feel like hanging around waiting for the weather to get even hotter, so I set off for the shop, tealess and unsettled. As I went out onto the Warwick Road, I'd have murdered for a drink. I was just rounding the corner when I saw a car pull up just along the road where the rubbish was always dumped. A tall, well-dressed man got out, looked around, then opened his boot and took out a black bin bag. Ha! Caught in the act! As I came closer, he dropped it on the pavement then went back for another. I put on a burst of speed and, by the time he'd straightened up and looked round again, he was virtually face to face with me, standing right next to the first bag he'd dumped.

He jumped, which was gratifying. Up close, he didn't look so well dressed. His shirt was creased and a little bit worn at the collar and he was sweating, his face shiny and high-coloured. He forced a smile. 'You gave me a start, there. Where did you come out of?'

'I come this way every day, but later on usually. After you've dumped your rubbish and gone,' I blurted, a little amazed at my bravery and trying to keep the tremor out of my voice.

He licked his lips and tried to smile. 'Sorry, love. Don't know what you mean. Dumped what?'

Normally, I wouldn't have started on him. Normally, I'd have been too worried about what he'd say, what he'd think. About what would happen if I saw him again. But today, with absolutely nothing to lose, I found myself ready for a fight. Though my mouth was dry, I put my hands on my hips, looked down with exaggerated attention at the bin-bag in his hands and the one he'd just dumped, then back at him.

'That's what I mean. That bag I just watched you dump. The bag you're just about to dump. The crap you leave every week on the street I have to walk down every day, picking my way round your rubbish because you can't be bothered to dispose of it properly. *That's* what I mean.'

He looked around, his eyes flicking up and down the street. I suspect he was actually hoping someone would turn up to save him from the crazy woman. 'I don't know what you mean. I've never been here before in my life.' He swapped the bag into his other hand and started to put it back into the boot of his car. 'That one's not mine. It's got nothing to do with me.' He nodded at the other bag wilting on the pavement.

I scented victory along with the stench of his smelly rubbish – and I wasn't going to give way now. So I pushed my luck. 'Well, as a matter of fact, there are other people on this street – shopkeepers, residents – who've taken on the unpleasant task of going through your trash and they found out your name and where you live, so I suggest you take that other bag away, too. The tip will be open in an hour or so and you can dispose of it there. Unless you want it emptied all over your front door step at home, that is?'

He grabbed the other bag and placed it, dripping something unspeakable, back into the boot of his car. He was muttering under his breath and wouldn't meet my eye and, as he drove away, screeching round the corner, I let out a whoop of triumph, my heart beating fast with fear and elation. I stepped carefully over the stinking trickle the bag had left behind and made my way to the Deli. This called for a celebration!

Sally was alone when I arrived, but it was before their busy time and there were only two men in there, both sitting on their own. She smiled, her eyes crinkling up at the corners the way they did when she was really pleased. 'You're early and you look like you mean it! What's the occasion? Or … are you a dirty stop-out on the way back from a night of depravity?'

One of the customers glanced up and stared at me, appraising me so blatantly that Sally and I burst out laughing. 'No occasion,' I told her. 'And no, I haven't been out all night,' I said slightly louder and stared at the man who'd been giving me the once-over. He smiled sheepishly and took a hurried swig of tea. I was starting to enjoy this. Something had definitely shifted in my attitude – a devil-may-care streak was bubbling to the surface – and people were responding. What a shame I only had a few days to enjoy it.

I was about to order my usual; in fact, I think Sally had even started steaming the skimmed milk, when I said, 'Sod it! Let's go for broke. Can I have one of those iced coffees with whipped cream on top and a lemon poppy seed muffin – that one, with all the icing?'

'Your very specific wish is my command,' Sally laughed. 'Why don't you have a seat for a change and I'll bring it over? There's something about you today that means business.'

So she saw it, too. I didn't pursue it, though, because Richard came in as I was turning away from the counter. He stopped in his tracks and raked his hand back through his hair, which I noticed was still wet from the shower. He looked me up and down in exaggerated surprise, followed me over to the table and sat down. 'And to what do we owe the pleasure of a visit at this ungodly hour? Are you coming to work, or on your way home after a night … er … camping? Dib dib.'

Ha! I'd been bang on. I swatted at him with a napkin. I could feel the mood lifting in response to his teasing – and to the heavenly iced coffee and muffin than Sally brought over to the table. He reached across and felt my forehead with his warm hand. 'Just checking,' he teased. 'What's brought on this uncharacteristic pleasure-seeking? What of the skinny lattes of yore? Are you celebrating?'

Well, I wasn't going to tell him, was I? I think I laughed a bit self-consciously. 'Nothing! Can't a girl give herself over to indulgence once in a while?'

'A girl most certainly can! In fact, I wish a girl would rather more. I might even drag you down to the boat next weekend if you're feeling reckless?'

'I er …' I stalled.

He shrugged quickly. 'Suit yourself. Oh well, must get on. That sister of mine – you know what a slave-driver she is.' He heaved himself up and stretched.

I felt awkward now, as if I'd hurt his feelings, but how could I have explained about Micah? Richard would have roared with laughter at my stupidity and crass gullibility. Something in me wished he's stayed and, feeling inexplicably disappointed, I picked up my half-finished drink and my muffin. 'Think I'll go and open up now, actually. Can you tell Sal I'll bring the glass back later?'

He nodded and I picked up my stuff and legged it. Richard's teasing had made me feel a bit self-conscious and I needed the solitude of the shop to compose myself again. But I wasn't alone for long.

It wasn't much after half nine and I was still drinking my iced coffee in the back room when the door jangled. 'Hello? Are you open?'

I swallowed and called out, 'Yes, I'll be with you in a moment.' And I stood up and smoothed the crumpled shorts over my thighs and went through. Well, I think my face must have fallen because it was Mrs No-Buy and she looked quite surprised.

'Hello – I was just passing and—'

'Oh, hello, again.' I smiled resignedly. 'Come in to try on a few things, have you?' I hadn't the energy to be cross.

'Well ...'

I shrugged. 'Help yourself. Nothing much has changed since the last time you were in. Or the time before that.'

'No, no,' she was quick to reassure. 'You always have such lovely things.'

Her face was so contrite and her enthusiasm so genuine that I couldn't resist asking her outright: 'Please don't take this the wrong way, but you seem to come in so often, and yet you never buy anything.' I noticed she blushed slightly. 'Is it the price that's the problem?' I asked gently. I could empathise with that. 'I'm sure we could come to some arrangement if there is something you particularly wanted. Or is it that you just like trying things on? I don't mind,' I lied hastily, 'but I was just wondering, that's all.'

She was blinking fast, staring at me in confusion, and suddenly I was worried I'd embarrassed her. I put my hands up and backed away. 'I'll be out the back if you need me.' I gave her a quick smile and left her to it, fairly confident that I'd hear the door open and close firmly behind her. In fact, I'd just licked my finger and was using it to pick up the last crumbs of my muffin when I heard her clear her throat. She'd come into the back room and was standing in the doorway with a pile of garments in her arms. 'I'll take these, please.'

Now I really felt bad. 'You don't have to. I was only ... I don't know. Look, I'm sorry – I'm in a funny mood at the moment. Really, if you don't want—'

'But I do. I do want them. I've wanted all of them all along but it's just so hard to choose. I'm terribly indecisive, you see.' She shrugged. 'But what you said sort of made me think. You're right. I want them but I keep putting it off. But what's the point in waiting?'

'You and me both.' I smiled ruefully and followed her over to the till, where I started ringing up the selection of separates she'd chosen – well over four hundred pounds' worth. Cash clearly wasn't the issue! 'It's true, isn't it?' I said thoughtfully. 'What *is* the point in putting things off? Because what are we waiting for? For everything to be just right? Cos that will never happen.' I separated the linen vests and full silk skirt with sheets of tissue and slipped them into my stiff bags.

She handed over her credit card and smiled sadly. 'You're very wise for one so young. I suppose you have to be – having your own shop and everything. I wish I had your confidence.' She sighed. 'At least I have your lovely clothes now, and perhaps some of your positive attitude will rub off on me. Thank you, dear. I'll be back.'

She picked up her bags and walked out of the shop. I stood watching her walk down the street. What was going on? Confidence? Me? Standing here in crumpled linen looking like Baden-Powell? I must be exuding something I couldn't see myself. I peered in the shop mirror just to make sure, but no. Same old Lucy Streeter, with no outward changes, except a glint of pleasure in my eye and four hundred quid in my till.

Tuesday nights were, without fail, supper with Mum and Dad. I'd go to their house on Sunday's too sometimes, but often Dad's golf or Nat's plans got in the way, and Monday was Mum's book club night, so Tuesday night it was. It was one of those odd family traditions that make up the framework of one's week. When Nat was younger, Mum could feel assured that I'd had at least one sensible, home-cooked meal in the week, and Nat could revel in the attention his doting grand-parents lavished upon him. I could sit in one of their overstuffed armchairs and indulge in a little nap, confident that someone else was doing the thinking, and my dad could play with Nat, enjoying the good fortune of having another little boy to play trains with. He really was a model grandfather. Later on he'd help him with algebra homework, but he could also indulge in his second favourite pastime: making little digs at me. Nothing overt, nothing I could call him on, just a drip, drip of asides that made the atmosphere tense.

As I changed out of my linen shorts into a cool shift dress, getting ready to head down to Archery Fields, I could barely believe that this might be the last time I'd ever go round there. I tried not to imagine Mum and Dad alone and, instead, focused on making the evening normal for them so, when I did get hit by the proverbial steamroller on Friday, they would at least have a happy memory to cling to. I vowed to steer clear of controversial subjects and not to react badly whatever provoca-tion Dad threw at me.

It was just before half past seven when I arrived at their front door, only slightly earlier than usual. On impulse I'd stopped off at the supermarket to get some flowers and some of Dad's favourite chocolate-covered nuts. Mum opened the door, as usual, wiping her hands on a tea towel, her face a little red from the steamy kitchen.

'Hello, love. You're nice and early. Oh, are those for me? They're lovely but you shouldn't have ...' She cast around, as if slightly thrown by this unexpected and slightly inconvenient gift.

'It's all right, Mum. I'll sort them.' I laid them on the work surface and set about finding scissors and a suitable vase. I peeped at her as she went through the familiar routine, saving the vegetable water to make gravy. Sensible, careful, caring. Just the way she'd always been. I trimmed the stems off the lilies and dropped them haphazardly into a tall, heavy vase she didn't use much.

'They're lovely, dear. Put them in the hall, would you? And go and have a read of the papers for ten minutes.'

'Isn't there anything I can do to help?' There never was – she didn't want or need intervention in the kitchen but I went through the motions every week.

She patted me on the cheek. 'No, thanks. You look tired, dear. Go and chat to your father.'

I left her to it and went into the long front room that served as a sitting room and dining room – a concession to retired living to which my dad had never really reconciled himself. As usual, he'd laid the table and put out the wine and that, as far as he was concerned, would be it until he sat down to eat. After all, the *Telegraph* wouldn't read itself and he was busy tutting and exclaiming over infractions and wrongdoings the world over, reading out bits of news to my mum that she couldn't hear out in the kitchen.

'Lucy! Come and sit down. Can I get you a little snifter?' He levered himself up out of his armchair and over to the drinks' cabinet and I noticed a slight stiffness in his movements. Why had I never seen that before? Was it new or was I just looking more carefully?

'The usual?' he asked over his shoulder.

Without waiting for a reply, he poured out a measure of Gordon's into one of the lead crystal glasses he had been presented with when he retired. Two – never three – lumps of ice and a slice of lemon. I would rather have had a glass of wine, but that would have thrown him so I let it go.

We stuck to issues like the weather and the cricket until Mum came through with the vegetable dishes and I jumped up to help her. During supper, which was delicious because my mum is a fantastic if traditional cook, we chatted about the usual. As our knives and forks clinked on the plates, I felt a surge of nostalgia and tried a few 'do you remember when' gambits, but my father deflected them, turning the conversation back to things *he'd* done in the week.

'How's business, then?' he asked eventually, as he carefully speared a segment of broccoli with the appropriate proportions of meat and mustard. 'Moving much stock at the moment?'

I hesitated. This was a bit of a trick question. If I told the truth about how slow business was, he'd come up with all sorts of strategies I should be trying – not that he really knows retail. His entire working life was in car components, but that's never stopped him. If I lied and said things were going well, he'd be asking why I wasn't expanding, and talking cash-flow and even – God forbid – offering to invest so he could be, as he put it, a sleeping partner.

'So-so,' I bluffed. 'I made a good sale today – Mrs No-Buy finally came up trumps – and new stock's on the way for autumn.'

'Already, dear? I swear the years go by quicker,' my mother tutted, but then she said the same thing every year.

We talked a bit more about the shop, about Chris and my nieces who'd each been bought a pony. We talked about the traffic on the Myton Road, the new supermarket. We even touched on the fairground incident that was all over the local papers but, as my stomach clenched, I diverted from the subject and told them about my trip to the cinema. They'd met Richard several times and, when I said I'd been to the cinema with him, I saw Mum shoot Dad a meaningful look. That irritated me, but I didn't say anything. That's how it always was with my parents. Maybe it's like that in all families. There are undercurrents but nothing you can grab hold of and really object to. Without making a tremendous fuss, that is. I told them about Tam's pregnancy with predictable results. My mother was delighted, my father made some comment about late motherhood being 'harder work than she'll imagine', which made me smile – how would he know that, for goodness sake?

Eventually the conversation turned to Nat and, as we chatted about the girlfriend and whether or not she was distracting him from course-work, the sense that this would be the last time we would sit here talking and wiping gravy off our plates welled up in me and I wanted to blurt out this awful, oppressive secret to them so they could take away the fear and make everything all right. As only parents can.

But that's when it all started to go wrong.

'Are they living together?' my father asked, looking over his glasses at me.

'No, although it might come to that!' I waved the question away, sensing what was coming. 'No, he's in halls and so is she.'

He snorted dismissively. 'That won't stop them!'

'David!' my mother admonished. 'Don't be so old fashioned. Nat's a young man now and, anyway, it's really none of our business!'

'Quite. What they do is up to them,' I replied, slightly defiantly but still determined not to rise to this baiting.

'Perhaps you should ask how serious they are,' Dad persisted. 'Don't want any ... unforeseen circumstances. That boy has a promising future. Tell him to be careful and to take responsibility for himself. And the girl.'

I should have let it go. I know I should, but would you have? 'Yes, well, we wouldn't want him to damage his future prospects like I did, would we?' I snapped sullenly.

'Anyone ready for seconds?' my mother almost yelped, jumping out of her chair and fussing with the plates. 'There's plenty more meat although we've got bread and butter pudding as well. I put in lots of cinnamon, just the way you like it, Luce.'

Dad shrugged and ignored her. 'If the cap fits, wear it. He's a bright boy. Good prospects. I just think it would be better for him not to get too serious about any girl at the moment.'

I felt hot with anger at this. 'But if I hadn't *disgraced* the family and got pregnant,' I took savage pleasure in seeing my Dad flinch slightly as I bit out the words, 'if I'd done everything according to *your* plan, he wouldn't even be here, though, would he? So maybe things didn't turn out quite so disastrously in the end, eh, Dad?'

'Yes, Janet dear, I'd love some pudding, thanks. Have you got any custard?' My father had turned very deliberately away from me as if the matter was closed and we'd moved on to dessert, but I wouldn't back down.

'Dad – I think that Nat is quite old enough to make up his own mind about what he wants to do and when. I trust him to get on with his own life.'

'Yes, well . . .' He folded his napkin carefully and placed it on the table. 'Unfortunately I trusted *you*, too, and see where it got us? Now, can we drop this conversation, please, before it goes any further? You're putting words into my mouth, Lucy, and I don't like it. Enough!'

I could feel a rising panic. I couldn't leave things this way, not now. 'But, Dad, I don't want to leave things like this,' I blurted. 'I want you to know how I feel – it's such a waste of time to hide your true feelings, to not do and say what you want.'

I caught the flash of triumph in his eye and realised I'd played straight into his hands. He pulled himself up to his full height. 'On the contrary, that's what makes the world go round – people doing what they know they *should* instead of what they *feel* like doing. That's what I was always taught, and your mother too. Our generation grew up with a sense of right and wrong. And a sense of duty. And if you'd shown a bit more of that spirit, young lady, you wouldn't be where you are today.'

There was a long silence and I could see my mum's face, pale and wide-eyed, beside him. She was willing me to drop the whole thing, but I just couldn't. It was a truth we had all been avoiding. I took a deep breath and said, as calmly as I could, 'And just what do you mean by that?'

I think he realised he'd gone too far but, by then, there was no way left to go but forward. 'I mean, Lucy, that you could have finished your education, got a decent job, settled down with a chap who was good enough for you and started a family when you were mature enough. You could have shown some responsibility and appreciation for all the sacrifices your mother and I made for you over the years. That's what I mean.'

I felt as though I'd been slapped. Here I was, thirty-nine years old, but the last twenty-two years might as well never have happened. And like the resentful teenager I'd been back then, I lashed out, hurt overcoming my good intentions.

'You've never thought I was good enough, have you? It didn't matter what I did. In fact, getting pregnant with Nat gave you the opportunity to come out and say it. You've been a good grandfather to him. You really have, Dad. But you've never accepted me for who I am, have you? You always wanted me to be more, to be better. Something boring and acceptable – an accountant like Chris, living in God-awful Godalming.' I knew I was right. Dad had always taken pride in his achieving son. 'But I'm afraid this is as good as it gets. And I'm never going to be the person you want.'

'You don't know what you're saying, Lucy.' He leaned forward on the table with his fists. 'But I won't be spoken to like that in my own house and I won't have you upsetting your mother. If you only knew the nights that woman has cried herself to sleep, fretting about you and the mess you made of your life. I think it's time you apologised.'

I glanced over at my mother who looked stricken and was shaking her head – either to deny it or to beg me to stop, I couldn't tell which. I knew this was hurting her, but I needed to lance this boil. These were feelings I just couldn't have left unspoken, no matter what lay ahead. I felt strangely calm as I stood up, although my mouth was dry and my voice sounded high. 'Actually, Dad, I think it's time I left. I didn't come here looking for a fight. I just wanted you to know how I feel, but it seems you're not really interested in listening to anyone's version of events other than yours. I'll see myself out.'

Of course, I didn't. Mum left the table and came with me, shutting the door behind her with a bang. 'I'm so sorry, Luce. I don't know what's come over him. He doesn't mean half of what he says.'

I hugged her tightly, my eyes now hot and my throat strained. 'I think he does, though. I really think he does.'

'Look, in half an hour he'll be regretting it. You will come over next week, won't you? Let him make his peace with you?'

My hesitation was fractionally too long and she mis-read it straight away. 'Please don't stay away, darling. I know it's gone wrong this time and I could bloody kill your father!' Her unaccustomed swearing took me by surprise and I laughed in spite of myself. 'But he looks forward to your visits – really he does. Since he retired ... well, he's not taking to it too well. All those things he planned to do – and all he does is watch the cricket and pretend to do the garden. Apart from that you and Nat are all he talks about. Oh, and Chris, of course.'

I remember I had to avoid her eye as I answered, 'I will come if I possibly can, Mum. I promise you that. I do love you, you know – both of you. And I'm sorry about the pudding.'

I pulled myself from her embrace and turned away, rushing down the path to my car with my head down, before she could see the tears pouring down my face.

Chapter Ten

I was far too keyed up when I got home to go to bed. I felt even crosser that I'd deprived myself of Mum's bread and butter pudding, so I resorted to eating cooking chocolate – always a mistake.

I watched a bit of a sit-com on the telly, aware that it wasn't even very good and a shocking waste of my time, then switched it off and put on my favourite CD. I slipped into my PJs and took out my list again, my list of things I should have done during the past thirty-nine years and would probably never get round to doing now. Maybe I was like my dad – full of good intentions but never quite fulfilling my dreams.

What I'd written so far, though, looked pitifully tame on the re-reading. Underwear! How radical was that! No one would even see it unless I waltzed about town in just my knickers and that would be a step too far. I was running out of time for the sex and the DVD rental store was shut by now so there'd be no furtive film-viewing for me that night. The internet – surely there would be a clip on YouTube of that love scene in *9½ Weeks* with Kim Basinger I'd heard so much about. I turned on my computer and made myself tea while it warmed up and there, sure enough, was the clip. It was vaguely disappointing and unpleasant, the Kim Basinger character seeming so powerless and passive. Feeling braver, I typed in You Porn – I'd heard Nat's friends talk about it, but after five minutes of deeply unsexy gyrating and jerky blow jobs, I closed the site, feeling slightly nauseated and quickly deleted my history in case anyone found what I'd been doing when I'd gone. This was a poor substitute for the real thing.

Idly killing time now, I began to Google things like 'clairvoyance' and 'fortune-telling'. I even searched Micah's name wondering if he was on Facebook but it was pointless – I didn't even know his surname and if I'd texted Tam to ask she'd have thought I'd gone mad. I don't know how I got into the chat room. Trust me, I've never done anything like that before (or since), but when it's dark outside and you've progressed from tea to a tumbler of whisky and you feel like you are the only person in the world, the internet can be an oddly comforting place. And, it turns out, somewhere you can say anything. Voice your deepest fears. Say things you wouldn't even tell your best friends.

Suddenly, just by searching using some random words that came into my head, I was online with the oddest bunch of freaks you can imagine. Charming, friendly freaks but freaks all the same. And all wonderfully anonymous and now, by signing in as ParadiseGirl (plucked from the recesses in my head), I joined their ranks. The discussion I'd stumbled upon seemed to revolve around clairvoyance, or at least people bumbling on about their destiny. This was more Tam's department than mine, but people were sharing experiences about things they'd been told – all of which had come true, of course. There was no place here for sceptics.

I simply observed for a while, amazed by how much these people passively left their fate in the hands of others and based their decisions on the pronouncements of fortune-tellers, until up popped Cincinnati63 with : 'Hi there ParadiseGirl. Welcome to the group. Not had you in here before. You have a great name.'

'Oh hi,' I typed back nervously. 'Thank you.'

A couple of others greeted me too, both with stupendous names like UnicornTail and RainbowSeeker, and the conversation carried on until, prompting me again, Cincinnati63 asked: 'Hey there ParadiseGirl. What brings you here? Had your tarot read?'

I remember I jumped a bit when I read the question, as if I'd been caught eavesdropping.

'Not exactly,' I typed back. 'Been told my fortune. Not too rosy I'm afraid.'

'Oh tell all,' came back UnicornTail. 'Was it from someone you know and trust?'

'No. Never met him before, but a number of things he's predicted have come true, including something quite spectacular that he couldn't have known about. I've never believed this kind of thing but now it's got to me.'

There was a delay before RainbowSeeker came back with: 'Ah honey. Tell us about it. It's good to share.' And so I relayed across the information superhighway all that Micah had told me. I even dropped in stuff about Tam, Fiona's dog, the car incident – without mentioning any names, of course – and finally the fairground. It all sounded more and more ridiculous as I wrote it, but what I hadn't anticipated was the immense relief in sharing this with somebody else, even if they were only virtual. The group were very impressed and that unnerved me. I think I had half hoped they'd poo-poo the whole overdramatic litany.

Cincinnati63 was the first in: 'Do you know where this character comes from? How long have you known him?'

'Only met him last week. No one knows him.'

Two schools of thought came out of this revelation. Cincinnati63 reckoned he was the real McCoy and relayed a similar incident they'd witnessed some years back. UnicornTail piped up with the idea that Micah might be a divine emissary.

'You are blessed,' he or she gushed from wherever they were in the world. 'Use this time to find the light in your soul and move towards it.' This is when I knew I was out of my milieu.

I didn't reply to this and no one posted anything for a while. Then back came Cincinnati63. 'Hey ParadiseGirl, it sounds to me as if you are at a crossroads. Instead of letting other people make your mind up for you, follow your heart for a change. None of us knows when our time is up, but – excuse the cliché – life is too short and precious to waste a second. Live each day as if it was your last and you'll get the best of everything.'

He or she was right – it was a cliché, but a curiously comforting one. There was a pause again, until RainbowSeeker added: 'That's sound advice, girl. You don't need a medium to tell you that. Sounds like it ought to be on a bumper sticker! Go for it!'

'Isn't there some quote?' came from UnicornTail. 'Something about regretting things we did can be tempered by time; it's regret for the things we didn't do that you never get over.'

I didn't know the quote but I understood the sentiment. 'Do things for yourself,' RainbowSeeker suggested. 'Maybe things you've never dared to do?'

'Hardly seems worth it now,' I countered but within seconds all three of them had replied.

'There's never been a better time!' they shrieked in various ways. 'If not now, then when?'

'Good luck, girl,' UnicornTail closed the conversation after a moment, 'and I hope we'll hear from you again.'

I signed out and slipped into bed, wrapping myself in a sheet and stared at the ceiling, pondering. That had been weird but then these were strange times.

Chapter Eleven

Wednesday

I woke ridiculously early again on Wednesday morning. The sun was streaming in at the window and I was tangled in the sheet, my legs sticky after the humidity of the night. What sleep I'd had was uneasy, plagued by odd dreams involving my father and a lawnmower that wouldn't start. Not sure what Freud would have made of that.

The neighbour's dog, a motley pedigree, had also decided it was time to get up and was scuffling around in the back garden having been let out, selfishly, by his miserable owners. What the poor thing needed was a walk, and the idea of an early walk on this scorching morning appealed enormously to me, too. Dog-napping is not my usual scene but I hadn't walked a dog since the Fred days, and I thought about last night's advice of my cyber-mates. Why the hell not? Shrugging into a T-shirt and shorts, I let myself out of the French window, crawled through the hedge, dropped my neighbours a note I'd scrawled on the back of my unopened electricity bill envelope (well, I wasn't going to bother paying that now) saying I was going to take out their dog, and lured the mutt back through the hedge.

Using one of Nat's old belts for a lead, we set forth down the road towards the park. I remember having a sense of unreality as I strolled along the pavement, as if I was watching myself in a film. And because of that, I felt as if I could manipulate myself.

I was both the film director and the lead role and could do what I fancied.

Our route took us past the Deli and, surprisingly for that time of the morning, the blinds were pulled up. The door was open and as I slowed outside, the dog tugging at my arm – I think a walk was a total novelty for the poor animal – I could hear the clanking of crockery out in the kitchen behind the counter.

'Yoo hoo?' I called, and it was Richard not Sally who popped his head out round the door, drying his hands on a tea towel.

I was surprisingly pleased to see him smile when he saw me. 'Bloody hell, Luce, it's only ...' he came to the door and squinted at his watch, 'ten to six. What in God's name are you doing up and what's with the hound?'

I shrugged. 'Couldn't sleep so I dog-napped Sky and thought I'd give him a treat. I don't think they ever take him out, poor chap.'

'Skye? As in the Isle of?'

'No, *homage* to their satellite dish, I think!'

Richard chuckled. 'I couldn't sleep either. It's too bloody hot. Thought I might as well get up.'

I paused for a split second. 'Want to join me?'

He glanced back into the Deli. 'Well, I ought to get this lot sorted.'

'Oh, come on.' I pulled at his arm. 'You don't open for ages. Come and enjoy the morning with me.'

He hesitated for a moment. 'Oh, go on then. The washing-up can wait.' He threw down the tea towel on the nearest table, and, taking the keys out of his shorts' pocket, locked the glass door behind him.

'No alarm?'

'I don't think it's really vandal time, do you?' he asked, smiling down at me – as always making me feel short. 'The lazy buggers have done their vandalling in the wee small hours and are now snoring away until it's time to go and sign on.'

'Vandalising is the word you are struggling for there, I think.'

'Oooh, get you, Mrs,' he laughed and, on impulse, I slipped my arm through his and let Sky pull us along towards the park. Richard didn't shake off my arm but I had to let it drop as we crossed the road, and I didn't touch him again. It had just been a friendly gesture and it might have seemed odd if I'd repeated it. Instead he slipped his hands in his pockets and, as we entered the park, we both slowed down to a stroll, enjoying the cool shade of the trees.

Sky, or Skye, did what comes naturally to a dog that's been shut in all night and, as boringly prepared as ever, I neatly scooped it up in a bag I'd brought in my pocket and then dropped it into the doggy bin.

'That has to be the rankest job on earth,' Richard observed drily. 'You see those earnest dog-walkers swinging their little bags of poop, all neatly tied up. Bleugh!'

'And so they should!' I retorted indignantly.

The park was empty and the grass, damp from the morning dew, made my flip-flops wet and slippy so I took them off and hung them from my fingers, letting my toes relish the coolness of the ground.

'You'd better hope everyone else is as fastidious as you!' Richard smiled. 'You don't want that squishing between your toes!'

'Thank you for the warning.' We wandered on a little and I let Sky off the lead, hoping that he wasn't the type to run off, but he pottered ahead of us, sniffing the new and fascinating smells frantically and lifting his leg proprietorially every now and then when something deserved to be marked. The birds were calling but, except for the odd car noise, everything was very calm and peaceful.

'Why have you never married?' The question was out before I could stop myself and I wasn't even sure where it had come from.

'Christ, that was from left field, Luce!'

'I know, sorry. You don't have to answer if you don't want to.'

He stopped and turned round to face me. 'Why do you ask?'

'Well,' I kicked the short grass with my bare feet making stripes out of the dew drops, 'I've known you – how long now? – ten years maybe, since I opened the shop, and I don't think you've ever held down a relationship that's lasted longer than about a fortnight.'

He laughed deeply. 'Crikey, you make me sound positively dysfunctional! I'm not that bad, you know.' He paused. 'But I'm not going to settle for second best. Anyway, I did have a life before you, you know! There was someone who came pretty close when I lived in the States for a short time during my hippy period – and hey, what about Katrina? I thought she was going to be around for ever.' He smiled sheepishly as we both recalled the little Polish dynamo he'd gone out with a few years back and from whom he'd eventually managed to disentangle himself before she moved in with her guitar and her two cats.

'Didn't we all! She had her claws well into you.'

He looked at me pensively. 'I guess you're right. I am pretty crap, aren't I? But I suppose women who don't mind getting drenched in a force eight or being shouted at to let out the jib are pretty thin on the ground.'

'Well, I haven't done much better. In fact, I don't think I know how to do all that going out stuff any more.'

Richard shrugged and then stretched in the sunlight. 'Perhaps we should get together, you and I? Save all the bother. You're pretty handy as crew, come to think of it.' I shot him a sideways look of alarm and his eyes crinkled into a smile. 'Only joking. You're far too grown up for me.'

'What? Cos I'm over twenty-five?' I nudged him with my elbow.

'Well, you've got Nat and you've had to be sensible, haven't you?'

'Too bloody right,' I murmured under my breath. I'd show him just how immature I could be and, dropping my flip-flops on the grass and preparing myself – could I still do it? – I took a little run-up and launched into a cartwheel, landing inelegantly on my backside.

Richard caught up with me and pulled me up with my out-stretched hand, a look of astonishment on his face. 'You feeling okay, Olga?'

'Olga?'

'Korbut, of course.'

I stood up, feeling slightly dizzy, but my face felt deliciously flushed with the joy of what I'd just done. Such a silly small thing, but I'd broken out of a straitjacket that I hadn't realised was there and, letting go of Richard's hand, I did another two cartwheels for good measure.

'Perfect ten.' Richard pretended to hold up a score card and hummed the national anthem before we both snorted with laughter. Picking up my flip-flops, we strolled on, Sky giving us an impatient and pitying look as he waited for us to stop messing around and concentrate on him.

At that moment I noticed a lad coming into the park with a dog that looked pretty close to the type they ban – all snout and front legs and built like a brick out-house. It too crouched down and deposited last night's supper neatly on the grass but, rather than pick it up, the boy ignored it and carried on walk-ing.

'Er ... hello! I think you've forgotten something.'

For a moment I wasn't sure it was my voice. The boy glanced across at me and carried on walking and I frowned, cross that he'd ignored me. Feeling infuriated now, and scenting – literally! – the opportunity to tick another item off my list, I ran over to him and handed him a spare bag. 'I'm afraid you can't leave that there,' I said, pulling myself up tall. 'It's quite dangerous, in fact, as well as disgusting. If a child touched that, it could catch an infection that can cause blindness.' His expression was sneering but the fact that he hadn't answered me made me feel braver and I thrust the poop bag at him again. 'You can use one of mine if you like.' He looked at it for a moment as if I was handing him a grenade. I held my breath then, slowly, he took it from me, turned back and picked up the dog poo.

I let out my breath. 'Thank you,' I said but he ignored me and marched off towards the bin.

Richard came up beside me. 'Christ, Luce, I thought you were going to get thumped – and all before breakfast.'

I had been a little bit more scared than I cared to admit. 'Would you have come to my rescue?'

'I doubt it.'

'My hero,' I laughed shakily.

'Come on, Mrs Daring, let's head back before you do anything else unwise. This isn't the quiet little Lucy we know and love.' This time he took my arm. 'We've both got a business to run, and you've got make-up to put on or you'll scare off the customers.'

I kicked him in the shins, affectionately, and we headed back across the park, chatting, but somewhere inside it felt as if the cork had popped off a long-sealed bottle with a fizz and that the contents were bubbling out.

I think it was the window of the dry-cleaner's that precipitated my next decision. After leaving Richard to his Fairy Liquid and rubber gloves, I headed back towards the flat and passing the shopfront, I glanced at my reflection. Dull T-shirt, dull shorts, dull hair. Nearly middle-aged woman with dog.

Had I really got what I wanted out of life? I had a beautiful son and a roof over my head but hadn't the rest been just a teeny-weeny bit disappointing? I had always been in the wings somehow, waiting to go on but without the nerve to actually do it. A life spent paralysed with stage fright didn't seem like much of a life at all.

Resolved now, I deposited the dog back through the hedge, to the astonishment of my neighbours who had just found my note, and made for the shower. I didn't exactly scrub away a layer of skin but I was pretty brisk and efficient, as if this was a new start, dried quickly and pulled open my chaotic knicker drawer. After much searching, I finally extracted from the back what I was looking for and held them up. They were wrinkled from two or three years left screwed up in a ball, but the cream and pink lace was, after a bit of pulling and rearranging, really very pretty. These knickers had been one of my very few impulse purchases – a rush of blood to the head when I'd first met Owen and was at that stage in a relationship where you present your best self: shaven legs, no root growth, freshly painted nails. I wasn't sure I had ever actually worn them but they seemed fitting for today. For now. For what was left.

I tugged them on, gave myself a little twirl in the mirror, then pulled out a small vest top and a floaty short skirt that had also been relegated to the back of the wardrobe. I only hesitated for a second before ignoring my bra. For all my boring normality, I have to admit to a very pert pair of boobs – being too embarrassed to breast-feed at the tender age of seventeen had had its advantages for me if not for Nat. And for today they were going to be permitted their freedom. Feeling strangely liberated – no wonder the women's movement burnt their bras – I grabbed my bag before I could talk myself out of it and headed for the front door.

Janine was only just opening up her salon when I got there. 'Lucy, how are you? I don't think we have an appointment today, have we?' She leaned across at the diary on the counter. 'No, I don't think I've got anyone in until Mrs Slater at eleven.'

'Can you squeeze me in now, then? And will that be enough time for a cut and tint?' I asked.

'That's not like you not to plan ahead,' she remarked. 'Yup, should be – but only the roots mind. No time for full highlights on hair your length.'

I breathed in hard. 'What if it was only a couple of inches long?'

She took some persuading – which was an odd change in the dynamic. Aren't hairdressers supposed to be the ones who try to talk *you* into something ridiculous? But after I'd pointed out a few pictures in the magazines by the sofa in the window and talked about Annie Lennox, I'd talked her round and thirty years of long-ish mid-mouse hair began to hit the salon floor.

The woman who looked back at me a couple of hours later was not Lucy Streeter. Well, the odd-shaped nose and rather non-descript eyes were hers but facing me was someone even I had to admit was quite foxy. Janine had lightened – okay, bleached – my hair an alarming ash blonde and with the help of 'product', something I'd always dismissed as fussy and vain, she'd created a short spiky look of a twenty-first-century punk. I couldn't help smiling.

'Wow, Lucy, you look fabulous,' she gushed.

I stood up, shook off the gown, and turned to her.

'Janine, you are a wonder girl,' I giggled, feeling the tears in my eyes and, on impulse, I kissed her on both cheeks.

The next bit was much more painful.

I'd passed the tattoo parlour so often, without giving it a

second thought. Tattoos were for builders and foolish eighteen-year-olds who'd regret them one day and when I'd spotted a small one on Nat's foot that he'd left exposed in an unguarded moment, I'd hit the roof, appalled at how he'd violated his body and been so sneaky about it. If I stopped and thought about it for a second I'd get cold feet, so I marched into the darkened basement shop.

Seated behind a desk was a short stocky man, totally bald, with a long beard and a ring through his eyebrow. He must have been the same age as me, but with his T-shirt and black waistcoat he looked older.

'Hello,' he grunted. Clearly I was not the normal clientele.

'I'd like a tattoo.'

'Well, you've come to the right place for that. What sort of thing?'

I hadn't thought about that, but I followed his gesture to the books on the table and opened them at random. Ying and yang symbols, skulls, Celtic crosses, daggers and serpents. 'Do you do anything a bit more ... feminine?' I almost laughed.

He sighed and pulled himself upright, handing me a book tucked under the others.

'Let me guess. A small rose on your lower back?'

He was taking the piss and I bristled. 'No. On my shoulder please. Can you do it now?'

By the time I left, half the day had gone and I was overcome with admiration for those people you see who are covered in the things. I thought childbirth was painful but the constant pricking of the needle almost had me begging for mercy. He'd told me to keep it covered for a while, but what was the point in that? Who'd see it if I did? So as soon as I was round the corner I whipped off the dressing. There it was – a neat little rose on the back of my right shoulder. Perhaps that was how I'd end my days – blood poisoning through neglect of a tattoo. Is that what Micah had foreseen?

I had to get home before my meeting with Neil, and I know that I purposely avoided walking past the Deli. It wasn't that I was embarrassed – I just hadn't had time yet to meet my new self, and I wanted to stand in front of the mirror in my bedroom and take it in. When I got there, I peered round at the mirror, not quite sure what I was going to see, as if I might have changed since I left the hairdresser's and morphed back to my old self. I turned my head this way and that; looked at myself from the back and sideways on. Then I pulled out some high wedges from the wardrobe – a sort of Dutch courage from the feet up – and slipped them on. I smiled at the woman who stared back at me.

I looked good. I looked very good. Why the hell hadn't I done this before?

Neil was late for our meeting, of course. He always had been, even in the old days, saying he thought timekeeping was for wimps, so I was halfway through my coffee before he walked through the door. I'd never been to this café before – I'd wanted neutral ground – and the two waiters hovered a bit, asking me every couple of minutes if I wanted anything else until I shot them a withering look and they backed off. Clearly a spiky blonde with a rose tattoo was better at getting the message across than mousy Lucy Streeter.

A woman I vaguely knew was sitting at another table with her friend, and I was gratified to see she did a double take, not sure if it was me. I waved boldly, not something I usually ever do, and stirred my coffee before licking the froth off the spoon. I had no idea what to say to Neil or how to say it. I'd just have to wing it.

I recognised him immediately when he eventually came

through the door ten minutes late and, whilst he glanced around the café trying to spot me, I had a few precious moments to assess him. He'd filled out from the rangy boy I'd last seen but still had the lank hair and dark eyebrows that met across the middle. And his likeness to Nat almost took my breath away. I suppose the memory of his face had faded for me, and in Nat's expressions I'd always found Streeter characteristics – his smile and his eyes like my mum's, his frown like mine – but the shape of Neil's head, the way his hair hung around his face was my son's. I realised that, though he'd been mine, he'd been someone else's too all this time.

He glanced appreciatively at me once, looked away, then shot a look straight back. I sat up a bit and smiled encouragingly, and after a moment's hesitation he came over to the table.

'Lucy?'

'Hi.'

'Bloody hell, you've … changed.'

'I know. What do you think?' I asked nervously.

'Very good, you look very good.'

He sat down on the seat opposite me and the waiter was there like a shot.

'I'll have a coffee please. Lucy?'

I indicated the cup in front of me. 'I'm fine, thanks.' The waiter melted away and Neil adjusted his position uneasily, resting his hands on his thighs as if he could push himself up to leave at any moment. He seemed so much more grown-up, which of course he was, but with a social grace he hadn't had before. How naïve we'd been then. Two silly young people barely started out on our own lives, let alone mature enough to create another.

I opened the batting. 'How have you been?' which sounded as though I'd seen him last week.

'Okay.' He smiled crookedly. His teeth still weren't great.

'I've got my own business, you know. Well, of course you do. You called.'

'Yes, I did. Family? I mean, are you married?'

He glanced down at his hands as if he was owning up to something that might upset me. 'Yes. Her name's Yvonne. We were at school together but you won't have known her ... ' He trailed off. *Because you were at the posh school*, was the underlying message.

'And you live in Leamington?'

'Warwick actually.' He named a big housing development on the edge of town.

'Kids?'

He smiled. 'This is like twenty questions. Yeah. Boy and a girl. Usual teenage nightmare.'

I looked him straight in the eye. 'Teenagers can be very stupid.' We both smiled sheepishly and there was a long silence.

'You?'

'Not married, no. I've got my own business, too – a shop in Paradise Street. You might have seen it. Clothes and things.'

'Good.' He nodded as if he approved. 'You used to say you wanted to get into design and stuff, didn't you?'

'I'm flattered you remember.' Another silence. 'I'm sorry about your dad,' I tried eventually.

'How did you know?'

'Your mum told me.' I paused then went on bravely, 'I went round to see her.'

'Of course. She said. She also said you wanted to talk to me.' He shifted in his seat, as he got to the nitty-gritty. 'Is it money you need? He must be an adult now – it's an odd time to come asking.' His tone wasn't harsh but I could tell he was being very cautious.

'No, Neil, I don't want your money – though there were a

lot of times I could have done with it. And yes "he" is an adult now.'

'Sorry. Nat.' The waiter brought over his coffee, and Neil took a sip and licked the froth off his lip.

'Er ...' He jiggled his knee nervously. 'How is he? Nat, I mean.'

'He's a very fine man.' I could feel a sharp pain in my throat and the tears beginning to fill my eyes and I looked away hurriedly. 'He's studying for a degree in Business Studies, so he'll probably do better than either of us!' I fiddled with the spoon on my saucer. 'Have you ever been curious to see him?'

He looked at me searchingly for a minute. 'Yes, Lucy, I was very curious.' But he stopped there and didn't say anything else, waiting for me to take the lead.

'I see.' This was going to be hard to say. Why should or would he care? So much time had passed and so many things had happened to us both. I screwed up my courage. 'Neil, I know he's an adult and he can care for himself and all that – but my mum and dad are getting older and when they die, well, there won't be anyone – except for me, of course – but if something were to happen to me ...' I paused and looked him straight in the eye. 'I need him to know that he could contact you if he needed to.'

There was a long silence as Neil weighed this up. 'Has he ever asked about me?'

I thought back to the day, the memory as clear as yesterday, when Nat had asked me outright in the car on the way to Wales for a holiday: 'Who's my dad?' He'd been thirteen and, though he'd asked me a few times before – usually on Father's Day or after he'd been to friends' houses and around a proper 'dad' – this time he wasn't going to be fobbed off with my usual line, 'Daddy and I decided we didn't want to be together but we both love you very much'. I'd held my breath for years waiting for the big question to emerge and there it was. So, as we meandered through the lanes towards St David's, I painted a not entirely untrue but heavily edited version of events: how we had both been too young; how his daddy wouldn't have been able to provide for him; how much we all loved him. Blah, blah. He'd seemed happy with this and never asked me again. I wonder why he'd settled for that. Perhaps he'd been trying to spare me pain. That would have been typical of Nat.

'Yes, of course he has, and I've told him the bare facts. He's a well-balanced kid, Neil, despite his parents.' I smiled wryly. 'But he has a right to know if he wants to. I can't stop him.' Would Neil buy into this? I realised now how much I wanted, needed, that connection to be made. 'Are you okay with that – Nat getting in contact with you if he needs to? I mean, I don't expect he will,' I added hastily, 'but I don't want to rule anything out.'

Neil sat back in his seat and drummed his two forefingers on the table in a rhythm. 'It does seem odd to be getting in touch – after all this time, I mean. You seem to have coped pretty well so far. Is there something wrong?'

Of course there was something bloody wrong! At this point I got a bit heated. My tattoo was stinging, and here was Neil getting funny about what I had hoped would be simple. I leaned forward earnestly. 'Neil, I may well have coped "pretty well so far".' I knew I was talking too loudly because people turned round to look at me quizzically, but I couldn't have cared. 'In fact, Neil, I've done better than "pretty well", I've done very well indeed, thanks very much. But this single-parent lark can be a bit of a burden. I've worked my backside off to provide for Nat, put my social life, not to mention my sex life, on the back burner.' That had the whole café looking round. 'In fact, there's a danger that I've completely forgotten how to shag – all to raise *your* son. Because he is your son, too.' Neil blushed at this point, clearly concerned that I was going to become hysterical.

'I never pursued you,' I said calmly and slowly, 'because what was the point? You didn't have two pennies to rub together then. And maybe in retrospect I should have done. I should have stopped trying to be a martyr and putting my life on hold, and chased you for a bit of financial support. Cos while you've been living your comfortable, middle-class life in your *executive* home,' I knew that barb would hurt – the old Neil would rather have died than think of himself as anything but muck 'n' brass working class, like his dad, 'while I bet you've been taking holidays abroad and living the life of Riley, we've had to battle. Some days we had to eat toast cos I couldn't afford anything else and I've had to buy Nat's shoes in Oxfam more than once. I think asking *your son* if he can get in touch if he wants to is hardly going to rock your neat little boat now, is it?'

I looked down at my hands then, a bit ashamed that I'd spoken so loudly, then back up at Neil, whose face was white, and then an awful thought occurred to me.

'Your wife doesn't know, does she?' He looked away. 'You haven't told her you have another child.'

'Yes, she knows. She's known all along – everyone knew,' he muttered eventually. Of course. I'd known kids at his school must have known, too, but I hadn't realised it would change his life as well. Had the stigma stuck to him? And how did his wife feel about the fact that he'd fathered another child?

'Sorry,' I said quietly. 'It never occurred to me that it would affect your life, too.'

Neil leaned forward at that point. 'You don't know, do you?' he asked urgently.

'Know what?'

'That letter you wrote to me.'

I rolled my eyes. 'Oh that – my dad dictated the whole thing to me.'

'Not as much as he dictated to me when he delivered it.'

I froze. 'What? Dad came to see you? I thought he posted it.'

Neil sat back in his chair and sighed deeply. 'Nope. He came round to the house like some sort of vigilante and, in front of my dad, told me that you never wanted to see me again and that, if I kept my nose clean, you wouldn't pursue for child support.'

'Fuck!' I gasped. 'I had no idea. I knew he'd—'

'I so wanted to see Nat,' Neil interrupted. 'That day when we bumped in to each other on Regent Street nearly killed me. He looked so perfect, and I just looked like a cheap mechanic. I wasn't ready to be a parent – neither of us were – but Lucy, I was also scared shitless. Terrified by what had happened, and terrified that your dad would kill me. He was really serious that day, and I was a coward – my dad told me to keep away, too, and I suppose I just did what I was told. Buried my head. Then, the longer you seemed to cope, the further away it all seemed, and then I had my own family and …'

I was stuck now. Livid with my father for his duplicity, but part angry and part sympathetic with Neil for his situation. That must have been what his mother meant about not coming over in the park to talk to me. She must have known Neil had been warned off. His side of the story hadn't even crossed my mind. He'd been in the past all this time, but in fact our lives had run parallel – inextricably linked but not actually touching. Was I being unfair asking him now about seeing Nat?

Then I reminded myself why I was here – to create a framework for Nat after I'd gone – and I couldn't leave without knowing that would happen. 'So can he get in touch?'

Neil thought for a moment but I knew what he was going to say. 'No, I don't think so. It's been too long to kick over the wasps' nest. I have to think about my kids, my wife, the impact it would have on them.' He stood up.

'And what if I can't stop him?' I asked desperately.

He shrugged. 'Well, that's up to him. He's an adult. But don't go putting ideas into his head, Lucy. I don't think I can start playing Daddy now.' He leaned down and, to my astonishment, kissed me briefly on my cheek, put money down on the table, enough to cover both our coffees, then turned and left the café.

Fired up and cross now, I headed home. So that was an avenue that had been closed off. There wasn't time to try to make Neil see sense or to persuade him to behave as he should, and I had my father to thank for that. Once again *I'd* have to sort things out. Like the grazed knees I'd soothed and the broken hearts I'd tried to mend, I'd have to make sure Nat was secure and confident if I wasn't there to offer tea and sympathy. How ironic – those words at the café were probably the nearest we had come to a row in all the short time Neil and I had known each other. This was a call to action to get my affairs in order, to go through the policies, the life assurance, all the boring ephemera of life (and death) so that I didn't leave an unholy mess for everyone when I'd gone.

Making myself a cold drink, ignoring the accumulating mess in the flat and throwing open the French windows to let in some breeze, I sat down at my desk. I'd taken out life assurance and made a will years ago – after much persuasion and lectures about 'responsibility' from my father – and I pulled the copy of it out of a drawer. Aren't wills a funny thing? A self-indulgent instruction that someone else will read and act upon when you are no longer around to care anyway. I really had nothing of worth to leave – except this flat – which Nat could either live in or flog. The shop was rented. I'd never had jewellery – though there is a pretty unattractive ring of my grandmother's – or valuable furniture; this place is merely a shrine to thrift shops

and imagination. No, Nat would really be no better off finan-
cially without me.

I pulled out a sheet of paper and a pen. I couldn't remember
the last time I'd written to Nat – if ever. Why would I? With
him living at home all the time, then emailable or textable, my
written communication with him had been of the 'Are you
there safely yet?' variety. I pondered for a long time, looking
out of the window. Then I began.

My darling Nat ...

Chapter Twelve

By the time I'd finished – or as close as I was probably going to get – the sun had moved round and the room was cooler, so I reached for a cardigan from the back of a chair and pulled it on. Then stopped and winced: I'd forgotten about the tattoo. Well, not forgotten, obviously, but the sting had subsided into the background until the moment I tried to shrug on the dark cotton knit. Hissing with pain, I eased it on over the tender skin, pausing to shoot a glance at the design once again before I covered it up. I wondered if I'd hate the sight of it in the morning and feel I'd made a huge mistake. But I could feel my mouth curving into an involuntary smile. I loved it. It was so completely not me and yet it felt more right than anything I'd done in quite a long time. Apart from the haircut, of course. I'd been ruffling my hands through my hair all afternoon and I loved the feeling of freedom it gave me. My neck felt cool. I didn't have to keep scraping the long strands off my face and into a ponytail or bun. It stuck up in lovely bold spikes and I couldn't stop looking at my reflection in anything even faintly shiny. And that was so not me either!

I actually *was* beginning to feel like a completely new woman, but would she have long enough to make her mark? Somehow not even the thought of that depressed me now. It was as if I'd crossed a line. Every moment felt like a gift and I was determined to pack as much living as I possibly could into the next few days.

And that meant not spending any longer trying to perfect my letter to Nat. I took one more look at it. I'd tried to keep it factual – particularly the details about his dad – at least at first, but then I'd diverted and began relating things from the past, some of which he was too young to remember. The memories of which I was the sole keeper. His first tooth. The time he'd put a piece of sponge up his nose and we'd spent four hours in A&E until he cried so much it had shot out of his nose with all the snot. His first day at Cubs, when I could have eaten him he looked so delicious in his new uniform, and then those peaks and troughs at school. In the team, dropped from the team. In the team again. GCSEs and his ear-splitting first band. I doubt the neighbours have forgiven me yet. There were bits I missed out, of course, especially that most challenging part of motherhood – telling him how great he looked with a curtain of hair and ridiculously skinny jeans, when in truth he look a sight.

Once I'd read it through again – making myself cry as much as I did on the first draft – I signed off. Then I folded it neatly, put it in an envelope, wrote his name on the front and propped it up on the mantelpiece.

That was when I noticed the invitation: Martin's launch party for the new tile range he was introducing. With everything else that had been going on, I'd forgotten all about it. Martin had been spending more and more time in Marrakesh over the last few years and had brought back the most wonderful range of ceramic painted tiles. Now there was an area in the shop that he'd created to look almost like a hammam, and it had even been featured in one of the Sunday papers. He'd teamed up with a local plumber and they were trying to start up a design service for Eastern-inspired wet-rooms. This party was intended to draw in the great and the good of South Warwickshire. Purely for decorative purposes, he'd invited the Paradise Street Crew – there was no way any of us could afford the kind of prices he'd be charging – but he knew he could rely on us to drink his booze and charm his potential clientele by saying all the right things. It was due to start this evening at half past six and a quick glance at my watch told me I'd have to get my skates on.

I wondered whether to change – I never would normally – but something made me pull out a dress I'd made a few years ago as a sample. I'd never actually put it on sale, perhaps because I never wanted it to sell, or perhaps because it had taken me so long to embroider the fitted bodice in red and gold silks that it would have broken my heart to have someone else enjoy it. Ironically, though, I'd never had the courage to wear it. It stopped above the knee, with a full skirt and stiff petticoats beneath and, when I slipped it on, my legs didn't look so bad after all. I'd caught a bit of colour in the sunshine and I almost looked acceptable. I had a moment's hesitation then stood firm. 'Nope, Lucy Streeter,' I chided, 'this is the new you. The you who isn't afraid of anything. You go for it!'

I grabbed a Burgundy-red cardigan and my bag and headed for Martin's. I could hear voices and laughter from the party even before I turned the corner. In the warmth of the evening, guests were spilling out of the shop and onto the pavement, and I could see that everyone had a glass in their hand. As I got closer, I recognised a few familiar faces I'd seen around town or at the theatre, and a little knot of those I knew well. Too shy just yet to enter the mêlée, I popped in to my shop briefly, wondering idly how much business I'd missed by not opening. Picking up the post, I had a quick look through the envelopes before stuffing them into my handbag. One was a bank statement and I'd got into the habit of opening it slightly and peeping at the total without actually reading the grim evidence. This month it was worse than ever because, even though there was money in the account, when Sayers' rent review came through it would all disappear into the ether. Then, in a flash of something that felt almost like relief, I realised death had its benefits – I wasn't going to have to pay it! What is it they say about death and taxes?

Locking up again, I squared my shoulders for courage but Tam caught sight of me, then did a pantomime double take and gave me a huge and enthusiastic wave. 'Look at you,' she screeched. And, sure enough, everyone did. This would normally have made me scuttle for the nearest doorway, but today I actually camped it up, slowing my pace to a confident strut. Tam looked utterly amazed. I never thought I'd actually render her speechless but my new look had evidently had a radical effect. Standing with her were her husband, Giles, the awful Sylvie and also Gaby from the pet shop, resplendent in a fabulous red kaftan that would have done Demis Roussos proud. I glanced into Martin's shop quickly to see if Richard or Sally was there, but I couldn't see either of them.

By the time I sashayed – that was the only word for it – up to the group, Tam had regained her voice, but I won't even attempt to repeat what she said, it was so fast. The gist of it was that I looked fantastic, years younger, stunning, sexy as hell, and why had I waited all this time to do it? Giles gazed at me, slightly goggle-eyed, looking as if he was trying to equate the mousy Lucy of his long acquaintance with the creature in front of him. He let out a satisfying low whistle.

'Bloody hell. You scrub up well!'

'My, thank you, kind sir,' I laughed back, in my best Scarlett O'Hara.

Gaby was less effusive – must be all those years of working with small, furry pets. 'What the hell's got into you?' She scrutinised me as if I was something new for the shop display. 'Are you feeling okay? Are you feverish?'

'Oh, leave her alone.' Tam nudged Gaby hard and she

wobbled like a large strawberry jelly. 'You're just jealous. She looks beautiful!'

'What brought on the metamorphosis?' Giles asked. 'Not that I'm saying you were a caterpillar before,' he added quickly. 'But you look like an exotic butterfly now.'

'Your wife isn't so shabby herself.' I leaned over and gave Tam a kiss. 'You're blooming, darling.' For someone who was barely six weeks' pregnant, she'd thrown herself into the role with predictable enthusiasm. In an extremely chic smocked dress, she looked almost six months' gone and was leaning back and rubbing her tummy in a way that was totally *de trop*. But I couldn't begrudge her even a second of her delight. This longed-for pregnancy was a role she was going to play to perfection and her sheer happiness was so infectious.

Sylvie, the self-appointed parenting guru, didn't look quite so thrilled, though. I realised that – not unintentionally – I'd ignored her so far, and without the limelight on her she seemed rather peaky. She looked at me with ill-concealed distaste. 'Yes, Lucy! Look at you! I hardly recognised you. You look – well, what can I say?'

I pulled myself up. 'I just decided I needed a change.'

'It's certainly a change,' she snorted, then turned abruptly back to Tam, trying to exclude me with some kind of talk about elasticated waistbands and nursing bras. I rolled my eyes, perhaps a little too impatiently, and started to talk to Giles, who was looking prouder than I'd ever seen him.

At that moment, Micah came out of Martin's shop, glass in hand. He stood on the step, surveying the group for faces he recognised. It struck me then that, despite his well-cut jacket and good bone structure, he was strangely sexless. He did nothing for me at all. Tam might have assumed that he was gay, but I wasn't so sure. Spotting us, he wandered through the crowd towards us before I could move away.

'Hello!' he boomed, slapping Giles on the back with huge bonhomie. 'How's the expectant father?' Giles smiled broadly and Tam squealed and gave Micah a hug that should have taken the wind out of him. Suddenly we made an odd tableau. There they were with news to celebrate, and I was standing observing, with nothing to celebrate at all. And all because of this man.

'Never better!' Giles laughed back at Micah. 'Done any more fortune-telling recently? Come up with the lottery numbers yet?'

Micah looked down into his glass and I waited for him to bask in the glory of his *pièce de résistance* at the fair on Sunday in the park. But, oddly, he didn't say a word and just brushed off Giles's teasing comments.

Then he turned to me. 'Lucy?' he asked uncertainly, and Tam butted in with the doesn't-she-look-glorious and isn't-she-brave spiel and my unease at seeing him again was thankfully buried in talk about my transformation (how long had the haircut taken? Did Nat know?). We talked pleasantries for a while until I noticed that Sylvie had managed to buttonhole Giles somehow and was banging on and on about her cervix in a revoltingly confiding way. Normally Giles, and Tam too for that matter, would be turning the whole thing into a joke, taking the mickey ever so slightly and generally having a laugh. That was one of the things I loved about them both. They never took anything too seriously. But today they seemed to be swallowing Sylvie's spiel completely uncritically. I moved a little bit closer, hoping to join in the conversation, as much to moderate Sylvie's almost Stalinist views on pain relief as to avoid any private conversation with Micah. This is where I came in.

'. . . so any form of pain relief diminishes the experience and, honestly, after everything you've been through, are you prepared to miss out on even the tiniest moment of the experience? Are you?'

Tam and Giles were nodding slowly, like the Churchill dog. I nudged Tam, hoping to distract her from Sylvie's lecture, but she seemed to be mesmerised. Perhaps it was time to present the counter argument.

'Well, when I had Nat, I was very glad of the old gas and air, I must say,' I butted in loudly. 'In fact, I think I asked if they sold it at the hospital shop so I could take some home with me. They don't, by the way.'

Sylvie glanced at me as though the buzzing of a fly had distracted her for a moment, then turned back to Tam. '*Modern* childbirth, you know, is an almost spiritual experience, actually. Or at least,' she shot me a dirty look, 'it can be. It all depends on how you approach it, of course, but the more preparation you do the better, obviously. By the time Pascal was ready to enter the world, my breathing technique was so well developed, I was able to consciously ask my cervix to dilate. I was genuinely in complete control all the time. The midwives were amazed. They said they'd never come across anyone like me before.'

'I'll bet!' It was out before I could help myself – rather like Pascal, by the sound of it – and Sylvie turned her best glare on me before morphing it into a slightly patronising simper.

'Yes, but I don't think your experience is all that representative, do you, Lucy?'

'Well, neither was yours, by the sound of it. You said yourself the midwives thought you were a bit of an oddity.'

'That's not what I said at all!' she spluttered. 'Anyway, your experience dates from so long ago, I'm not even sure it's relevant these days.'

Wow! She was quite an operator. I'll just *bet* the midwives were amazed by her.

'Hmmm, yes. I did have Nat very young, that's true. In fact, it was the same time you had Harriet, of course, wasn't it Tam?

I seem to recall we managed pretty well just breathing in the old-fashioned in-and-out sort of way, didn't we?'

'Yes, but he wasn't altogether *planned*, I gather,' Sylvie persisted, and I shot Tam a look. Who else had she shared my past with? 'So you probably didn't really make the best of those early months, in particular. But Tamasin here can give her baby the very best start. In fact, I'm starting up one of my chanting groups again soon. It's a way of really connecting to the baby. You'll love it!'

An immense feeling of sympathy for poor little Pascal swept over me. Let's hope to God Mr Sylvie had a sense of humour and that the blessed child would inherit the gene that meant he could laugh at himself. There was no sign of a Mr Sylvie tonight – either he was at home cowed by his wife's fecundity and tied to the sharing the childcare or, if he had any sense, he'd run for the hills the moment her amazing performing cervix started to do its business.

'Actually, Sylvie,' I said gently, trying not to appear too amused by her pomposity, 'I think you'll find that generations of women have managed perfectly well without chanting and breath control, cooperative cervi – if that's the plural – and all those other things you *modern* mothers know so much about. Otherwise how would the human race have survived? And amazingly, Nat has all his limbs and his faculties – as far as I know – despite his mother's irresponsible behaviour as a gal.' I could see a little smile on Micah's face and even Giles was looking supportive. But Sylvie was outraged.

'But there's been so much *research*!' she spluttered again.

'Maybe, but to what end?' I asked. 'What kind of pampered generation are we raising? And do you think all that guilt that we didn't breast-feed till they went to school or make placenta fricassee has really made us happier women? Tam, just go for it the way you think is best, I say. Things haven't changed that much since Harriet was born. You don't have to listen to all this bunkum.'

I breathed out loudly. It felt so good to get that off my chest at last, and to pick Sylvie up on all the little digs she'd made over the years. She was virtually speechless, just huffing and puffing and looking like a bullfrog in Fenn Wright Manson.

At last she spoke. 'Bunkum! I've never been so insulted in my entire life. I'm not staying here to be spoken to like that.'

'I could murder a glass of Pimm's,' I giggled apologetically, planning a fast exit. 'Scuse me, everyone.' And I scuttled into Martin's shop. Behind me I could hear Sylvie's outraged voice.

'Now, Tamasin! Lucy's obviously just trying to get attention for some reason, and you really shouldn't be exposed to that kind of negativity. Why don't you and Giles come home with me now? I've got some lovely herbal tea you can have, and I can show you the latest pictures I've put up on my website.'

'No, thanks, you're all right,' I heard Tam reply, her voice clear as she followed me into the shop. 'I think I'll stay here for a bit. I want to catch up with Lucy. See you around, Sylvie.'

I stopped but didn't turn round. To tell you the truth, it mattered a great deal to me whether Tam would decide to stay with me after what I'd said. I felt all jangled up. I was trembling but I couldn't work out if it was anger at that stupid, irritating, patronising woman, or exhilaration that I'd at last said what I'd felt. The thing is, I'd spent all my life *not* saying what I thought and keeping my feelings under wraps, that the last few days, when I'd actually spoken my mind – to Dad, to the boy in the park, to the bin bag man, Mrs No-Buy – it had made me feel extremely peculiar. It was as if I'd taken some truth drug and couldn't stop myself. Although I was being truer to myself than I'd ever been before, it was so unlike me to reveal my feelings that I was starting to wonder which one the real me actually was. But I knew which Lucy Streeter I preferred.

Inside the shop, the crowd – and really, it was fairly packed in there – seemed to part for me and I remembered how different I looked. I was used to making discreet entrances, coming and going with as little fuss as possible, but with my new hair and the dress I'd chosen, that wasn't an option. I squared my shoulders and strode on in, making for a rough marble table with drinks set out on it. I helped myself to a long glass of Pimm's, took a swig and turned round. As I scanned the room, through the ranks of red-faced men in pastel shirts with straining buttons and identikit blonde-streaked wives, I saw Sally. She was wearing a strappy maroon-linen dress – one of my designs, I was pleased to note – and making her way over to me, a look of complete astonishment on her face and her eyes as round as gobstoppers.

'Lucy?' she said cautiously. 'Is it ...? It is you, isn't it? We couldn't work out where you were today when you didn't open up the shop. So this is what you've been up to! Darling, you look amazing. Like a completely different woman. That dress is exquisite! Is it one of yours?'

At that moment Tam joined us and gave me a tight hug that made me gasp with pain as she connected with my tattoo.

She let me go quickly. 'What's wrong? Have you hurt yourself? What is it?'

Looking from one to the other, I slowly slipped off my cardigan, lifting it carefully from my newly-embellished shoulder.

'A *tattoo*! What on earth made you do that? God, it looks fantastic.'

I felt myself starting to grin rather sheepishly. Sal, at Tam's insistence, circled me like an amiable vulture, examining my clothes, touching my hair, exclaiming over (but not touching, thank goodness) my tatt and asking, over and over again, what had possessed me to make such a change. Well, I could hardly tell them, could I? And although it was strange to be the centre of attention, I must admit that I was quite enjoying it.

Gradually they calmed down, but Sal kept shaking her head in wonder. 'What on earth will Richard say?'

I'd expected him to be there, and had slightly dreaded the prospect, but now I felt curiously let down that he hadn't witnessed the new me. What *would* he say, next time he saw me? And, strangely, that same thought was at the back of my mind for the rest of the evening, distracting me even from the succession of completely unknown and very expensively dressed women who sidled up to me and asked about my dress – and then, ever so discreetly – about my tattoo. Where I'd had it done, whether it hurt much, and whether the tattooist could do nice little fairies or butterflies, and – mystifyingly – whether I was planning on staying in the area for long. A very odd experience, but it just shows: you can't really go by appearances.

A very boozed Fen gave me a wet kiss on the cheek and peered down my cleavage, which, thanks to my high heels, was almost at his eye level. Fortunately we were joined by Martin who, until now, had been busy schmoozing his guests.

'Lucy, I wouldn't have recognised you. Honestly, you're transformed. Anyway, thanks for coming. You really made the party. Once you made your appearance, the whole place livened up. I've had loads of orders – and people asking me if I knew who you were. Seems most people are putting their money on you being an actress but I heard someone saying he'd seen you singing with a rock band. I'm afraid I've lied shamelessly and said I was helping to refurbish your manor house in the Cotswolds. Oh, and your place in St John's Wood.' He grinned mischievously. 'Sorry! But you do literally look a million dollars.'

It was late when I finally left, much later than I'd intended. I'd never been much of a party animal. To be honest, I hadn't had much of a chance. But that night I'd thoroughly enjoyed myself. I'd met loads of new people, especially after Sally and Tam had both left. The fact that most of them thought I was a demi-celeb made it all the more fun and I must confess that I camped it up something rotten. The dress was almost more of a wow than I was. I could have sold it twenty times over, but what would have been the point in giving out my details? By the time they found my shop, I'd be stitching celestial robes or mending holes in the clouds. In my slightly tipsy state, the thought made me giggle. One woman, in pink-framed glasses, a short white bob and a full-length coat that made her look like Merlin, had asked Martin to introduce us and had then examined my dress in detail, quizzing me about my techniques. I had jabbered away, self-absorbed in my inebriated state, not making much sense, but enjoying talking about something I loved to someone who was clearly interested. I don't really remember what I said, but I do know I didn't ask her a single question about herself and, looking back on it, the thought makes me blush.

Eventually, though, Martin started tidying up and trying to get the shop ready for what he probably hoped would be a flood of new customers. I took the hint and, kissing him goodbye and begging him loudly to find time to start on my new suite of wet-rooms, I set off into the dark. I've always felt safe walking the streets of Leamington, even at night, and anyway it was only Wednesday. I had nothing to fear, it seemed, until Friday, so I walked on the dark side of the road with no anxiety at all.

Chapter Thirteen

Thursday Morning

The curious thing about these changes was how they exhilarated me. You'd think I'd have been full of dread. If this had been happening to someone else, I'd have imagined them curled up in a corner waiting for the sword to fall. Instead I found myself running my fingers through my shortened hair before I had even opened my eyes on Thursday morning, smiling. I winced slightly as the tattoo had stuck to the sheet but that too made me content. It was a liberation, as if I'd shaken myself out of a straitjacket and spread my arms at last.

There was an occasion when I was small – perhaps nine or ten – when we'd been playing in the park, my brother, Chris, and I, and a couple of his friends. I was little sis – the pain who'd had to tag along because my mother had insisted. I'd been bored at home, kicking my heels and the furniture and she'd blown her top – or at least by my mother's gentle and serene standards. The boys had been showing off, of course, locked in a competition to see who was the bravest, and they set up a bridge over a small stream, an off-shoot of the river. It was rudimentary to say the least – some sticks and a plank that Chris had found and held up with triumph. Enid Blyton would have been proud of us. If the reason for it hadn't been so ruthless.

'Dare ya, dare ya,' Chris's friend Tom had chanted, a nasty

sneer on his face and, one-by-one, the boys had walked the plank, wobbling precariously as they negotiated the stream. I was last to try, of course, and by that time the makeshift bridge had virtually collapsed. The boys were lined up on the other side, waiting and watching. I can feel the pain now of trying to hold back the tears. I looked over at Chris but there was no fraternal sympathy in his eyes. I hated him at that moment – I've never much liked him anyway – but I felt betrayed that he put camaraderie above his sister's agony.

Shame, pride, bloody-mindedness – whatever it was, it stiffened my resolve and I tentatively began to make my way through the challenge. I suppose being lighter than the boys helped and, despite the water seeping into my Clark's sandals and a moment when I had to wave my outstretched arms like a tightrope walker, I managed it and hopped on to the opposite bank.

There was no welcoming congratulation, just a resentment that I hadn't fallen flat on my face but, as I watched them run off laughing, I felt an overwhelming sense of achievement and release. I'd faced a demon. I'd stepped outside my comfort zone.

Now I opened my eyes slowly. The curtain was billowing in the slight breeze and letting in flashes of morning sunshine. It was very early, again, but I wanted to stretch out the day for as long as I possibly could. I had things to do. I threw back the bedclothes, dropped my nightie onto the floor and pulled a shocking-pink shift dress from my wardrobe. It was crumpled, and I wasn't even sure it would still fit me, but it was one of the first things I'd ever made and somehow it represented the beginning of my career – or at least what I saw as my career, though my father had made it plain he didn't agree. He had always referred to sewing as 'my little hobby', never comment-ing on the growing number of orders for alterations that people asked me to do. At first it was Mum's friends who staunchly supported me; then, when I had proved that I could sew a straight seam, they recommended me to their friends. Though they never said it, I think it made them feel better – there but for the grace of God went their daughters, who were now safely sitting A levels, as I pushed a pushchair with my hopes of a future evaporating in my wake.

It was my art teacher, Mrs Downing, who 'commissioned' my first dressmaking project – a Butterick pattern for a skirt that was fairly straightforward. Though she'd never admit it, I think she asked me on purpose to help me along. In any case, something excited me when I opened out the tissue-thin pattern. I know some people can pore over plans and not understand them, but I got it immediately. As more people asked me to run-up a 'little something' for them, I started to get braver and add extra details – some binding, perhaps – or adjust the pattern slightly. I'd make things for myself – it was cheaper that way – and poor Nat had to suffer homemade trousers and jackets. He probably looked a sight but it was that or charity shops or cast-offs.

When I could afford to, I'd pick up vintage clothes – or persuade my mother to ransack her wardrobe – and I'd pick apart the dresses and jackets to see how they were put together, cutting new patterns from the remnants. Nat didn't exactly help his mother's burgeoning career. Once he was crawling around our tiny rented bedsit, his big nappied bottom in the air, he'd do his best to rearrange the precious scraps of material or demonstrate his special knack for finding pins. It was a wonder he wasn't taken into care!

It was Mrs Downing who talked me into the shop on Paradise Street, too. 'You have to come and see it,' she urged. 'It's just round the corner from a friend's house and it would be perfect for you.' There was she on one side, already imagining how it would all look, and there was my father on the other, determined to put me off the idea. I showed him the business plan that I'd put together for the bank and even tried to take him to see the premises, though he refused to come and look and, when he realised he couldn't actually stop me taking on the lease of the shop, advised me imperiously to make sure I stocked clothes 'that would sell'.

His advice was right, of course, though I was too stubborn to admit it and he was too angry with me to see that, though it was hand-to-mouth and some months I wasn't sure I'd make the rent, the shop was my achievement and in a precarious sort of way, it worked. What he never knew is that there had been a couple of months when Mum had 'lent' me the rent, on the quiet.

It was because I'd invested so much time and energy in the place – and because I knew that none of the Paradise Street Crew would be able to survive the rent hike we were about to have foisted on us – that I determinedly ironed the funny little shift dress and slipped it on, then headed out of the door. I swung my bag as I walked along. I felt no fear. I felt buoyed up by an emotion that was deliciously new. I felt feisty and I had a mission.

'Bloody hell.'

Richard's face was a picture of disbelief as I waltzed into the Deli. He stopped midway through pouring milk into a jug and simply stared.

'What do you reckon?' I asked, for a moment hoping he didn't think I looked stupid.

'I …' he spluttered. 'Well, I …'

Sally walked in behind me carrying some lemons. 'Looks pretty fabulous, doesn't she?' she smiled broadly at her brother. 'That pink is gorge. Not regretting the hair, are you?' she asked me. 'Don't you dare change your mind.' She dropped the lemons on the counter and laughed at Richard, who was still speechless. 'Close your mouth, brother dear. You should have seen her at Martin's last night, Rich – she walked in and took everyone's breath away.'

Richard seemed to have recovered himself. 'I'll bet she did,' he said, and blasted hot steam into the milk jug. A wave of disappointment took me by surprise. Had I wanted him to say more? Perhaps he thought I looked ridiculous or, worse, like mutton dressed as lamb.

'Want your usual?' he asked, handing over a tall latte to a customer and taking their money.

'No, thanks.'

'Oh. Taking another day off, are we?' He frowned slightly.

'Not exactly.' I found myself apologising. 'I'll go in later. I've just got some things to do first.' I turned to go, my bubble a bit deflated, but Sally intercepted me by the door.

'Think you might have made an impression,' she muttered in my ear and I looked round hopefully but Richard was busy putting out sandwiches into the fridge cabinet. 'Over there.' She jerked her head towards the window where a man, a boy really, not much older than Nat, was sitting at the counter that looked out onto the street and appraising me with all the arrogance of youth.

I stopped and, smiling now, gave him the biggest wink I could summon before flouncing out of the Deli.

The landlord's office was in the same area of town as Micah's flat: the grubby end. This time I walked. The motley collection of shops was beginning to open and set up for the day and it took me a while to find the office doorway. The rent had always vanished out of my account by direct debit and I'd never met the elusive Mr Sayers of Haynes Sayers. For rent reviews he'd always sent round a weasely little man with arms too long for his sleeves and a strong smell of stale sweat, who'd talked to my tits and not my face. The reception area smelt musty and was narrow and pokey with a half-glazed door off it, the glass obscured. Two hard chairs covered in a grubby red weave were pushed against the wall and, between them stood a low table with a few well-thumbed copies of *Heat* magazine. I looked around for a bell or some way to alert someone that I was there but could find nothing. I sat for a moment, perched on the edge of the hard chair, but since I had no time to waste sitting around I got up and knocked tentatively at first on the glass door, then harder as I heard voices. It was opened suddenly and violently, knocking me backwards.

'Hello?'

The woman was short and round, with a hairstyle like a man's and hard eyes behind plain rectangular glasses. She wore an ugly shirt that you'd call a blouse with a navy blue skirt and sensible shoes. She looked me up and down in my little pink dress.

'Can I help?'

'I've come to see Mr Sayers?'

'Is he expecting you?' Her attitude was hostile and suspicious.

'No. No, he isn't, but I wonder if I might be able to have a quick word with him.'

'I doubt that, dear. He's a very busy man,' she said, pulling herself up to her full height, which wasn't far. Her tone implied that the elusive Mr Sayers was really too important to be interrupted at any cost.

The fight began to seep out of me. 'I'm sure he is but I really don't have much time and I'm one of his tenants. I just want to talk to him about the imminent rent rise in Paradise Street.'

At that she sighed. 'We have had several representations about this and we have responded to them accordingly and through the proper channels. I really don't think he will talk to you, Miss er … The letters have gone out, as you know, and that is the end of it. I think his intentions are fair and been made utterly plain—'

I peered down at her from my heels and tried to look as intimidating as I could. 'Are you the landlord too, Miss er … ?'

'Well, obviously not but—'

'Well then – as one of his long-standing tenants, I would very much like to see Mr Sayers. I don't think that is unreasonable, do you?' And, in an impressive side move, I scooted past her and through the glazed door.

The room beyond wasn't much bigger than the lobby but into it were squeezed two desks and a very busty, very middle-aged platinum blonde with a cleavage you could drown in and who was typing on a computer keyboard behind one of the desks. Beyond her was a further door and behind it I could see a man. On the assumption the busty blonde wasn't Mr Sayers, I carried on past her, leaving her spluttering, her red-taloned nails poised over the keys, and let myself through the glass door.

'Mr Sayers, I presume?' I did my best to purr.

His head shot up. He was about the same age as my father, but balder and stouter, his round belly squeezed behind a desk that took up most of the room. A big glass window looked out onto the railway line and the room smelt of cheap aftershave. On his face were a series of large moles and he peered at me over those half-moon spectacles that give people an intimidating air. And it worked for Sayers. There was a harshness about him that was chilling. No wonder those two outside worked for him. It was unlikely he'd attract anyone with half an ounce of charm. The battleaxe, panting, had followed me in.

'So sorry, Mr Sayers. I did try to stop her—'

'Not a problem, Miss Dryden.' He smiled slimily at me. 'Is it polite to storm into someone's office, my dear?'

Now, if there is one expression I can't tolerate it's 'my dear'.

It's patronising and superior. The bitch of a school secretary used to address all of us like that just before bollocking us for some shortcoming, and since then it's always put me on my guard.

'No, *my dear* Mr Sayers, it probably isn't.' His eyebrows had shot up so at least I had a reaction. 'But nor is it polite to hike up the rent on Paradise Street to an extent that will bring the small businesses that have existed there for years to their knees. Nor is it polite to ignore letters we've sent you, or to refuse to see our consortium spokesperson.' Martin would like that title.

Mr Sayers leaned back in his chair and took off his glasses, slipping the arm into his mouth to reveal crooked and stained teeth. 'Ah, this again. Which shop is it that you rent, Miss ... ?'

'Streeter. Lucy Streeter. And I run number seventeen.'

He nodded. 'Yes, you've been there a while, I believe?'

'Ten years, so that's why really this recent decision to massively increase the rent is so unreasonable. We have all been good tenants and deserve better than this. You haven't even carried out our repairs, despite several requests.' I was warming to my theme but I wished Richard was with me. He always argued so much better than I could. 'My leaking roof has already caused damage to my stock. It's because of people like you that there are no independent shops left on the high street these days – we just can't afford it – and every high street looks the same. You could be anywhere in Britain. Are we to become a nation of chain stores with no place for the enthusiastic artisan?'

'Ten years?' he interrupted ominously quietly. 'Then you will understand why this very reasonable rent rise has to take place. We have to keep abreast of inflation and rising costs, and the previous increases were not adequate.' I opened my mouth like a fish but he ploughed on. 'These properties are highly sought after, Miss Streeter, and the rents need to reflect that. I am sure you will understand when I tell you that I am approached by some national chains wanting these properties and I want to be supportive of local business people but ...' He shrugged as if it was beyond his control and placed his glasses on the desk, laying them on what I could see now were a set of architect's plans.

It's always been a talent of mine to be able to read upside down and I squinted at the wording on the bottom corner. It definitely said 'Paradise Street'. Was that his game? Kick us all out and redevelop?

'Mr Sayers, I don't think you want to support us at all. Can I?' I put my hand out and before he could stop me, I pulled the plans out from under his glasses and turned them around so I could read them properly. For a moment I thought I must have got it wrong. This drawing was of Paradise Street but it was barely recognisable. The façades were the same, but soaring above them were more floors in glass and steel, with Juliet-balconied windows and shops on the street level. And, sure enough, in the corner of the plans was an architect's name and 'Paradise Street Retail Development Drawing 1' written in black capitals.

Mr Sayers' expression was so unabashed I wanted to slap him.

'I see,' I said slowly. 'So you want to back us into a corner and force us to quit when we can't meet the rents, then you can build this monstrosity and turn the whole street into Same Street, UK, with the same old, same old high-street chains taking units. Is that it?'

He put out his hand patiently to retrieve the plans as you might to a small child. He shook his head sadly. 'Miss Streeter, what must you think of me? I wouldn't be doing my job if I didn't explore all the possibilities, but you do me a disservice. I only have the best interests of the town at heart and, either way, you really have to understand that this rent increase is in line with recommended guidelines – as you know, two tenants on your street have already seen sense. So it can't be that unreasonable, can it? I think you'll find I'm in the right here.'

I dropped my shoulders in defeat. I wasn't going to get anywhere here. It didn't matter about my shop. After tomorrow my stock would probably be taken away – where to, I wondered? Divied up amongst friends? I had a momentarily hysterical vision of Richard in one of my dresses. But all this mattered terribly to Martin and Gaby, Fen and Deepak, and especially to Sally and to Richard who had worked so bloody hard to make the Deli a success. This would be the end of the line for them. They barely made the rent as it was, despite having a reputation for the best muffins in town. They'd have to sell them in industrial quantities to achieve what this bastard was asking.

'Well, I think it will probably be the end of the line then, Mr Sayers.' I made for the door. 'Don't worry. You'll crowbar us all out and make lots of money from someone else, and you'll be able to buy a lovely new house and car and maybe even get some decent offices. You might even be able to hire some polite staff – but I hope you never have a restful night's sleep for the rest of your life.' And I sped – no, flounced would be a better word for it – out of the building, leaving Shorty and Busty with their mouths wide open.

My heart stopped thumping with anger and indignation somewhere down the street. Well, I'd really blown it now for everyone. He'd be so angry he'd probably double what he'd already demanded and insist we were all out by the beginning of next month. I'd better keep my mouth shut to Richard or he'd lynch me. If I wasn't dead already.

I was, frankly, out of breath and I slowed to a stop, realising I'd walked quite a way down the road but in totally the wrong direction. In fact, I didn't exactly know where I was. I looked around. A scruffy mix of residential – flats, mostly – and commercial. A charity shop, a kebab takeaway and bookie. Nothing to distinguish it. Then, as I squinted, I spotted the little, rotund figure of Fen hurrying out of a shop to my right. I was going to call hello and tell him about my meeting with Sayers but he scurried across the road before I could attract his attention. He jumped into his van and drove off.

Twenty minutes later I still wasn't home. I was hot, out of breath and my shoes hurt. I was even crosser when I saw Fen's van outside his shop – I could have cadged a lift back if only I'd shouted louder and got his attention. The issue of Mr Sayers had plagued me all the way back. I hadn't achieved anything by going to see him and now what options were left? Writing a letter to Sayers wouldn't help. We'd tried that. Perhaps I should have him killed, or kill him myself? That option was tempting and seemed a little drastic. Should I leave Nat with the reputation of having a murderer for a mother?

Nat. My heart did a painful leap. It was leaving him that was the most agonising part of all this. He'd be fine. Children always are, but that wasn't the point. I fished out my phone to send him a message – since he's been at uni I've sent him one every morning to say hello. It's become a sort of ritual. Sometimes he'll reply and sometimes he won't, depending on what he's up to, or how hungover he is, but it means I can be there in his life without being too invasive. Oddly there was a message from him already there this morning.

Thought might pop back on Sunday to collect some CDs.
Full roast?!

Cheeky bugger. I smiled, then remembered with a lurch that I wouldn't be there. How odd to imagine Nat at the flat and how terrible that he'd be there to sort through the remnants of my life. I felt curiously detached and, as I let myself in, I looked around with fresh eyes, trying to imagine what would greet him. Chaos that's what. Piles of washing-up and laundry that I'd ignored over the last few days, under the illusion that it didn't matter anyway. But should my poor son really have to sort through Tuesday's cereal bowl with the crusty remains of my bran flakes, and my dirty clothes?

As I loaded the dishwasher and scraped toast crusts into the overflowing bin, I stopped for a moment. What broke my heart about Nat was a result of the immense and immeasurable love I have for him. In fact, I realised that I had never told anyone I love them. Not my parents, not Neil – because I didn't love Neil, or a boyfriend since. And not even Nat, because I'd always assumed he just *knew*. I remembered a theory I'd read somewhere that real love shouldn't need to be said out loud, because we only ever say it to seek assurance from the other person that they love us back. A woman in the article had explained how she'd berated her husband for never saying he loved her, to which he'd replied, 'I told you I did on our wedding day and I'll let you know if that changes.'

But was that wrong? Didn't we have a duty to let people know how we feel?

Walking over to the mantelpiece, I took down the envelope and pulled out the letter. Crossing out my name, I added a paragraph telling him very specifically and deliberately how much I loved him. By the time I had finished, it was not just an information sheet about his past, but a love letter to my son. Satisfied now, I slipped it back into the envelope, and propped it back on the mantelpiece.

It wasn't until later, as I tried to create some semblance of order, that something Sayers had said popped back into my head. Hadn't he said two tenants had 'seen sense'? Hadn't his letter only mentioned one?

Chapter Fourteen

I was chewing over all Sayers had said, thinking about the plans, and trying to formulate some sort of solution – though I couldn't think what – as I moved furniture and filled bin bags with rubbish, ruthlessly chucking worn pillowcases and shredded towels that had sat in the back of the linen cupboard for years. I didn't want to go down in history as the slackest Alice in town. But this was so much more than a spring clean – it was the emergence of years of accumulated *stuff* that I hadn't needed any more. What I hadn't expected was how much it would reveal about my life and who I'd been. An autobiography in garments.

I pulled open cupboards and rummaged like a slapdash archaeologist, unearthing milestones in fashion – leggings the first time round, shoulderpads (ditto). Almost embarrassed to find it, I pulled out a poncho that I'd known was a mistake when I bought it. The tassels where crimped from having been jammed into the back of the cupboard and forgotten. Even some of my own designs were woefully outdated – far too much teal and shapeless linen for layering; a look that women love and men hate. And out came items that had become lost somewhere in the back of drawers. Stuck behind a knotted clump of tights, which I pulled out like intestines and discarded, I discovered the pink and green velvet scarf that Tam had given me Christmases ago and which I thought I'd left at a party in London. It was beautiful and, in spite of the heat, I wrapped it round my neck in an attempt to make up for not wearing it, as I carried on with my task.

I worked on like a dervish, filling bags for the dump and bags for the charity shops – maybe dungarees would eventually come back into fashion. Though let's hope not. Then, from beneath my bed, I found an old teddy of Nat's and, right behind the headboard, an old sock that must have been Owen's. These two things stopped me in my tracks.

I slumped down on the floor and brushed the dust off the teddy. I think Nat had called it Roger for some inexplicable reason and that made me smile, though my throat felt tight with pain, and I rubbed my cheek against its soft fur and studied the old dusty sock as it lay dejected on the carpet in front of me. Boyfriends. The word sounds awkward at my age; it smacks of carefree, and that was something I'd never been. There hadn't been many over the years, and I hadn't exactly beat them off with a stick, mind you. But at the same time, I realised I hadn't ever really made myself available either. I'd stopped things before they had a chance to start. Not returned answerphone messages. Not made eye contact. Not taken hints. And I'd always told myself that it was because of Nat.

But now I had to wonder if that was really true. Though he hadn't asked about his father directly by then, Nat had gone through a bit of a phase, while he was at primary school, of saying he wanted a daddy – mostly to play football with, I think. And you can imagine how that made me feel. But I wondered how I'd made Nat feel by my rather defensive, jolly replies that we were much better off, just the two of us. Eventually, he stopped asking. Was it really because he didn't feel the lack of a man about the house, or had he picked up on how I felt and tried to protect me? I wouldn't put it past him – he was always a thoughtful, observant kid.

He'd taken well enough to the odd boyfriend who'd lasted

long enough to be introduced to him; and there had been one, Clive, who'd stuck around for a few months. We did the visits to the park and 'family' outings, but I remember in the café at Longleat he'd scolded Nat for slurping his drink through his straw.

'For Christ's sake,' he'd hissed, bursting the bubble of pretence; and at that moment I'd known it wasn't going to work. Nat had looked from me to Clive and back again, and suddenly it was me and my son versus the rest. No boyfriend had a hope.

After a while I got bored with my sorting-fest. It wasn't really the recommended way of spending one's last precious moments, so I pushed the bags into a corner and stood in the French window overlooking the garden and cooled down. What now? My stomach rumbled, reminding me I'd achieved a ridiculous amount on an empty stomach and, as I munched an impromptu elevenses of chocolate digestive biscuits and a can of Coke that Nat had left in the fridge, I planned my next move.

I still wasn't sure what Sayers had meant about two tenants 'seeing sense', but I did know he wasn't going to get a penny of my hard-earned cash when I was gone. I needed to make sure now that there'd be nothing left for him to get his sticky hands on and, anyway, I could think of much better ways to spend that money.

There was a small queue at the bank as always and I joined the end, quite calmly. I'd spent some scary times in this place over the years – initially trying to persuade the manager that more designer casuals were essential to the prosperity of Leamington Spa, then having to account for why sales of wrap-over cardigans were not quite as buoyant as I'd predicted. When I'd been allocated a faceless business manager in a call centre far, far away, it had almost been a relief, although it had coincided with my first year of profit, so the whole relationship suddenly became easier from then on. I was definitely not one of the types that lament the demise of the personal relationship with their bank. I was only too happy to keep them at arm's length somewhere in Birmingham. Now I had nothing to fear.

At last it was my turn. The polyester-suited teller beamed professionally. 'And how can I help you today?'

I was still looking worriedly at her shiny lapels and logo-encrusted shirt and had to consciously bring my attention back. 'I'd like to withdraw some cash, please.'

'Certainly. Do you have your cash withdrawal card with you?'

I fumbled in my wallet and handed over my business payment card and she checked the details before tapping some numbers into her keyboard.

'And how much would you like to withdraw today?'

'Well, *today* I would like to withdraw everything, please.'

She frowned slightly. There was a slight pause as she checked her screen.

'Do you know the balance of your account?'

I shrugged. 'Roughly, but can you just take it to zero?'

'Do you have any direct debits due to go out, Mrs er ... Streeter, that need to be covered?'

'*Miss*, actually, and I'll be taking care of those.' I drummed my fingers on the counter, not wanting her to thwart my plan and, after a few more questions, she finally handed me back my card, followed by a neatly rolled-up wodge of notes, secured with a red elastic band. 'Is there anything else I can do for you today?'

It was a lovely solid log of cash and my fingers tingled with anticipation as I put it carefully into my handbag. 'No, thanks. Not today.' And probably not ever again.

Out on the high street, the shoppers were starting to get into their stride and the bus stops were thronged. I picked my way through and headed determinedly down to Jephson Gardens. The place would be heaving any minute when the workers from the local offices made their way there for their lunchbreak, but for now it was quite quiet and sunny. On the benches close to the fountain, I could see the familiar group of winos and homeless, and could hear them laughing and joking with their cracked, indistinct voices before I'd even halved the distance to them. There were a couple of older men, hairy and toothless, but amongst them were some young lads, no older than Nat, painfully thin and purposeless. It wasn't for me to say if they were wasters or victims of society, but what did that matter? I'd never seen the point of the campaigners who wanted them hounded out. They had nothing and, to me, that was terribly sad.

The group gave me a friendly, if incomprehensible, greeting as I approached. They seemed a cheery lot, and I stopped and smiled.

'Afternoon, gents. How are you?'

There was general astonishment at being addressed politely, but they soon recovered. 'Very well, very well, thanks, lassie,' replied one in a strong Glaswegian accent. 'And how about yerself?'

'Fine thanks. I was wondering, Mr – er …'

'You from the Social?' another asked suspiciously.

'Gosh, no!' I laughed. 'Do I look like it?' For a moment I faltered – not really sure what someone from the Social would look like, but I didn't think it would be a compliment. Then, before I could change my mind, I pressed on. 'Um. I was wondering. I'd really like to help you.'

They exchanged glances. 'You from one of them charities? God botherers? You know.'

'No, no!' I said hastily. This was a bit awkward. I reached into my bag and pulled out the notes I'd separated off as I left the bank. 'No, I just wanted to give you a sort of gift.' I held the money out tentatively, aware that I was offering it as you might food to a dangerous animal. 'There's enough here for you all to get some shoes or some blankets, maybe. I don't know ...'

They didn't take much persuading. The man closest to me snatched the money from my hand with dazzling speed.

'God bless you, luv.' The most vociferous lad toasted me with his can of Tennent's as the other fingered the notes, scuffling slightly as they made sure they got their share of the crisp tenners. 'God bless you, and keep you in good health.'

'Please buy yourselves something you need, won't you? Something ... nourishing?'

'Oh, you can count on that, love!' he called reassuringly as I scuttled away, a warm feeling of benevolence suffusing my body as I left the park.

Chapter Fifteen

Thursday, early afternoon

I knew the moment that I slid into my baking car that what I was about to do could well be a pointless exercise, but as soon as I left the park the urge to see Nat had overwhelmed me. I had to see him, to reassure myself that he was happy and healthy and safe. I tried to call but it went straight to answerphone so I snatched up my car keys and simply left without thinking.

The weather was clear and glorious, the sky a cerulean blue without a breath of wind, and I wound down the windows to make up for the lack of air con. I pulled out on to the main road, my skin sticky against the car upholstery and, as I drove past Clarendon Square, a meaty convertible car driven by a woman with large dark glasses swept past me, her blonde hair blowing out behind her. She looked so cool and carefree and I felt a surge of pure envy. Lucky cow. That's what I'd always hankered after: a little sporty number I could jump into and screech off in. The traffic lights turned red and, as I waited, I tapped the steering wheel. Why not! If I couldn't do it now I never would – but where do you hire a sports car at the drop of a hat?

Five minutes and one phone call later I had done a U-turn, and not just in the road, and was heading in the other direction. To Neil's garage.

'You want what?' he'd asked when I'd been put through to him on the phone. 'What, now? It's a bit short notice.'

'I know, I know,' I'd urged, 'but you're the only person I could think off and ... come on, you owe me!'

'Come over then,' he sighed, but I could hear a smile in his voice. 'I might have something.'

I found the garage after asking directions twice then, in-between industrial units and car body repair shops, I spotted his forecourt, the signage matching the card I'd been given by his mother. There were several small hatchbacks laid out in shiny rows with prices in their windscreens and my heart sank. These weren't much better than what I was in already! Sensible little runabouts. I locked up and went in to the reception, Neil's secretary looking up curiously at this spiky blonde who had walked in off the road.

'Can I help?' She smiled.

'It's okay, Carol. I know this lady already.' Neil came out of an office at the back, jingling a set of keys. 'This way.'

I did as I was told and followed him back around the work-shop to the car park behind. There, roof already down, was a silver Mazda MX5. My eyes widened with glee.

'Wow!' I breathed. 'Are you sure?'

Neil smiled broadly, clearly delighted he'd made an impression. 'No, not at all sure. Call it a guilty conscience. Just don't scratch the bloody thing. And don't put too many miles on it. It's nearly sold.'

Spontaneously, I gave him a peck on his cheek before slipping into the leather driver's seat and adjusting the rear-view mirror. He dropped the keys into my outstretched hand.

'Thank you.' I smiled up at him. 'I'll have it back before bedtime.'

'You do that. Put the keys through the letterbox. And Lucy,' he added as an afterthought, 'wherever you're going, drive carefully.'

It wasn't until I was on the dual carriageway heading towards the M69 that I realised what I'd been missing all my life. Forget Prozac. Driving an open-topped car should be available on the NHS. In fact, I can't be sure I didn't actually yelp with glee as I opened the throttle, but I know I sang along ridiculously loudly to some cheesy Tina Turner on the radio that was cranked up full volume. At the traffic lights by the A45, the man in the car next to me looked over appreciatively. No wonder they're called pulling-cars. I should have got one years ago, along with the hair and the tattoo – how different life could have been!

I'd done this drive a few times now but it still fooled me. Part of getting older, isn't it, suddenly becoming unsure of routes to places. I used to think my parents were daft for fussing over maps before they set off in their neat little caravanette to the West Country or the Lake District, but now I understood. After a couple of false turns – okay so I wasn't really concentrating quite as much as I should have – I found Nat's faculty and pulled up in a designated 'no parking' area, hatched with yellow lines, in front of the building. I tried his number again, and as I listened to it going straight to answerphone, I watched people pushing in and out of the wide glass doors – all looking the same in their shorts and T-shirts, all tall and lanky, all wonderfully young. A wave of sadness threatened to overcome me – they were so optimistic, had so much to look forward to in the naïve way young people have, and there was I on the edge of a precipice.

For the first time through all this, I thought about God. In fact, I sat on the 'no parking' area for a good fifteen minutes thinking about God, which was fifteen minutes longer than I'd ever given him before. As the sun beat down on my head, and as students poured in and out of the building, it crossed my mind that tomorrow I might well have the answer to the question that the whole planet was asking: is there a hereafter?

I might be met at some fancy wrought-iron gates by a bloke with a long white beard and flowing robes, and welcomed into a paradise of endless chocolate and happiness – like perpetuity spent between a spa and a sweet shop.

I wasn't sure what I believed really. I'd had Nat christened, of course, but not out of any desire to make sure he was entered into the Church. I had simply caved in to my father's insistence. He is a fair-weather churchgoer – funerals, weddings, Easter Sunday and Christmas Day. Like many Church of England people, he attends as much to be seen as to go down on bended knee. But to have Nat baptised was an imperative for him, as if not having him 'done' would confirm his illegitimacy and, as I stood in the musty-smelling church in Warwick with a wriggling Nat, uncomfortable in the silly family Christening gown that was too tight and pinching his arms, I felt like a hypocrite. Perhaps tomorrow St Pete would pull me up on that, as well as my other indiscretions: late bill payments; the odd white lie; that night I'd slept with Klaus, the rep from Gamel, the Scandinavian clothing brand. That had been stupid, embarrassing and most annoyingly, it had meant I'd had to stop stocking the range in the shop because afterwards he wouldn't leave me alone. Instead of telling him it was a mistake, I'd compromised. Again.

Yes, that's what St Pete would pull me up on: being a wuss.

But what if I never made it through the gates? What if it was the Hell option for me? It seemed a bit harsh – perpetuity in a fiery nightmare just for having had unprotected sex with Neil Bartlett when I was seventeen, but who knew what the admissions policy was when it came to the 'other side'?

I was being facetious to jolly myself along but, as I watched the comings and goings of the students, I felt a wave of fear. What if the atheists were right and there was nothing afterwards at all? There was little comfort in thinking I might well find out the answer tomorrow.

'Hey, you can't park here, love.' An official with the university crest on his uniform towered over me as I sat in the car. 'This is for deliveries only.'

'Are you expecting one?' I asked. If I had to go and find a car park, I'd be using up precious minutes.

'Well, they come and go all the time. We'll clamp you if you don't move.'

I put on my most winning smile. 'Would it be okay if I left it here for the minutest second? I just need to drop something off for my son over there?'

I clearly hadn't lost all my charms because he looked brazenly at my legs, straightened up and said: 'Two minutes and that's it.' I slipped out of the car and flashed more teeth at him.

'Thanks sooo much,' I cooed. Another thing for St Pete to add to his list: flirtation with intent.

As I pushed open the heavy glass doors, it crossed my mind that I'd been a bit rash. Nat hadn't even replied to my text and I had no idea where he might be today. I looked around at the noticeboards covered in faculty meeting notices and torn posters for gigs in the JCR, hoping perhaps I'd find some sort of timetable, but this wasn't school. What did I know about how universities functioned? A boy passed me, all jeans hanging off his bum and oversized beanie. His head must have been roasting.

'Excuse me?'

'Huh?' he grunted. His chin had a thin beard – more fluff than stubble – and he looked so achingly young in his coolness.

'I'm trying to find Nat Streeter. Do you know him?'

He shrugged. 'Nah, sorry.' And loped off.

After all the frantic activity, the reception area was suddenly empty. I looked at my watch – it had just gone past the hour so perhaps lectures had changed over and the students were all in classrooms now. I headed through some double doors and down a long corridor. There were rooms off it on either side, loads of rooms all with porthole windows in the doors. I had to go up on tiptoes to see in. Some were empty and some contained varying numbers of students, some in rows, some in a circle around the lecturer, all writing on notepads or looking bored. I scanned each one, then went up to the next floor, a replica of the one below, growing more and more frantic that I wouldn't find Nat at all.

Then there he was, a dark head bent over a book and hidden behind a girl with long hair and a large bust barely contained in a vest. Without thinking I burst through the door.

'Nat!'

The lecturer, a tall man with wire-rimmed glasses and a loose open-necked shirt, jumped as I stormed in, noisily breaking his flow, and all the students jerked up their heads as one and looked at me. And Nat, too, looked up.

Only it wasn't Nat. This boy wasn't even close to resembling my beautiful Nat.

'I'm so, I'm so ...' I mumbled, backing out of the door and closing it quietly behind me. My face was on fire with embarrassment and I scuttled back down the corridor, bobbing up every now and then to peer through the next porthole. It was no good and I headed towards the exit. As I pushed my way out now, heart thumping, I almost collided with a woman, older than me and efficiently dressed in pink shirt and black skirt. She was missing the studied grunge of student and lecturer so had to be administrative staff.

'I'm sorry – I'm looking for my son, Nat. He's third-year Business Studies?'

'Mmm.' She paused for a second. 'Yes, I know that group. I don't think they have a lecture this afternoon. Have you tried his room?'

I thanked her, jumped back into the car and squinted at

signs to find my way to his halls of residence, a charmless brick building that looked like a mental hospital. As I clambered up the stairs and navigated my way down corridors of doorways plastered in stickers, lit by strip lights, I took in the atmosphere: a mixture of the smell of cup-a-soup and the thub thub of music emanating from different rooms. This was one part of higher education I wasn't sorry to have missed.

The loudest music was coming from the room of my studious son, who was obviously studying for his exams with the help of some drum 'n' bass, and I had to bang quite hard before he finally heard me and the door was flung open. It is quite probable that I was the last person on earth he was expecting to see, but his expression of horror and incredulity was made all the more comical because he had to assimilate not only that his mother had tipped up mid-afternoon on a weekday, but that his mother did not look like his mother at all.

'What the f—' he managed.

'Well, nicely put, darling.' I smiled, and touched my hair self-consciously. 'Do you like it?' He came out into the corridor and inspected me, then nodded cautiously. 'Yeah, it's quite funky.' I put my arms around him and he hugged me close. 'It'll be a tattoo next.' I kept quiet – he wasn't ready for such a change – and simply inhaled the familiar scent of his boyish skin.

'Sorry to turn up like this.' I swallowed. 'I did try to call. I just fancied seeing you. Are you busy?'

He looked back into the tiny room, the floor of which was entirely carpeted in clothes, and shrugged. 'Just finishing an essay. But it can wait,' he said loudly over the music. 'Sorry, I've forgotten to top up my phone.' Then a doubtful expression crossed his face. 'Er ... Do you want a coffee?'

I smiled. 'No thanks. Not sure my immune system could cope with the inevitable unwashed mug. How about we go and get an ice cream like we used to?'

He picked up his keys and, turning off the music, pulled the door behind him. 'We haven't done that since I was about seven.'

'Oh well,' I tried to sound as jolly as I could, 'you're never too old for an ice cream.'

His eyes were even wider when I slipped into the car and patted the seat beside me.

'Christ, Mum! New hair, new car. Have you come to tell me you've found some new bloke – am I going to have to call him "Daddy"?'

'Ha ha.' I forced a laugh, and made up something to cover my fluster. He seemed quite happy with the explanation that I'd 'borrowed it from a friend' then, after ten minutes of tracking down an elusive ice-cream van, we parked and found a spot under a tree in the park.

As he licked his cone, catching the drips as they ran down the side, I studied him intently. His hair needed cutting and he could have done with a shave, but to my biased eyes he was as perfect as any man could be, yet no different from the boy who'd sat on the beach in Devon aged five arranging shells he'd collected into colours and shapes. He could obviously feel my eyes boring into him and he shot me a sideways glance without moving his head.

'You're being weird,' he grunted, a small smile on his lips. 'Take a photo; it'll last longer.'

'I've got enough of those. Do you remember that holiday in Woolacombe when you were about five?'

'I was six!' he said in mock indigence. 'Was that during my shell period?'

'Yes, one of your many obsessions. I think it was trading cards after that.'

'Sure was.'

'Shells were cheaper.' I smiled, remembering how he'd tapped me for a pack of cards every time we went in Woollies.

Nat thought for a moment. 'Was that the holiday when the air ambulance landed on the beach?'

I leaned back against the tree. 'Or was that Watergate Bay?'

Nat shook his head as he licked his lips. 'No, pretty sure it was Devon.'

He was probably right and we were both silent for a moment, me lost in reflection, him concentrating on his 99. 'Did you have a happy childhood?' I asked.

His head shot round. 'Now you are being weird!'

'Well, did you?' I pushed on. 'Do you have good memories? I mean, was it the childhood you *wanted*?'

Nat snorted with laughter. 'I don't remember putting in an order for any particular kind of childhood! Shit, if I'd known you could, I'd have requested being the son of the Sultan of Brunei. Then I could have had one of those scaled-down Ferraris we saw in Harrods that time. God, how I've wanted one of those!'

'Sorry, I clearly failed as a mother.' I smiled back. 'You didn't even have a Scalextric, did you?'

'Nah. Practically neglect on your part.'

'You poor, deprived boy. I clearly didn't work hard enough to provide for you.' I pulled my knees up and watched some students playing football a few yards away. Nat wiped his hands on his shorts, then rolled over onto his front and looked at me.

'Come to think of it, what *are* you doing here? I mean, not that it's not lovely to see you but I'm coming home at the weekend – and shouldn't you be in the shop?'

I searched his face, realising that my impetuous behaviour, my need to create a last memory for him, had obviously un-settled him, so I threw my hands up in a 'who cares?' way and chuckled, hoping I sounded convincing. 'Do you know, I just walked out? The sun was shining and I thought, Sod it! I'd rather see my son. My boss is a bitch anyway!' From nowhere

I could feel a sob building so, quickly, I jumped up and pulled up Nat after me. 'Come on then. It's supposed to be us old folk who are boring farts. Let's go and have some fun.'

The next hour or so was the most carefree I'd had in ages. With cash burning a hole in my pocket, I spoilt Nat in a way I'd never been able to. In the past I'd had to count every penny, but that afternoon in a shopping centre I parted company with a couple of hundred quid on my son. A new pair of Converse in bright red tartan, some skinny-fit jeans and a T-shirt that was ridiculously overpriced. I even topped up his phone for him. Giddy now, we tried on silly sunglasses and laughed at our reflections, had an ice-cream soda (because I'd never had one before – and won't bother again) and had a game of tennis on a demonstrator Wii in a gaming shop, which I lost embarrassingly – but it left us breathless and laughing and whenever I could, I feasted my eyes on my son. Just enough to register every feature but not enough to freak him out.

By the time I dropped him back, I was only just holding it together. I wrapped my arms around him far too tightly, but he tolerated it with a good-natured 'all right, Mum. I'll see you in a couple of days.'

'Yes, yes I know.' I touched his cheek. 'I just miss you sometimes, that's all.'

He pulled away gently and headed towards the front door of the halls of residence, then turned and gestured with his arms full of shopping bags. 'Thanks for all this, Mum. I'll see you shortly.'

'Don't call me Shortly,' we both called in unison as he turned and I watched him disappear. 'And I love you,' I added quietly.

The tears that poured down my face as I travelled back were worse than the rain shower that came from nowhere. By the time I'd worked out how to pull up the soft top, my clothes were soaked and sticking to me, and I steamed my way back to Neil's garage. I must have looked a fright, my hair flat on my head and my eyes puffy from tears, and I was relieved that it was after closing time and I didn't have to face him.

I left the fun little car on the forecourt, with a thank-you note scrawled on an old receipt I'd found in my handbag, and climbed back into my own tatty little car. Feeling deflated and wrung out and reluctant to go home to my empty flat, I headed for the Deli, hoping there was still somebody there.

Chapter Sixteen

'There was someone looking for you.' Sal smiled as I walked into the Deli, her face still fresh despite a long day.

I slid gratefully onto a bar stool. My stomach rumbled and I realised I'd had very little to eat – except ice cream – since breakfast.

'You look bushed. Have you got hay fever? What can I get you?' Sal leaned against the counter, a tea towel over her arm. I looked at the clock. It was long after closing, but I took liberties with her friendship and hoped she wouldn't mind.

I thought for a moment. What did I really fancy? 'A hot chocolate with whipped cream and a flake and a brie and grape sandwich please.' I might be about to croak but I wasn't going to starve to death. Plus, I might as well go out on my favourite sandwich.

'Watching our weight, are we?' Sally teased, as she took down a tall glass mug from the shelf above the machine. The Deli's coffee machine is Richard's pride and joy – not for him the classic espresso machines in every Starbucks on the planet. This was a gargantuan, shiny steel coffee monstrosity that stood three feet high on the counter and off it came pipes and dials, handles and nozzles. It summed up everything he did. He'd never settle for the standard – the Deli chairs had to be the most unusual and match those he'd seen in a café in San Gimignano. The coffee they sold had to be the very best from Vienna. No wonder the place was so popular.

'So, anyone we know – this person looking for me? Was it that oddball friend of Tam's?' I hoped it wasn't Micah. I didn't want to see him again. He was a living reminder that I soon wouldn't be.

'It was a woman, actually. Quite plump, about fifty, I'd say.'

'Oh Christ – not Mum's friend Hilary Bellingham?' Mum used to walk the dog and do keep-fit classes with Hilary who, since she'd been widowed, was permanently trying to persuade my mother to take interesting and improving cruises with her to learn about ancient history and gardening from resident lecturers. I felt sorry for her in her hearty attempts to fend off her loneliness but right now, I didn't really need her.

'No, I've met Hilary, haven't I? This woman was dressed a bit wackily. In fact, I think she might have been at Martin's launch party but I can't be sure.'

I did a mental sweep of the guests at the party – or at least the one's I hadn't offended. 'White-grey bob, long coat and pink glasses on top of her head?'

'That's her. Friend?' Sally pushed the flake into the whirl of whipped cream and slid the glass across the counter towards me. 'Fill your face with that then, Miss. A moment on the lips ...'

I smiled. The lifetime on my hips would be momentary. I pulled out the flake and licked off the cream that had stuck to it. The chocolate melted against my tongue and felt smooth and creamy.

'I'll just nip out and make your sarnie. Hold the fort for me. Rich isn't here. He's gone out for a bit to get some stuff for the weekend. He's off to the boat.'

'Alone?' I'd asked the question automatically. I don't know why it mattered.

Sally raised her eyebrows very slightly. 'No, he's meeting Jerry down there. He's that old mate from college – do you remember you met him at Rich's birthday party?'

I did. A tall, lanky wine merchant, with bright smiling eyes behind his glasses, he'd engaged me in conversation most of the evening and I'd spent a delicious time flirting with him. Not because I particularly fancied him, but because I could. Richard kept coming over to us, to hand Jerry another drink mostly, and Jerry had teased him about the crap Rioja he was serving, though, being Richard, it hadn't been bad at all.

I laughed airily now to Sally. 'The latest bird not up to crewing then?'

'No, she's more the decorative type – besides, she might chip a nail. Come to think of it, he hasn't mentioned her recently. But that doesn't mean much – getting anything out of him is impossible. It makes running a business together a challenge at times!' She slipped through to the kitchen at the back and I was alone. A wave of tiredness came over me and I leaned my elbows on the counter and rested my head in my hands. I had a headache but that wasn't really a surprise after the amount I'd cried on the way home from seeing Nat. No wonder Sally thought I had hay fever.

'Hello, stranger.'

I hadn't heard Richard come in, but there he was, leaning on the counter beside me. 'Aren't you getting any service? Crap joint this anyway. You'd have better luck at McDonald's.'

It was so comforting to hear his voice and I looked up, hoping to cover my tiredness and puffy eyes. 'Yeah, I've been sitting here for hours. I think the owner has buggered off to do his shopping. It's very poor show!'

'Yes, but look what he's bought!' He whipped out his phone and scrolling down the keys with his thumb, opened an image and handed it to me. There was a shot of a long, traditionally built boat with wooden hull, two masts and a cabin.

'I don't understand. I thought you'd gone to buy *things* for the boat not to buy another boat altogether!'

'Sssh – I didn't want to tell Sal because—'

'Didn't want to tell Sal what?' Sally appeared out of the back, a fat sandwich on a plate that she put in front of me with a napkin. She peered over my hand at the phone.

'Oh, Richard, you haven't.'

'Yup, I have.' He smiled widely, unashamed, like a small boy. 'She was over the other side of Southam and I saw her advertised online yesterday. Isn't she the most beautiful thing you ever saw – present company excluded, of course?'

She was. She looked like *The True Love* in *High Society*, the one Grace Kelly sailed on the swimming pool the night before her wedding. How wonderfully spontaneous he'd been! I'd never done anything like that – fallen for something and just bought it, whether I could afford it or not.

'She really is lovely, Richard. What's she called?'

'*Serenity*. It's a bit of a cliché but I can't change it. Bad luck and all that.'

'No, no, you mustn't change it. It's a lovely name.' I looked back at the boat. He'd have such fun in it, out in the Channel with the wind in the sails as the waves crashed up over the bow. I knew because of the times Sally and I had crewed for him and we'd been soaked with spray and had returned home, late and exhausted, our hair matted with salt and our faces stiff and glowing from the sea air.

'Want to crew her for me?' He smiled down at me.

I didn't know how to reply. 'Yes, maybe. Who knows?' I sank my teeth into the sandwich, the grapes sweet and delicious with the salty cheese, and chewed thoughtfully. What did I have to lose? I grabbed the opportunity. 'Look, Richard, what are you up to this evening? Why don't we celebrate the *Serenity* and do something silly?'

'Something silly? You?' He smiled. 'I thought you liked to think things through before taking the plunge.'

'Yes, well, people change.' I probably sounded a bit sullen. 'So, *are* you busy?'

He smiled at me rather disconcertingly for a moment. 'Are you asking me out, Ms Streeter?'

'Don't push your luck,' I laughed back, glad the mood had lightened.

'Well,' he pulled himself up straight and walked around the back of the counter, 'as it happens, my date with Claudia Schiffer has had to be postponed, so I expect I could oblige. What did you have in mind? A mad outing to a Chinese take-away? A riotous night at the Bingo?'

Enough of his teasing. He'd made his point – so I hadn't been the most spontaneous when it came to taking risks but I'd show him. This would be a last night to remember.

'We'll see, shall we?' I swallowed the last of my sandwich. 'I'll pick you up at eight.' I slipped off the stool, thanked Sally and made for the door.

'Luce?' Richard calling my name made me turn back.

'You've got lettuce on your teeth.'

I didn't actually have anything planned for our night out. What would you have done if it was your last night on earth? I suppose we should have headed for London or the centre of Birmingham for some late-night marauding, but Richard would have to be at the Deli by seven in the morning so that wouldn't delight him. As I showered and surveyed my depleted wardrobe for something to wear, I scanned through the possibilities in my mind. Dinner? Too dull. A film? Definitely not. I'd spent enough evenings sitting in the cinema next to Richard and not even another rerun of *The Shawshank Redemption* would be enough for a night like tonight. I pulled out a soft silk vest in aqua-green as I pondered the options. (Another creation from years back with a bit of spare silk from a jacket lining, but it made me feel good.) Richard and I had always disagreed about our Best Five Movies of all time. He'd put *The Godfather* top, and we'd both been allowed a sexual-stereotype movie to include on the list, so mine had been *Brief Encounter* – oh, the lost opportunities! – and he'd been permitted *Pulp Fiction*. The yardstick had been how often you could watch it again, but I hoped he was lying when he said he'd seen it seventeen times.

As I ironed my top, slipped it on and pulled on some cropped jeans to go with it, it crossed my mind that we rubbed along pretty well, Richard and I. It was fraternal really, wasn't it? And it's fine to ask brother-figures to mend taps for you or investigate mouse droppings behind your kitchen cupboards, isn't it? He should be married really, a man like him. Perhaps he had some fatal flaw I hadn't noticed.

I picked out some drop earrings Tam had given me for my birthday – pearls with a clear green stone – and surveyed the result. With my spiky hair and the bright colours, I looked ... funky. Too late, Lucy Streeter had finally got funk.

I knocked at the front door of his house at almost exactly eight o'clock. Curiously enough, I didn't come round here often – the odd party – but after a day at the Deli surrounded by food, Richard didn't go big on entertaining, and suppers in the past were usually around my kitchen table with Nat there, and Sally and her boyfriend, Karl. They'd put up with my repertoire of chilli, or moussaka if I was being really brave, just content that they hadn't had to prepare it, and we'd spent quite a few evenings just shooting the breeze. Somehow I'd avoided inviting any girlfriends of Richard's – I used to tease him that some of them must be on a curfew at their age – but perhaps my real reason was that I didn't want an outsider to break up the group. We were all good together, shared in-jokes, had mutual friends, and I knew I'd studiously avoided allowing someone who'd be all over him to elbow in on the fun. What a bitch I'd been! But Richard had never pursued it or insisted, so perhaps he hadn't minded.

He pulled open the door in just his shorts and holding a hand towel. His hair was damp from the shower and, though I'd seen him numerous times without a shirt, either at the boat or on the odd days we'd all gone to the beach, this was different and I looked away now in embarrassment. 'Come on in – won't be a moment.' I followed him down the hall. 'There's some wine in the fridge. Pour us both a glass. I'll just put my face on.'

'Get on with it,' I called back as I took a couple of glasses down from the cupboards. 'We haven't got for ever!'

'Cheeky.'

We didn't have for ever and I didn't want to waste a minute. I poured us both a glassful, and took a long sip from mine. Richard's kitchen is that of a true foodie. Not for him the minimalism and stainless-steel surfaces of a bachelor pad. His is always mildly chaotic with utensils everywhere: well-used chopping boards leaned up against the wall, tagine dishes and bottles of fancy oils he'd bought on one of his cook's tours of Europe or North Africa, and a long bookshelf on one wall of cookbooks, from Jane Grigson to Nigel Slater. Recipes torn from magazines and newspapers poke out from between the copies. This is the business end of things, where Richard tests out the dishes they serve in the Deli, and it was warm and welcoming that evening. No wonder he teased me about my culinary skills. 'You do the sewing,' he'd say. 'I'll do the baking.' And baking he did well. The times I'd watched him prepare food at the Deli or cook something here on the odd occasions we didn't decamp to my place *en masse*, he'd move with assured confidence. I knew he'd trained in professional kitchens where speed was of the essence and there was something reassuring about his competence – whether he was chopping an onion or navigating a boat through a gale.

'Right, will I do?' He appeared at the door in a loose shirt and shorts. Weekends on the boat over the last couple of months had given him a deep tan, except in the creases around his eyes where he'd obviously squinted in the sunlight.

'S'pose.' I smiled and handed him his glass. 'Knock that back. We're burning twilight.'

'What's the hurry? You shouldn't rush a good Sauvignon Blanc.'

'Just things to do, that's all.' I realised at that moment I wanted to dance. 'First off, are your shoes comfortable?'

Looking back now, I don't know how it rated as last nights go. I know we did things I'd never done before and I know I did some things I shouldn't do again, but by the time we were heading back homeward, I felt some sense of achievement. I don't suppose that standing on a table singing karaoke is top of everyone's 1,000 things to do before they die, but belting out Guns 'n' Roses at the top of my voice ticked a box I'd secretly wanted to tick forever. Imagine me, Lucy Streeter, three or four glasses of wine ahead of the game, microphone in hand, stomping out the rhythm to a pub full of bemused people.

By the time we'd found the club, I must have been six glasses ahead. Richard and I have totted up many years in this town between us, but we both had to think hard about where best to go dancing and, when we eventually heard the pavement-vibrating boom boom emanating from a basement, we knew we'd found the right place. It was sweaty, it was crowded, it was frankly vile, but who cared? I didn't. I took his hand and pulled him through the perspiring mass of youth, and we danced for what felt like hours. He's a good mover, is Richard, though that might have been just my benign haze of wine, and I wouldn't have minded anyway if he'd danced like Orville the Duck. I swayed and gyrated, occasionally stumbling into the people around me who kindly put me back upright.

'What has come over you, young Miss Streeter?' Richard gasped, when he eventually persuaded me over to the bar. His face was glowing, and mine was red hot. My tattoo stung a bit where I'd been bashed by fellow dancers lunging into me, but my smile was wide. In fact, my face hurt with pleasure.

My head was spinning in a mixture of booze and adrenalin from the dancing. 'Oh, I just thought I'd live a little. Hey – are you hungry?'

'I'm always hungry. What did you have in mind? From your mood I wouldn't put it past you to want to eat oysters out of the belly button of a mermaid? Grapple a shark to death with your bare hands before cooking it on a spit?'

'Er ... what about a doner kebab?' I giggled.

Richard looked down at me in the light from the bar and didn't say anything for a moment. He was being jostled by people trying to get the attention of the barman but he ignored them and didn't move. 'Okay, if that's what you want.' He didn't sound cross exactly, but he was frowning slightly as if he was confused.

'We don't have to. Would you prefer a Chinese or a take-away pizza?'

'I'd positively loathe a Chinese or a takeaway pizza,' he said after a moment and, taking my arm, guided me through the throng and out to the door. The night was warm but the fresh air hit us both after the stifling heat of the club. I had no idea what time it was and didn't want to know. As we wandered down the road, bumping into each other occasionally, it struck me that crap food is very easy to come by late at night. I was too drunk to explore the correlation between the two factors, however, and happily swayed into the open doorway of the chip shop and came face to face with the old bag who ran the place: the very one, who never smiled, from my List.

'Chicken and chips,' I ordered brazenly and Richard, after trying to cover his distaste at the menu, opted for just chips. She turned her back on us and wheezed over to pick up the chip scoop. I hardly dared look at the globules of yellow grease that would soon be pasted to my arteries, but couldn't help watching in fascination as she slapped the soggy offering onto the paper and grunted, her lips downturned like the cod she served. My self-imposed challenge surged to the fore and I couldn't stop myself.

'That colour really suits you, you know,' I gushed and she hesitated momentarily in her task to look slowly down at her stained blue and white nylon apron, then fixed me with an expression of utter contempt.

'Vinegar?' she grunted.

'Oooh, yes, please,' I continued, unabashed. 'Chips without vinegar is like … is like …' I waved my hands about and made myself wobble alarmingly as I searched tipsily for a suitable metaphor. I looked at Richard for assistance.

'Assault without battery?' he suggested, and I shoved him affectionately.

'Nooo, silly,' I snorted nasally. 'Like … gin without tonic.'

Richard smiled, and shook his head. 'Well, you'd know all about that. You could have done with a bit more tonic in yours tonight! How about marriage without love?'

I thought about it for a moment and nodded. 'Good one. What do you think, Mrs …?'

'I think that's five pounds sixty,' she wheezed, banging the two wrappers down on the counter and thrusting out her hand. Richard did the honours, and I picked up the hot packages, realising I was beaten. She was a lost cause.

I wheeled round towards the door too fast and, slipping on

something greasy on the floor, executed a triple salchow that would have done Torvill and Dean proud, landing flat on my arse.

As Richard put out his hand chivalrously and I staggered to my feet, I distinctly heard a deep and strange grating noise emanating from behind the counter. Could it be ...? I turned to see the old cow shaking with amusement, her face contorted with glee at my discomfort. It hadn't been quite the way I wanted, but it would do! Result!

We headed to the park (me still giggling but unable to explain why, of course) and after toasting the *Serenity* again – this time with warm Sprite – we sat down under a tree, leaning back against its thick trunk and, without speaking, consumed our feast. Have you ever played that game at dinner parties – choose your last meal before the electric chair? Mine was always going to be spaghetti alla Puttanesca, or maybe langoustine and garlic butter. Chicken and chips eaten out of a polystyrene box with a small plastic fork wasn't quite the culinary swansong I'd envisaged, but hey. My lips tasted salty from the chips and my fingers were sticky from the chicken. I wiped them on the grass, made the palest green by the clarity of the moonlight. I felt mellow and carefree, which was odd in the circumstances. I picked up the last crispy remnants at the bottom of the box and sighed.

'Give me your rubbish then.' Richard held out his hand and as I passed it to him, our fingers brushed. I pulled away so suddenly that the box fell onto the grass between us.

'Oooops!' I laughed, stupidly embarrassed all of a sudden.

'I haven't got leprosy, you know,' Richard replied and, pulling himself up, he wandered over to the litter bin. I watched him in the moonlight. I remember thinking, this is my friend, in the soppy way one does when one is half-cut, and I knew that there was no one else I'd rather spend my last night with.

So, yes, as we meandered back up the road, feeling a little

sick after our haute cuisine, I did feel content. I tucked my arm through his and I rested my head on his shoulder. He smelt sweaty but not in an unpleasant way, and he let me stay there without saying a word. I don't know what possessed me next but as we passed the church, I looked up at the scaffolding that had been set up against it for weeks now.

'Are they ever going to take that down?' I asked, peering up and feeling a bit dizzy.

'They've had some issue with bats, I think. Deepak said they've had to down tools for a few days while the conservation people come and assess it,' Richard replied. 'I'm amazed that sodding bell doesn't drive the bats out. Never mind blind as a bat, they must be deaf, too.' The church bell was an ongoing issue with the locals, chiming in the hours and quarter-hours throughout the night. One got used to it after a while, but there were regular letters to the local paper asking that it at least be changed just to the hourly chime. The very zealous priest, however, had been most un-Christian in his response and the battle carried on between Church and town.

Then it struck me, pardon the pun, that I could at least make some contribution towards everyone's welfare before I went off and played my harp in the clouds. 'Wait there,' I called back to Richard, as I ran through the church car park and up to the scaffolding. At first I couldn't find a way to get in – the bottom of the scaffolding was surrounded by security fencing, which was padlocked and heavily papered with warning posters and health-and-safety outlines. I was about to give up on what was a stupid idea anyway, when I noticed that a small Fiesta was parked with its bonnet up against the fencing.

'What the hell are you doing?' Richard had joined me now at the fence.

'Just wait there, and if the old Bill comes, duck!' With that, and feeling very adventurous, I clambered up on to the car bonnet – it didn't cross my mind that it might be alarmed and thankfully it wasn't – and performed what can only be described as a gate vault over the top of the fencing. I landed painfully on the other side and had to stagger to find my feet. I'd grazed the inside of my leg on the bar at the top and checked quickly that it wasn't going to bleed everywhere.

'Luuuce!' Richard hissed from the other side of the boarding, and there was laughter in his voice.

'Won't be a minute! Stay there!' and in the shadows and darkness I looked around for the ladder.

Now you have to admire builders who clamber up and down ladders all day. The scaffolding was a series of platforms at each level joined by a ladder and, three levels up and out of breath, I was finally on a level with the bell tower. I didn't dare look behind me. I was unsteady enough as it was. Perhaps this was the ending Micah had in mind – I'd fall off, pissed, from a bell tower. What a way to go!

I checked my watch. If the bell rang now I'd be deafened. I had about ten minutes until it was quarter past two. I hadn't realised until now that midnight had passed. It was Friday. *The* day. I stepped gingerly off the scaffold on to the bell tower and yelped as three pigeons I had disturbed fluttered and took off into the night. Had it been bats, I would have screamed so loud, the bell ringing would have been but nothing.

The light up there was worse, and the inside of the bell was in complete shadow. At first I couldn't see how it worked. I suppose I'd imagined that it had a clapper that banged out the time, but when I peered around a bit more I realised that it was hit by a hammer on the outside. I wasn't even sure it was possible to unfasten it and I had to stretch round and up on tiptoes, blindly feeling how the hammer was attached. After a moment's fiddling, it became clear this was an impossible task and I was about to give up and clamber down again when I had a flash of inspiration. Struggling out of my jeans, I wrapped them around the end of the hammer, knotting the legs to keep it secure.

This made the karaoke seem tame. There I was at two in the morning standing in a bell tower in my vest top and knickers – fortunately one of my better pairs. With no time to lose. As I pulled the leg of the jeans into as tight a knot as I could, I heard the mechanism of the bell begin to grind alarmingly. Shit. It was going to chime. I stepped back just as the hammer pulled back then ... thub. Nothing. The only sound was the straining of the mechanism and my squeal of delight. I stretched out my arms with glee and for the first time took in the view. The town spread out before me, a sparkling patchwork of street lights that surrounded the park. I could see rooftops and the odd glimmer of light through a bedroom window – people who couldn't sleep or who had just got in from work or a night out. The occasional car sped up the road, and in the distance I could hear and then see a police car. Had someone seen me? I stiffened but then relaxed as it shot past the end of the road heading up the Parade.

Tentatively, I put my feet back on the ladder. The air was playing around my bare thighs and my flat shoes slipped every now and then when I hadn't secured a firm foothold. As I dropped virtually soundlessly to the bottom of the last ladder, I squinted into the darkness. What I hadn't worked out yet was how I was going to get over the fence. Surely there would be a box or something? I heard a scuffling behind the boarding.

'Richard? Is that you?'

'No,' he answered in a deep, deep voice. 'It's the Chief Constable. You're surrounded.'

'I'm not sure how I'm going to get out,' I whispered loudly back.

'You should have thought of that before you got in.'

'Oh, help me. Think of something.' I felt ridiculous now. Behind me was a large builders' merchant's bag of sand, and behind that I spotted the handles of a wheelbarrow. Inspiration. 'Look, if I stand on this barrow, can you lean over and pull me up?'

'God, the things I do,' I heard him puff and I smiled to myself as I dragged the barrow over to the boarding. I could hear Richard clamber on to the bonnet of the Fiesta. The barrow wasn't that stable but it might hold steady if I stood still enough with my leg slightly apart. As I clambered in and stood up precariously, I could see Richard's head appearing over the top of the boarding. He peered down at me.

'Lucy.'

'Richard?'

'You are standing in a wheelbarrow in the dark on the wrong side of a builder's boarding ...'

'In my knickers!' I snorted a giggle.

'What!' He peered over harder.

'Don't ask. Just get me out of here.'

Leaning over as far as he could, he reached down as I reached up and once he had hold of my hands he pulled as hard as he could. It was incredibly painful, and I had to abseil up the boarding until I was near enough to the top to swing my leg over. 'Ouch, shit, God, careful, that's my thigh.'

I could tell Richard didn't know quite where to put his hand, but eventually he settled on the back of my thigh as very slowly, so as not to leave half my skin on the top of the fence, I negotiated myself over, trying to ignore the tingle of pleasure from his warm hand. It didn't make things any easier that I was laughing helplessly, tears pouring down my face with mirth. I landed inelegantly on the car bonnet with a worrying crunch and I could feel it denting.

'Gosh, I hope this doesn't belong to the vicar!'

We both jumped down as quickly as we could and Richard brushed off his shorts as I checked my legs for major lacerations. My silk vest was slightly torn under the arm.

'So, Luce, silly question I know, but where exactly are your jeans?'

When I told him, he roared with laughter so loud I was certain we'd be caught and I quickly put my hand over his mouth. 'You can't walk back like that, lovely though your legs are. Here,' he started to unbutton his shirt and pulled it off. 'Wrap this round your waist.' It felt warm as I used the arms as ties and fashioned a skirt.

'Let's get you back home.'

We wandered up the road, Richard snorting again with laughter every now and then as he thought about what I'd done. 'They'll find them on Monday, of course – I think Deepak said the builders come back then, but at least we can look forward to a weekend of peace and quiet.' He hesitated as we got to the corner where we'd have to part, but only for a moment. Then he put his hands in his pockets and set off down Warwick Road towards my place. 'Come on, I'll walk you all the way home. A lady shouldn't be walking the streets alone at this time of night in her knickers.'

'Hang on.' I stumbled after him, my legs stinging a bit now, and took his arm to steady myself. 'You walk too fast.'

He slowed down and we walked on in silence until we reached my front door. Then I began to panic. I didn't want to be left here on my own. Not tonight.

'Cuppa?' I asked, retrieving the key from its hiding place under the stone frog and fumbling to get it in the lock.

I remember he took it from me, opened the door and I fell inside.

'Just need a wee,' I muttered, and headed off to the bathroom.

Once relieved, I caught sight of myself in the mirror as I washed my hands. My make-up was halfway down my face and I was flushed. I removed as much as I could with some loo-roll then splashed my face with cold water, hoping it would make a difference, but you can't sober up that quickly. By the time I emerged, blinking, having slipped on some pyjama bottoms I'd found on the back of the bathroom door, Richard was stirring a teabag in a cup. I noticed he'd only made one and that he'd thoughtfully only put on the gentler, under-cupboard lights.

'Your shirt,' I said, handing it back. 'Thanks for protecting my modesty.'

'Here, drink this, you old soak.' He handed me the mug carefully, as if I was infirm, and slipped on his shirt again. 'This place smells very clean.' He peered through to the sitting room and put his hands firmly into his pockets. 'Are you …? I mean, what's this all about, Luce? The hair, the tattoo, the dancing on tables, not to mention clambering up bell towers. Are you having some sort of mid-life crisis?'

'I don't know what you mean,' I said airily and took a swig of tea to cover my unease, scalding my mouth so badly I had to spit it back into the mug quickly. 'Sorry.' I wiped my mouth with the back of my hand. 'A girl can have a little bit of fun, can't she?'

'Of course, and it was fun tonight. Actually, I haven't had such a laugh in ages. Made me forget about overdrafts and rent reviews and that's got to be good. But it's not your usual night out, is it? Has something happened? Nat okay and everything?'

His gentle questions were too much and, as I blew into my steaming mug, tears plopped into the liquid. Carefully Richard took the cup out of my hand and pulled me into his arms in a warm embrace. I turned my head and rested it against his chest.

I steeled myself to ask the question. 'Rich?' I mumbled eventually.

'Uh huh?' He smelt so good, and I could hear his chest rumble as he spoke and his heart beating fast under my ear.

'Would you please kiss me?'

I shouldn't have said it, and he pulled back, holding me out in front of him. His expression was unreadable. 'Why?'

'Look, I know you've had lots of girlfriends and stuff,' I gabbled, suddenly mortified by what I'd asked, 'and I know we're just friends and all that. But I haven't actually been kissed for ages, and sometimes I'd like to be because everyone needs to be kissed occasionally, don't they? That physical contact—'

And probably to shut me up, he leaned down and put his warm lips on my mouth.

Then he pulled away slightly, too quickly, and because I didn't want him to go and because this might be the last time ever, and because he smelt so delicious, I put my arms up round his neck and pulled him down to kiss me again. I couldn't have cared that he may or may not have had a girlfriend, or that he wasn't mine to kiss. He was my friend, wasn't he? And that made it okay. We had just our lips together for a minute and then, brazenly, I slipped my tongue gently between his lips. He didn't respond for a moment and I felt his body tense beneath my arms, but then he relaxed again and, as the kiss deepened, he put his arms around me and pulled me gently towards him. I felt like I'd come home. There was nothing here of the fumbles I'd had with Owen, or garlicky snogs with Danish clothing reps. This felt soft and warm. And so right.

'Luce,' he mumbled against my mouth. 'We shouldn't be doing this.'

'Why not?' I gasped for breath and kissed him again and he made a sound that was like a groan. I let my hands drop from his shoulders because I wanted to drink this all in. If this really was going to be the last time, I was greedy for every sensation and I slipped my hands up the back of his shirt so they were against his bare skin. It felt taut and yet soft, this back I knew so well but had never touched. Richard groaned again, and cupped my face in his hands, kissing me intently now. As I slipped my hands round his body to feel his hard stomach, he gently pushed the straps down off my shoulders. His hands were firm on my skin and I know I gasped as the fabric fell away, leaving my breast bare and exposed and tingling with anticipation. Still kissing me, he rubbed his thumb against the nipple then, as suddenly, pulled away, breathing hard.

'What's the matter?'

'I can't do this.' He ran his hands through his hair and turned away. 'This isn't right, Luce. You're drunk. We'll regret it, and I don't want to spoil ... everything. Look, I'm going to go.' He leaned down and kissed me briefly on the lips again. 'I'll see you tomorrow.' And with that he swept past me, and left the flat.

It was very quiet and I sipped my tea distractedly. How stupid I had been to do that. I blush now thinking about it. What had got into me? I'd virtually thrown myself at him. But then, would it matter? Would he mind that his abiding memory of me would be a kiss in my kitchen in the middle of the night? I wandered through to the sitting room, illuminated only by the shaft of light coming through from the kitchen, and slumped down on the sofa. I pulled my legs up under me and rested my head back against the cushions. The problem was that once it had started I had wanted it to go further. I wanted to feel his body, not just because he was a man and I wanted to experience sex for the last time, but because it was Richard. He had felt so warm, so good. Touching him had been both sensual and horny, and surprisingly tender, too, and I couldn't remember the last time I'd felt that. If ever.

I could see my letter to Nat on the mantelpiece, the envelope now also stuffed with some of the cash from the bank, tucked behind a picture of him I loved. His hair had been caught in the wind and he was smiling broadly at the camera, full of confidence and hope. We'd been on holiday and he must have been just seventeen because he'd driven me for the first time down to Dorset where we'd taken a cottage for a week. It was probably the most terrifying journey of my life – my baby driving a car – but I remember it had been a lovely week. I'd read books, and gone blackberry picking and sketched ideas for absurd clothes I would never make and no one would want to buy, and he'd mucked around with friends who'd come to join us and slept on the floor, littering the house with lanky teenage bodies. My boy.

That was the last thing I remember.

Chapter Seventeen

Friday

I jolted awake, my heart pounding. I wasn't sure if it was a sound that woke me or just pain from the awkward position I'd slumped into on the sofa, and I stared around the room in confusion. It was only six o'clock. If I'd been tucked up in my comfortable bed, I wouldn't even have been stirring but that sofa was not designed for a good night's sleep. I blinked my eyes to try to clear them and started to piece together what had happened the previous night.

Oh God! My thumping head was testimony to the many, many drinks I'd had with Richard. My feet were aching from those hours of dancing, and I had a strange bruise on my hip. I stood up carefully and winced, aware of a stinging on the inside of my thighs. At least I was warm in my pyjamas. Pyjamas? I'd been wearing jeans. Then the whole bell adventure took shape in my mind. Had I really climbed up that scaffolding and muffled the bell with my ... Then I remembered. I'd walked around the town in my knickers. In. My. Knickers. Okay, Richard had given me his shirt but still. The CCTV cameras would have some priceless footage from that little incident.

Then we must have come back here. And—

The memory of what had happened with Richard came flooding back to me and I virtually fell back on to the sofa, a flush of embarrassment sweeping through me. Had we really kissed like that? Yes, my slightly swollen mouth proved it. Had I really pulled him to me? Yes, I undeniably had. I shivered and looked round for a cardigan to cover the thin silk top. And remembered in a flush of heat how Richard had pushed it down and … a tingle ran through me. I felt buzzy and alive in a way I hadn't for literally years. And then I remembered what day it was.

It was very quiet in the flat. There was no sound from the street outside and, for a crazy moment, I wondered if I had died already. I can remember thinking, bizarrely, that I couldn't be dead because my neck felt stiff, my thighs were sore from what I realised now was my mountaineering and my head was still thudding with a pulse that was all too physical. I wasn't going to spend my last day nursing a hangover, so I found a couple of paracetamol and downed them with a glass of water, then made myself a cup of tea and sat at the table trying to remember more about the night before. Richard. He'd left. I hadn't wanted him to. I'd tried to make him stay. I'd tried my hardest, in fact, but he hadn't wanted to. He'd walked out on me.

Wow! That was quite a rejection. I'd offered myself on a plate and – very politely, I'm sure – he'd turned me down. If I hadn't been scheduled to die that day anyway, I'd have been ready to die of shame. I was struggling to remember what he'd said as he'd gone but I soon gave up. There was no point analysing the minuscule details of what he'd done and said and what it might mean, because it actually didn't matter at all.

What counted was that I would never make love again. Richard had been my last chance. I wondered what he thought of me now. I really wasn't the Lucy he thought he knew. No wonder he did a runner. It shouldn't matter what Richard thought of me now. But it did, very much.

The tea and painkillers were kicking in as I showered quickly, avoiding rubbing the painful bits too vigorously. I had things to do. Lots of things to achieve before the axe fell – although I'd never noticed many precariously balanced axes around Leamington Spa. I looked at my watch. Nearly seven o'clock and I was on borrowed time. I felt a mixture of determination and fear, and I found myself getting dressed with care. I didn't want to die tripping over my knickers. I'd already chosen an outfit for my final day. I was definitely going to wear my best underwear. When I was younger, it had been a sort of joke between me and my mum that, if either of us was going out, we'd remind each other to put on our good knickers, in case we were run down by a bus. She hadn't said it again after I became pregnant. Maybe she thought my best knickers were to blame for my downfall. As I dressed – short cotton skirt, virtually new white T-shirt and my favourite pink cardigan with the fancy buttons – I felt a wave of sadness about my mum. What would she do when they told her? Would she remember the last time she'd seen me, when I'd argued with Dad? I swallowed hard. I had to see her again.

First, though, I had to go to the shop. I had to be there for the delivery from Derbyshire. I couldn't have it left sitting on the doorstep when I'd gone. I'd made the arrangement what felt like ages ago now – and I had to honour it. As I set off for the shop, giving up the search for my purse and 'stealing' some cash from Nat's envelope, locking the house door carefully behind me and wondering if I'd ever have a chance to open it again, I tried to work it out. Was it only just over a week since I took that phone call and wrote the delivery in my desk diary? So much had happened since then, it was hard to believe. You're probably wondering why I was bothered if the fabric was delivered or not but the company had been good to me over the years – even offering ridiculously generous extensions on my credit when times were really hard, and I didn't want them to go short.

As I got closer to Paradise Street, my feet started to drag a little. I was getting perilously close to the Deli and I wasn't brave enough to go in and see Richard. Not yet. Maybe not at all. I felt a wave of loss.

I picked up my pace again and took a diversion, turning left before I reached the corner and walking round the block to approach my shop from the other direction. Chicken? Yes, I suppose I was. But it was my last day on Earth and I wasn't going to give myself a hard time so I pushed all thoughts of Richard away. I remember consciously focusing on the shops instead, seeing them with fresh eyes this morning.

The outside of the Parade was starting to look very dilapidated. Sayers' spell as our landlord had already taken its toll on the little Victorian terrace, which needed constant attention if it was to remain in good order and looking spruce. In just a few months, weeds had taken root in the gutters, patches of green had appeared around weak joints in the downpipes and the paint on the windowsills was starting to peel away. No wonder Fen had a big new 'Sale' sign in his window. Sayers' plan was more and more obvious. Once he'd forced everyone out, the slimy creep would have no trouble presenting his lovely glossy plans for redevelopment to the Planning Department as a viable alternative to the grotty row of deserted shops. If only there was something I could do to help – one last heroic act.

I opened up the shop and had only just gone through the mail when the delivery van pulled up outside. Wassim was always prompt and he brought the boxes in cheerfully, and waited, whistling softly, while I checked the contents against the delivery note.

'You look different,' he said brightly. 'Felt like a change, did you?'

'Yes.' I smiled back. 'Good as a rest, they say, don't they?'

'It looks lovely, if I might say so,' he added, slightly

embarrassed, as if he'd been too forward. 'You should have done it years ago!'

'There a lot of things I should have done years ago, Wassim.' I handed him the remainder of my cash. He frowned.

'Don't we usually raise an invoice?'

'Yes, but perhaps they'll knock off the VAT if I pay in readies?'

He paused for a moment, then shrugged and countersigned the form, tore off my copy, handed it to me and left with a wave of his hand. I watched him go, thinking hard about lost opportunities. I'd tried to jump Richard's bones last night – had I always wanted to, maybe without admitting it to myself? Too late now. I looked at my watch – I had some important goodbyes to say and I needed to be sure I'd left enough time to do it. I locked up the shop, put on my bravest smile in case I encountered Richard, and headed down to the Deli. I wanted to appear carefree, as if last night had been a moment of madness. I didn't want to witness the look I feared might be in his eyes: the look of disappointment and embarrassment. The look that said I'd overstepped the boundaries and he'd remember me as some desperate nymphomaniac.

Sally was looking a little bit harassed. There was a queue at the counter and one of the students that do part-time work there was clearing tables. 'Oh, hello,' she called as she snapped the lids onto takeaway coffees. 'What did you do to Richard last night?'

'What?' Shit! Had he said something?

'He was supposed to be working today but he left me a message saying something had come up. Either he's gone down to the boat early or it's a mammoth hangover. You're looking a bit peaky – so I'm putting two and two together ...'

'Well, we did go out dancing,' I began cautiously.

'You see! Leading him astray. Oh well, I shall get my revenge when he reappears. I'll take a duvet day one of these days and see how he likes it! Anyway, what can I get you? You'll have to join the queue.'

'Nothing, it's okay.' I didn't have any more money on me. 'I was just passing by. Um – say hi from me if you speak to him. Oh, and ask him if he can remember what I did with my purse, will you?'

'I shall say more than that,' Sally exclaimed. 'He's turned his blasted phone off. Either that or he's fallen overboard. The way I'm feeling, that might be the best end he can hope for. See you later.'

'Thanks, Sal,' I answered, then, before I rushed away, I went around the counter and gave her a quick hug. 'Be happy,' I muttered into her hair, 'and you should marry Karl.' Leaving her open-mouthed, I fled, relieved I'd missed Richard entirely.

Rushing back now, I collected the car and headed down to Mum and Dad's, driving too fast and shouting expletives at agonisingly slow pedestrians on the crossing and the lights for being too slow to change. I had a real sense now that the sand in the hourglass was running out. I knew Dad would be out because it was his day at the golf club. He's nothing if not predictable, my dad. Mum was surprised by my sudden arrival, and almost gasped at the change in my appearance. Her face, as she answered the door, was pale and shocked.

'Oh, Lucy! What have you done?'

I had forgotten that she hadn't seen my hair. 'It's just a haircut. And colour.' Did I sound like a sulky teenager to her, I wondered? I certainly did to myself.

'Is everything all right, love? There's nothing wrong, is there?'

Thank goodness the tattoo was covered by my cardigan! Hopefully she'd never know about that. 'No, no – I'm fine. I've just had a new look, that's all.'

'What about Nat? Is he all right?'

A small part of me wanted to fall into her arms there and then, tell her everything. Instead, I tried to reassure her with a bright smile. 'Don't worry, Mum. Everything's fine. Things are a bit slow at the shop. Haven't got long but I thought I'd come to see you and show you my transformation!'

She nodded. She understood all right. She knew I knew that Dad would be out and a look of sadness entered her eyes. 'Well, that was nice of you, darling. I miss seeing you in the week, when you're so busy.' She then walked around me, assessing my haircut and running her fingers through it. 'You look like you did when you were a little girl. You were white blonde then, do you remember? And it was always sticking up! You were such an adventurous little thing.'

'Was I?' I felt strangely satisfied to hear her say that.

'Oh, yes, you were much braver than Chris. I used to think I'd got you two the wrong way round. Want a cuppa?'

'Er, no thanks, Mum. I can't stay long; I just wanted to see you.' I hope that didn't sound too lame or like receiving a scary telegram. My throat hurt with trying not to cry.

'Well, that's lovely. I'm off out to play tennis with Hilary any minute, as it happens, but I'm so glad you popped by, especially after last time. I was worried. I don't want you to think ...'

'What, Mum?'

She crossed her arms. 'That you can't come when your father's here. He does love you, you know, your dad. He's just not very good at showing it. If things aren't done his way, it makes him feel ... sort of out of control. That's when he speaks out of turn. Like the other day.'

I sighed, and rubbed my face. Now I was here, I wasn't sure what to say. 'I suppose I know that, really. But I just feel he's waiting for me to slip up all the time. So he can say, "I told you so".'

'No, love. It's not like that. He's not a dog-in-the-manger

type, your father. It's just ... through everything that's happened to you, you've been very private. You've coped so well on your own, Lucy.'

'But isn't that a good thing?'

'Maybe it is in some ways. But there's such a thing as being too independent. I know you had to grow up fast, love, but sometimes ... I think your dad feels you don't need him and that upsets him. You're still a little girl to him and he wants to protect you.'

I was about to snort in disbelief, but something stopped me. Perhaps there was some truth in what she was saying. My dad hadn't really changed either – he still saw himself as my protector. Only I wouldn't let him protect me. Hadn't wanted him to since those first awful days when he let his disappointment in me overrule everything else. A wave of sadness washed over me. Relationships were so complicated and there was so little time left to sort them out – even if I knew how to.

I turned to the door. 'Listen, can you tell Dad I'm sorry about the other day?'

She pulled me close and I allowed myself to relax in her embrace just for a moment. 'I will, Lucy love. He'll be so relieved. I know he regrets saying those things.'

'Me, too.'

'Maybe,' she began cautiously, 'you could come and see him yourself and have a chat. Just give me a bit of time to prepare him for your hair, eh?'

I laughed and hugged her close, squinting my eyes tightly to try to stop the tears from falling. I breathed in her scent – vanilla and Imperial Leather soap. 'I love you, Mum,' I managed, then let her go and turned away quickly.

I hurried back to the shop. There was another loose end I had to tie up – almost literally. I had Tam's coat to finish.

Chapter Eighteen

Lord only knows why I'd agreed to stitch such detailed embroidery for Tam. The swirling design, adapted from my youthful drawings I'd found the other day, included birds and white roses (a theme a barmy friend of hers had told her meant bridal happiness and prosperity), and it was a bugger to get right. It didn't help either that I was trying to hurry. The thread became knotted a few times, and I had to unpick one area entirely. My neck was stiff from tension and from being arched over the work, and I ignored the couple of times I heard someone trying the handle of the shop door. Today, and forever more, I was officially closed.

I kept having to glance at my watch because – oh, how ironic – there were no chimes from the church clock to tell me what time it was. Had other people noticed the silence, I wondered? Or would it be as if a friend had shaved off a long-worn moustache. You know something is different but you can't put your finger on quite what it is. I had the radio on low, and a mellow piano concerto was keeping me company. I didn't want inane DJ chat today.

'Ouch!' I flinched as the needle jabbed my finger. Perhaps that was the way I'd go. I'd contract blood poisoning and fall off my chair, or fall into a deep sleep like in the fairy tale. I liked the sound of that. But would any handsome prince bother to come and kiss me awake?

The phone rang and I ignored it, then whoever was trying to

get hold of me became impatient and my mobile buzzed on the workbench beside me. Tam's name came up on the caller ID.

'I know you're in there,' she said without preamble.

'Where are you?' I smiled.

'Outside the door, you silly cow. I can see the light on in the back.'

Sure enough, as I walked into the front of the shop she was on the doorstep, hopping from one foot to the other, and I unhitched the chain.

'Have you given up being a shopkeeper?' she breathed, pushing past me as I re-locked the door.

'No. I just have your coat to finish, so I thought I'd deter visitors.'

'But the wedding's not for ages. You'll have plenty of time.'

I gulped. 'Well, I'm quite busy with ... things next week so I thought I'd get ahead.'

'Oooh.' She dropped some shopping bags on the floor and rubbed her hands with glee. 'Can I take a peek or is that bad luck?'

'I think that only applies to the groom seeing the bride's frock. Mothers-in-law don't count.'

'Oh, think of it, Luce! I'm going to be a mother-in-law and a new mum all within months of each other!' Her eyes had filled with tears and she embraced me in a perfumed hug that I returned even more warmly than I usually would.

'I know, Tam. It's simply wonderful. Now put on the kettle and make us both a cuppa – but don't put the mugs down anywhere near the coat!'

'Oh, Lucy, it's so beautiful.' Gently she touched the embroidery I'd done so far. Now I looked at it, it wasn't half bad. 'Even better than I'd hoped – your best yet! You're so clever and so patient. I couldn't do that kind of thing. I'll look fabulous. Oooh, I can't wait.'

She jabbered on as she fussed around the kettle, sniffing the carton of milk pointedly as she went. Bless her. Tam has always been a curious mixture. She will boss me around, clucking about my lifestyle, or the amount of coffee I drink or wine I down, but she is entirely enthralled by other people and their fads. Introduce her to the latest dictat and she will make a radical U-turn in her habits, eschewing butter or coffee or fish or whatever has been declared harmful, and religiously follow the new and trendy regime. She consumes magazine advice or the weekend sections of the papers as if they were gospel. The most recent had been lemon and water acid/alkaline but, now she was pregnant, heaven only knew what she'd be talked into doing or not doing. This was my last chance to tell her.

'You are going to be sensible about this pregnancy, aren't you, Tam?'

'What do you mean?' She pulled up a chair on the other side of the table and sipped at a mug of hot water. I glanced at the cup she put down at a safe distance from me.

'I mean, you're not going to get sucked into the latest pregnancy "thing", are you?'

'Well, you can't be too careful, Luce!' She did have the decency to look a bit bashful.

'Oh, crikey, what have you done now?'

'Well, my friend Melody has read about this Indian masseur in Bridport who reckons that your central energy pools—'

'Don't go any further!' I snorted. 'And don't tell me, he charges two hundred quid for a personal consultation and profile, with full chakra analysis and an MOT on your car thrown in.'

She looked down and I wondered if I'd been too harsh. 'Three hundred quid, actually,' she said quietly.

'Oh, Tam!'

'I know, I know; but I just want everything to be right. This little chap,' she touched her stomach, 'he or she only has one beginning, one life, and if I can, I want to make it the best. That's kind of logical, isn't it, giving it my best shot?'

'Yes, of course, but don't let people bully you into doing what they think is the right thing.'

She smiled. 'You're one to talk. You're not exactly Miss Assertive yourself, are you? Look at how you let your dad dominate you. You told me so yourself.'

Maybe I had, but I was younger then and things were different now. 'Yes, I know I've given in at times when I shouldn't have but, come on, Tam, you've brought up a child before. We both have. We do the best we can, but you have to be sensible and trust your own judgement sometimes. Okay, so I didn't exactly watch what I ate when I was having Nat.' I remembered being in denial and filling my face with burgers and chips in some sort of defiance, challenging this baby inside me to thrive. 'But look at him now. Six foot and with the constitution of an ox.' Let's hope he has the emotional strength, too, I thought to myself.

Tam sighed and dropped her shoulders. 'You're right, I know; but these people I meet – they can be right sometimes. Look at Sylvie.'

'I try not to.'

Tam ignored this. 'She swears that Pascal's eczema is because she ate too many grapes when she was having him.'

I snorted again. 'It's more likely to be caused by the stress from having to be the perfect child and having such a smug mother.'

'And look at Micah.' Ah, yes. Micah. I thought we'd get round to him. 'He's been right.'

'So far ...' I mumbled, pretending to concentrate intently on my stitching.

'But he *has*. I know you're cynical but I keep hearing things again and again. He was right about Di's granny – she was rushed into hospital on Wednesday: suspected stroke. He told Melody that she ought to go to the doctor and apparently she has a seriously low calcium problem—'

'That'll be too many beans in her diet, I expect.' I snipped off a thread.

'Maybe, but he *knew* she had to go, didn't he? And then, and *then* …' She leaned forward urgently and my stomach clenched. I didn't need more evidence. 'The other night I saw him – he came by the theatre – and we were talking about stuff and he mentioned something about a bomb in Madrid and I said, "What bomb?" And he muttered something and changed the subject and then, what do you know? That one goes off on Thursday – yesterday – killing all those people.' She sat back in her chair and breathed out slowly. I hadn't seen the news or read a paper. I knew nothing about it. I did know, though, that my skin had gone cold and I felt sick.

She eventually left me alone around five. I hadn't wanted to hurry her away but time was precious. However, as she closed the door behind her, after I'd hugged her hard and she'd called over her shoulder about making some arrangement for next week, I felt different. Being with her had made me feel safe. No one could get to me with her there, and if anything had happened to me, she'd have been with me. Now the shop was silent again, I held up the coat and checked the quality of the stitching. It was never good enough, of course, but this would be okay. She really would shine at the wedding and I felt proud that I'd stretched myself to make this piece truly special. I don't know what made me do it but, instead of hanging it on a rail at the back to be collected when … when everything else was collected and taken away, I took the dress from the mannequin in the window and replaced it with Tam's coat. A self-indulgent memorial to me for any passer-by to enjoy.

I didn't bother clearing up my mess and, as I locked up for what I thought would be the last time, I glanced back at my workbench covered in snippets of fabric and colourful thread. It reminded me of *The Tailor of Gloucester*. Dad used to read that to me as a child and I, in turn, had read it to Nat. Perhaps I hadn't been such a bad mother after all.

Cautiously I stepped out on to the pavement. I must have appeared very eccentric to anyone passing by as I looked up to check nothing was going to land on top of me. What a way to go, splat under a pile of bricks or sliced in half by a roof tile. What should I do now? Go and get drunk? I glanced at my watch. Why not? My headache from last night had come back after the tension of the afternoon and, besides, the nearest bar, Henry's, was in the other direction from the Deli and I didn't want to go *there* again.

I'd never actually been inside Henry's bar. There was nothing classy about it, and as I suspected this early in the evening, the place was full of dross, most of it sitting outside on the pavement smoking. You're more likely to die from secondary inhalation just walking down the street these days. The men looked like navvies and the women were busty and too old for the short skirts that pulled tightly across their fat thighs and backsides. All of them bore the vestiges of too many hours spent in places like this.

Under normal circumstances I wouldn't have dared cross the threshold but that day I couldn't have cared. As I slipped through the door, ignoring the curious glances of the other customers and clambering on to a bar stool, I chuckled to myself. That was it. Lucy Streeter was going to end her days saturated with whisky and keeling off a bar stool. What a very fitting end to an unremarkable life!

'What can I get you?' Henry, tall and stocky with strong arms covered in faded tattoos, came over to me.

'A double Scotch, please. No ice.'

He didn't comment at all, pushed a glass up into the optic on the bottle behind the bar, and put in down in front of me. I took a sip, the liquid first numbing my tongue before slipping smoothly down my throat.

'Aren't you from up the road?' he said.

'Yup. The dress shop.'

'You're not a usual Friday customer.' He smiled patronisingly.

'Ah! But this isn't a normal Friday.' I took another sip. 'Tell me – this rent increase. Do you know anything about it?'

Henry stood upright and pulled up his trousers by the belt loops, which was pointless because they remained firmly under his bulging stomach. 'Nope, except that it's a bloody disgrace.'

'I happen to know that two people have agreed to the rent increase and everyone thinks one of them is you.' He raised his eyebrows in surprise.

'Do they now? Well, it weren't me, love, because my rent review isn't until October. Best look at that snotty tile seller with his overblown prices, or the Deli. Have you seen how much they charge for a cup of coffee? You get one for half that out of my machine.'

'It won't taste half as nice, though,' I said, bristling. 'No, it's not Martin and it's not the Deli. I know that.'

'Then what about the flats or that empty place – the one that was the daft shoe shop? Perhaps he's got a new tenant lined up for that and he's set a higher rent?'

One of the men from outside came in and slid on to the stool beside me. He was so close I could smell that he reeked of cigarette smoke.

'On about that bastard landlord then? Henry was telling me about him.'

But Henry just shrugged. He looked tired and, even though

he was making little effort to be friendly, I felt sorry for him. It must be hard work for him, too, to keep things ticking over. His business might not be my kind of thing, but it was his livelihood. Would he be able to cover the rent hike just through servicing the addiction of the town's alcoholics, especially when they could get hammered for a third of the price if they bought their booze at the local supermarket?

I knocked back the remains of my Scotch. 'Yes, he is a bastard and he's not going to walk over us all.' I put my hand in my pocket to pay then remembered about the elusive purse.

'Henry, bit embarrassing but I haven't got any cash. Can I ...?'

He raised his eyes heavenward. 'Glad you're not a regular. Drop it in tomorrow.'

He'd be lucky. I put out my hand and Henry, smothering his surprise, shook it.

'Thanks, Henry. That's generous of you. Nice to know you and good luck.' I flashed him my most winning smile and marched, as determinedly as I could after a double Scotch, out of the bar and made my way across Paradise Street, and in to Fen's shop, the windows displaying big red 'Sale!' posters. He might have some fresh ideas about who else the snake in the grass might be.

The bell dinged as I went in and the smell of tools and hardware hit me again. The shelves seemed quite low in stock and there was an atmosphere of defeat, as if Fen had given up in the face of Sayers. Behind the counter was a young girl in a pink hoody top with a logo in sequins. She couldn't have been more than about nineteen and I couldn't imagine she knew much about DIY. She was serving an elderly lady who was buying a metal bucket and they were disagreeing over the change. I waited as patiently as I could until the old dear was happy and shuffled out.

'We're closing.' She slammed the till drawer shut and came around the front of the counter.

'I'm sure you are, but I only make it twenty past.'

'Yeah, well, the owner said he'd be back by now. I told him I had to go at quarter past or I'll miss me dance class.' She'd clearly missed the class in customer relations, too.

'Oh, right. He's out, is he?'

'Yeah.' She turned the sign on the door. 'He said he was only nipping over to the other shop and that was hours ago.'

'The other shop? I didn't know he had another shop?'

'Yeah,' she said again, without moving her mouth. 'Two actually – just opened. One at the top end of town and one up West Street.'

'Oh?' Crikey – if he was struggling in Paradise Street, how the hell could he afford two shops elsewhere?

'Yeah, he's closing this shit-pit down, which is why everything's so cheap. No money in hardware anyway, he's always saying. Mobile phones he's doing. Really cool stuff.'

Slowly, slowly a penny began to drop. Hadn't I seen Fen in West Street? 'Thanks,' I said and let myself out of the shop. I might be too late – Sayers' battleaxes had probably left the office for the weekend at five but I frantically got the number from directory enquiries on my mobile and was put through. The phone rang and rang. Damn. I was about to give up when at last it was picked up.

'Sayers' Properties?' It was the same woman who had greeted me so warmly before.

'Hello,' I breathed. 'Sorry to call so late but I need to get hold of one of your tenants.'

'We've very many tenants, Madam, and I'm afraid we are about to close up for the day.'

'This one has a mobile phone shop on West Street, and

another property with you. You must know who I mean. He's just down the road from your office.'

There was silence at the end of the phone. It was obviously not company practice to reveal information but I had to know. I cast about for some way to persuade her to give me the information and spotted a large pile of cardboard boxes waiting to be picked up. 'It's the Council recycling department here and we need to make arrangements for recycling. It's all part of our Responsible Landlords Incentive.' It was feeble.

'Yes, we do have a new tenant on that road I believe.' There was a rustling of paper. 'Mr F. Gates. Number seventeen.'

'Thank you soo much,' I gushed, in a very non-civil-servant way, and clicked off my phone.

So Fen had another business with Sayers as his landlord, and that was why I'd seen him on West Street. He'd kept that very quiet. Why hadn't he mentioned it at our meetings? How odd to take on another property with the same landlord if he wasn't happy with the way he operated in the first place. Something wasn't right and I had a strong feeling Fen had done the dirty in some way. I suppose I was so deep in my thoughts that I wasn't looking where I was going and only looked left when I crossed over by the post box. A small Fiesta screeched to a halt and the young lad behind the wheel shouted angrily out of the window.

'Are you trying to get yourself fucking killed?'

I was going to reply, 'Yes, possibly,' but I thought that would get me pulverised, which isn't a nice way to die, so I just waved sheepishly. I think he flicked his middle finger at me as he screeched off again, but I didn't care. Instead I stood on the little traffic island wrestling with all the facts. Fen was closing down. He had a new place and Sayers was his landlord. Henry had denied he'd agreed to any higher rent but Sayers had let slip there were *two* people who'd given in. It can't have been

Deepak or Gaby – she'd rather die than give in to the man. Martin? No, and I knew it couldn't possibly be Richard and Sal.

There was only one person left.

I knew where Sandy lived because she'd invited us all over to a rather excruciating garden party a couple of years back when we'd had to endure a drumming band, incense and crystals hanging just low enough from the trees to bang you on the head as you passed. It was after Richard had knocked one off for the third time, and then spotted the strips of tofu being put on the barbecue, that he really started to lose his sense of humour.

'Fucking vegetarian barbecue!' he'd snorted and I'd had to put my hand over his mouth and look around to check no one had heard. 'What's the point of having a fire if you don't cook real flesh?' he'd mumbled. 'It offends the caveman in me!'

There had been a funny moment when Sandy, in droopy cheesecloth, had nearly gone up in flames as she passed a garden candle – not the kind of barbecue Richard had in mind – and I know the Paradise Street Crew had all stumbled home paralytic on organic scrumpy consumed on virtually empty stomachs. There's only so much courgette you can dip before you want to gag.

Even though it was only a ten-minute walk, I was quite warm by the time I turned into her road, but for a moment I thought I'd got the wrong house, or she'd moved. She hadn't mentioned it the other day at the fair. A large and silver Mercedes was taking up most of the narrow driveway and I had to squeeze past. It can't have been Sandy's – she's always poured scorn on executive gas-guzzlers. It was hardly likely to be her husband's, unless painting and decorating had suddenly become hugely profitable. Perhaps they had visitors, which I hadn't even considered, or that she might not be at home.

The expression on Sandy's face when she saw me on the doorstep, though, confirmed the suspicions that had been gathering in my head over the last half an hour: that her abrupt departure from her shoe shop in Paradise Street was connected with Sayers' bid to move us all out.

'Lucy?' Her tone of voice was almost as if she had been expecting me, but she certainly didn't invite me inside.

'Sandy, sorry to arrive unannounced but I wondered if I could have a quick word?'

She didn't say anything, just folded her arms, so I coughed and carried on, hoping I wasn't wildly off the mark.

'The thing is, I've had some contact recently with Mr Sayers, you know, our landlord.' Something unreadable flitted across Sandy's face and she seemed to focus on something over my shoulder. It reminded me of how she'd reacted when she saw me at the fairground. 'And he seemed to suggest that *two* tenants had agreed to a higher rent. Now I've discovered one person who I think may be – how I shall I put it? – may be cooperating with Sayers by taking a shop somewhere else, and I'm pretty sure it's no one else on the street. So that really only leaves … you.'

Sandy shook her head and fussed with her hair nervously. 'I don't know what you're talking about. It was uneconomical, that's all. I just couldn't go on.'

'But you didn't even have a closing-down sale to get rid of the stock. You didn't even say goodbye.' Sandy frowned at this, and, uncomfortable now, tugged at her T-shirt, another garish design like the one she'd been wearing at the fair. I began to compute the information in my small wooden head – new look, possibly new flash car and, unless anything had come along in the last few days, no work apparently. I plunged right in there, feet first.

'Sandy, did Sayers offer you money to leave and to go quietly?'

She looked at me for a while, then sighed and rubbed her eyes. 'Oh, God. Ever since that bloke at the fair – you know, the fortune-teller who saw the accident coming – I knew I'd be found out.' I waited for her to go on. 'Sayers made me such a good offer, Lucy, I couldn't refuse. I wasn't doing all that well, and there's no way I could have afforded the rent rise, so when he said he'd "help me out" I sort of grabbed at it.' She spoke faster now, as if an explanation would excuse her. 'Things haven't been too great for Barry – everyone's been hit by the recession, you know – and a bit of extra cash has been so useful.'

'How much did he give you?'

Sandy opened her mouth about to tell me then closed it again. 'Um, I can't tell you that. He made me promise not to tell anyone.' Suddenly she looked frightened and put her hand on my arm. 'Lucy, he said that if anyone found out, he'd make things very difficult for us. Those were his actual words. He said he was powerful in this town and he'd ...' She almost sobbed at this point. 'There are some things you don't know about Barry – some stuff about his business, silly tax short-cuts he took. Sayers found out somehow and said he'd make sure Barry never worked again. Lucy,' she pleaded, 'I'm only telling you cos I like you – and cos of that bloke at the fair.' She looked down. 'What he said about loyalty sort of got to me.'

For a split second I felt sorry for her. Sayers had blackmailed her and she seemed genuinely afraid, but then it passed like indigestion when I thought about Martin and all his efforts to make his shop beautiful, and Deepak, the newsagent on the corner, who was open every day from some ungodly hour, and Gaby with her gerbils and noisy parakeets. Then I thought about Sal and Richard. All my friends.

'Yes, Sandy, it damned well should have got to you.' I felt really angry and her head shot up at my tone of voice. 'You've pretty much sold us all down the river, haven't you? You and Fen.'

'Fen?'

'Yeah, I reckon he's the other one who's done the dirty.' I looked at my watch. 'I've got to go. I'm running out of time.' I started to walk back up the drive. 'I hope you're happy with what you've done – with your leather sofa and your big car and you're principles in shreds.' And I left her standing on the doorstep to chew that one over.

It took me a while to get home because I let my feet simply take me, and as I walked I thought about Sandy and all I'd heard today. I realised now that I wouldn't have time to put the situation right for everyone in Paradise Street, but if I wrote down all I'd found out I could at least warn them of my suspicions. That would give them enough to challenge Sayers and prevent him getting his own way and wrecking Paradise Street for ever.

Evening was falling, warm and windless, when I found myself heading down to the park. As I wandered along the footpath, I watched the dragonflies darting over the water in the evening sunlight, having a feast from the clouds of midges that diced with death around them. People were walking their dogs or sitting on the grass chatting, or heading out for dinner in restaurants I knew. In a town that was mine. The weekend stretched out in front of them. There were couples holding hands – some young and some not so young – and I realised that I'd missed out on all this. But as lives go, it hadn't been so bad. Across the road I spotted some of the winos. I hoped they'd used the money on something useful. I felt a glow of satisfaction that I'd done something good. I even felt a deep sense of peace.

'Bring it on,' I challenged, as I walked back up the Parade, passing the statue of Queen Victoria that had 'jumped' in the War when a bomb fell close by and was now a few inches off-centre. On up past the shops I went, all closed now for the evening, ever hopeful that tomorrow would be a better day, and around the corner at the top into tree-lined Clarendon Square with its magnificent Georgian townhouses – the Belgravia of the Midlands. And then past the Georgian villas and down Beauchamp Hill and then out opposite the shop where I'd bought my first armchair to furnish my little flat for me and my baby.

As I walked, I thought about why Sandy had changed herself so radically since Sayers had paid her off. All her eco ethics had gone out of the window with her cheesecloth smocks, and I was sure her new handbag wasn't mock-croc. How sad that all it had seemed to take was a large wodge of cash to part her from her convictions. Would I have done the same? I hoped not, but now I'd never know how shallow I could be persuaded to be!

When I got home, I dumped my bag and, with every minute feeling like a bonus now, I started to write down what I'd unearthed during the day. If I left it somewhere obvious, then when Nat or Richard found it they'd understand. But as I wrote, I grew more and more angry, and answered my own question. I *did* have conviction and somehow a letter handing the responsibility on to someone else wasn't enough. In fact, it felt like a cop-out, and I wanted some sort of closure before I was closed down for good! So I folded up the letter, left it on the desk and headed for the little shed in the garden.

'Little' is an overstatement – it is closer to the size of a dog kennel. I bought it from one of those small magazines that comes inside the Sunday papers and which promise innovative products you can't live without. The door was stiff and cobwebbed and I had to crawl on all fours to get inside. In the darkness and with a bit of careful feeling – a pretty unpleasant sensation – my fingers landed on what I was looking for. A can of emulsion paint. I'd have preferred gloss but I'd have to make do with the remainder of the shocking pink from when I'd painted my bedroom last year. This would do nicely. I picked up a brush too.

I waited impatiently for it to grow dark – that's the trouble with summer. It gets dark so late and what I needed to do would take darkness, so I passed the time stuffing the last of my clothes into plastic bags, then I got into my little car and, driving recklessly and far too fast through town, I pulled up first in the supermarket car park. It was busy, of course – people shopping at all hours (what did we do before twenty-four seven was invented?) and, one by one, I put the clothes bags in the tray and tipped it. For once it wasn't full and I heard them drop with a thump into the depths of the recycling container. Jumping back into the car, I headed towards town and pulled up on the double yellow lines outside Sayers' office. Then I set to work.

By the time I had completed my task and had returned to Paradise Street, I felt exhausted by the tension – the tension of the whole week. Things were going to end soon (and it must be soon because there wasn't much of the day left). I dumped the empty paint can in the nearest wheelie bin, wiped my hands on my jeans and headed home.

I let myself in and glanced at the clock. I'd been out longer than I thought and was grateful that I'd had enough time to accomplish what I'd set out to do. I remember I stood for a moment in the middle of the room, and pondered the one last thing I wanted to do. Of all the things I'd done it would take the most courage. Then, calmly, and yet with my heart beating hard, I picked up the phone and dialled the number. When the answering machine kicked in, I left the strangest and most heartfelt message I have ever made in my life.

'Hi, Richard, it's me. Lucy. I know it's a weird time to call and I know you're not there but ... I hope the weather's nice on the Hamble. I'm really excited by *Serenity*, by the way. She'll be lovely.' Oh come on, get on with it, Lucy, I chastised myself. 'Anyway, the reason for my call is ... well, to tell you two things, actually. And I'm not going to see you again, for reasons that you'll soon discover, so I thought I'd better leave a message.' I cleared my throat. 'I think that Fen might be up to something with Sayers. Have you noticed he's got a sale on? Well, it's a closing-down sale apparently, and I've discovered that he's opened two shops on West Street and that Sayers is his landlord. Odd when he was being so rude about Sayers at our meetings – don't you remember he was trying to blame Henry? But I'm sure it isn't Henry. I met him, by the way. He's quite nice really. I owe him for a double Scotch so if you're passing ... Anyway, it made me wonder if Fen is getting a lower rent on the new shops in exchange for agreeing to leave Paradise Street. And Sandy. Remember how she left so swiftly? I've confronted her and it turns out she was offered a huge bribe by Sayers to go – but Rich, I think Sayers has threatened to get nasty if she lets the cat out of the bag. You might want to look into this – it might help when we – you – go to arbitration. It might even be illegal what he's done, but I haven't time to find out.'

I paused and swallowed, hoping I wouldn't run out of answering machine time. 'But the other reason for my call is that ... is that I'm sorry about last night. I shouldn't have – you know. But what it made me realise is that, Rich ... I think I am in love with you, and what's odd is that I think I always have been.' I laughed drily, blushing into the phone. 'I know you don't feel the same – you made that very obvious last night – and I'm probably too boring and unglamorous for you anyway!' I hoped he would hear the smile in my voice. 'You're actually responsible for screwing up my love life. No one even came close to you, and the funny thing is, I didn't realise I was even comparing.' I speeded up now, sure I'd run out of time on the machine any second. 'You're my best friend. You're the only person I want to go and watch obscure *film noir* movies with. I love sailing with you and drinking wine with you. I love the way you laugh and hug me ... And I loved the way you kissed me last night. I wish we had gone all the way and made love, because I think we'd have been good together ...' I seemed to have rambled on for ages, and the machine had probably timed-out, but I just carried on, unable to stop, cradling the phone in my shoulder. 'I wish we could have been together and I could have woken up next to you every morning. We would have been *so* good. I'd have made you happy. I love you, I love you, I love you.'

I put down the phone, tears of happiness and immense sadness pouring down my face.

Then I waited.

And I waited. I switched on the TV and turned it off again. I made tea and hardly drank a drop.

And nothing happened. And at eleven forty-five, remembering to slip on my best underwear beneath my clothes, I went out into the dark, and into Warwick Road, and out into Dale Street, and I stood in the middle of the road.

And nothing happened. Cars full of teenagers simply swung past me, horns blaring. I stayed where I was, hands outstretched until they ached.

I looked at my watch. Twelve ten.

And that was when I realised, as I stood there in the middle of Dale Street, that Micah had got it wrong. I wasn't actually going to die just yet.

I've asked myself so many times since then what my feelings were at that moment of realisation. I remember I looked around me just to be sure I actually *was* still alive, and hadn't sort of evaporated like Doctor Who. I checked that I still had a body and pinched myself. Which hurt. A group of girls, pissed and tottering in high heels, came around the corner shrieking with laughter, and only just veered out of the way in time before actually colliding with me. Clearly I hadn't disappeared.

Oddly – embarrassingly even – I think I felt a tiny bit disappointed. All that emotional build-up! All the expectation that I'd see a flash of light and hear a host of angels as I ascended heavenward. And all I got was nothing. This wasn't heaven, it was just another Friday night in Leamington Spa. Then my legs began to tremble, a reaction I suppose as if I'd gone into shock. I started to walk, and then I started to run and run. I was acutely aware of the tingling in my fingers, the cool air rushing over my lips as I breathed in. It was intoxicating, yet it was absolutely normal. I was alive and this is what life feels like. Relief and exhilaration flooded over me and I laughed manically as I ran down the pavement, tears at my own stupidity pouring down my face.

I'd believed Micah – well, wouldn't you have done on the evidence? – but, for once, for one glorious time, he'd got it fantastically wrong! I was alive!

I must have run quite a long way and after a while I had a stitch, so I sat down on the kerb and breathed deeply – all the tension of the last few days pouring out of me. I felt a mixture of utter stupidity and total elation, thanking God – or someone – over and over again that I wouldn't have to leave Nat or Mum and Dad, that I would still be here with my friends and see Tam's baby born. And I vowed that I would grasp every second of life now and make the most of it. It felt like a gift. And most of all, dear reader, I thanked my lucky stars over and over that I hadn't mentioned Micah's 'prediction' to a living soul. How much of an arse would I have looked then? Like those experts who confidently predict the end of the world then are left standing on the mountain top at zero hour looking like idiots.

As I got my breath back, I glanced about me. Somehow I was down by the Pump Rooms, and surrounded by the evening's debris of chip paper and polystyrene cups. It was terribly late and I glanced at my watch. Why hadn't I heard it strike my midnight reprieve? Why hadn't the church clock told me?

And then, as I began to come down to earth, a cold chill ran from the top of my head downwards settling somewhere around my stomach. Of course the church bell hadn't chimed. It couldn't because my jeans were tied round the hammer. And worse still, I now remembered where I'd left my purse. It was in the pocket. And in it, my address details, there to tell whoever found them exactly who'd silenced the bell.

And that wasn't all.

What about everything I'd been up to this evening? All the things I'd done, confident in the knowledge that I wouldn't be around to have to explain them, or apologise for them. As I remembered each irresponsible and incriminating action, I felt my heart beat faster in fear.

And worst of all, I thought about my phone message to Richard!

I jumped up, not sure exactly where I was going to start putting things right, but one thing was very clear. I needed assistance and there was only one person on Earth who could help me. And bloody hell, he owed me!

Chapter Nineteen

The early hours of Saturday morning

Galvanised by my anger and my panic, I stormed down the road in the direction of Micah's flat. It was a longish walk but it gave me time to work up a head of steam and, before I was even halfway there, I was hitting the livid-level on the barometer. The consequences of my still being alive were gradually sinking in with every footstep. I know it sounds ungrateful but look at it from where I was standing: I'd thrown away all my clothes. I'd given valuable hard cash to a bunch of winos in the park, thinking I wouldn't need it. I'd blown the rest of it on a shopping spree for my son – not that he didn't deserve it, but I definitely couldn't afford it. I'd also paid up front for my new stock. I'd done things over the last few days that, in retrospect, seemed like lunacy. I'd walked around town in my pants, sung in public, and hurled my half-naked drunken-self, embarrassingly, at my best friend. And then I'd called him and opened my heart! I was suddenly aware that my heart was pounding and my face was hot, despite the cool night air.

This was all Micah's fault. He had seemed so compelling, so convincing. He'd predicted a fairground near-disaster, for goodness' sake, but I'd let my heart rule my head and hadn't listened to the quiet little voice of reason that had squeaked: Don't believe him!

When I arrived outside his building, I could see light from

the windows. It hadn't even occurred to me that he might be asleep, but I don't think it would have made any difference if he had been. I was too fired up to think about anyone else. I still hadn't worked out which bell was his so I pressed all of them at once, and eventually the door buzzed and I let myself in – although I could hear a torrent of sleepy abuse through the intercom from whomever had let me in. I didn't even care.

Nor did I care when I thumped on Micah's door with my fist. I waited in the silence and was about to bang on it again when it opened, slowly.

He was rubbing his eyes and looked as if I'd woken him, although I could smell food and hear music from inside. 'Yes? Can I help you?' He sounded almost irritable.

'Micah, it's Lucy.'

'What? Shouldn't you be …?'

'Dead?' I pushed past him into the sitting room. 'Well I'm not, look!' The place looked suspiciously neat. A large rucksack, half-filled with clothes, stood open on the floor. 'Going somewhere?'

He closed the door slowly and stared at me. 'I don't understand.'

'No, me neither – though I do realise I've been a total arse. But clearly, not quite as much of an arse as *you*.'

'Oh!' He shuffled his feet and looked down. 'Oh!'

'Yes – oh, bloody oh, just about sums it up. Have you any idea of the mess I'm in, thanks to you?'

'Shouldn't you be grateful? I'd have thought you'd be pleased. Not to be dead, I mean.'

'Micah!' I screeched. 'Yes, I'm thrilled, obviously, but we've got a tiny problem. After you'd convinced me that I was about to die – deluded fool that I was – I did some things I probably shouldn't have done.' Once again the enormity of my recent activities crashed in on me. 'Things that are going to cause some real problems, because I'm still going to be around to face the consequences. They need undoing – and quickly. And I can't do it all on my own and, since you're behind this whole mess, you are damned well going to help me sort it all out.'

'Oh – right,' he said more calmly than I was expecting. 'Well, just let me finish my cheese on toast, and we'll see what we can do. What exactly do you have in mind?'

So, in a surreal tableau, I sat bolt upright on Micah's sofa, jiggling my leg in impatience and running through the list of social gaffes, petty crimes and acts of sheer madness and irresponsibility that I'd carried out over the last few days, as he munched calmly on his late night snack. The thing is that each action seemed perfectly sensible at the time. It was only now, as I described them all, that they sounded like the work of a mad woman. What I did carefully edit out of my report, though, was Richard – about last night in my kitchen and the message I'd left for him. That was way too embarrassing to admit to just yet.

Micah listened carefully, leaning forward in amazement at times, covering his mouth in shock and even laughing, which didn't please me at all. He licked his fingers clean of crumbs and stared at me. 'Well, you have been busy. Why did you do all that stuff, though?'

I felt as if I was going to explode. 'Because,' I answered through gritted teeth, 'you told me I was going to die.'

Micah paused. 'Yes, I did, didn't I?' From the top of his rucksack he pulled out a small black book and opened it slightly to peep inside. He frowned. 'But I didn't tell you to do any of that stuff.'

I was almost too angry to reply, so he went on in a slightly puzzled voice, 'I mean, you must have *wanted* to do some of those things or you wouldn't have done them. That's one thing I've noticed with people, Lucy, they mostly do what they want. It's rather interesting, actually ...'

'Micah!' I growled and jumped up. 'We've got to go. Time's running out.'

He had the good grace to look embarrassed and stood up quickly to take his plate out to what I assumed must be the kitchen. I could hear crashing and rummaging and, after a short while, he reappeared with a bucket of steaming water and some cloths. 'Come on, then. I don't think we can carry a ladder without attracting too much attention – and I haven't got one anyway – so we'll have to improvise. Let's go.'

I was flummoxed once again by his abrupt change of tack, trotting behind him as we headed into the night. Out on the pavement he stopped and turned to me. 'So which shop is it, then?'

I pointed up the road to Fen's new shop window, newly decorated by me and my pot of pink paint. Micah stared at my handiwork, then a smile spread across his face.

'Oh dear! I see what you mean. You *have* been busy this evening. What did this bloke do again to deserve such abuse from you?'

'He's been a ruddy traitor, that's what! He's shafted us all, sold us down the river to the landlord just so he could get cheap rent on this place and another on the other side of town. In the old days he'd have been tarred and feathered.'

'I've not had many dealings with traitors. We don't see many of them where I come from.'

'Sorry?'

'Never mind. Well, grab a cloth and let's get going. "Two-faced sneaky bastard", hey? Well, that's telling it like it is. And I didn't think there were two 'p's in "unscrupulous".'

'I think you've given me quite enough grief over the last week or so. Don't start on my spelling, too.'

So, shooting furtive glances up the street to ensure no one was coming, we scrubbed and scrubbed at my graffiti, which urged passers-by not to buy their mobile phones from Fen. I didn't really want to wash it off, to be honest. I think he deserved every word, but it was in the same colour I'd used on Sayers' windows and on my own. Best to get rid of all the evidence that could link me to this rampage of misspelled and probably defamatory graffiti. But removing it wasn't nearly as easy as applying it and, though we managed to get rid of the words, the window and our clothes were left with streaks and smears, as if the shop had been closed down. Let's hope people thought it had.

And after we'd finished that one, we set off for Sayers' office up the road, the water bucket now pink from our rinsed cloths. Micah chortled as he read my pink scrawl squeezed on to the landlord's narrow doorway. 'I wouldn't have thought that was physically possible. And are you quite sure he only has the one? The bit about fixing rents, that I can believe. But unless you've followed him into the gents, I don't see how you can be sure about his shortcomings in the trouser department. And lying is a sin, Lucy.'

His serious tone was so out of keeping with what we were doing, I felt the start of a bubble of laughter deep down inside. Maybe it was the elation of simply being alive, but I was feeling almost as mischievous as I had when I'd painted the blasted doorway in the first place just hours before. As we shot into the side alley to hide ourselves from the odd passing car, I had to cover my mouth to stop myself snorting with giggles.

As we gradually rid it of my carefully painted caricatures and rude comments, Micah and I became more and more splattered with watery paint. Our arms ached and we must have looked a sight but, checking my watch, I could see it was already two o'clock. And that reminded me.

'Come on,' I grabbed his arm. 'I've got some climbing to do.'

He smiled vaguely and, dumping the bucket outside his front

door, he followed me unquestioningly through town until we reached the church, the scaffolding still shrouding it. Though it was still the wee hours, it gets light so early in summer and I could feel a sense of urgency. I had to get those jeans back by Monday when the builders resumed their restoration work or they'd know exactly who'd been up there. Was there a punishment for doing the opposite of disturbing the peace?

I surveyed the scene quickly. It looked a bit different stone-cold sober and someone had improved security since last night. Worse still, the Fiesta had been moved.

'Oh, Micah, give me a leg up.'

'How do I do that?'

What planet had this man been on? I had to explain urgently how to give me a bunk-up over the fencing and, catching my stomach on the top painfully, I eased myself down and scuttled to where I'd climbed up before.

Micah was as puzzled as Richard had been by what I was up to and kept calling to me as I made my way to the tower, asking me where I was and telling me to be careful. Believe me, I didn't need any encouragement on that score. Last time I'd climbed this scaffolding, I'd been so certain of my own invulnerability. I'd been so confident I couldn't fall then, because I'd believed Micah's prediction that Friday would be my last day. I'd practically floated up there on wings of alcohol and crazy courage. But now that it was most definitely Saturday and rumours of my demise had been exaggerated, all my bravery had seeped away. I stood at the bottom of the tower, next to the ladder I'd scaled, stared upwards and wondered how I'd ever managed it. I gulped, then took hold of the ladder with both hands and stepped up on to the first rung.

It seemed much further to the first platform than I remembered. Although, to be honest, I didn't actually remember all that much. I cautiously pulled myself upright, holding onto the scaffolding poles carefully as the planks shifted under my weight.

'Lucy!' I could hear Micah call in a hoarse stage whisper. 'Are you all right? Can you hear me?'

I whispered back, leaning out just a little so he could see me. 'I'm fine – won't take long.' I wished now that I'd asked him to come with me but those long, stringy limbs of his might have been a liability in the confined space of the bell tower. I took a deep breath and braced myself for the rest of the ascent. The next two levels went relatively well, although it was dark and I had to feel my way along, holding onto the poles to steady myself.

'Lucy! Lucy!'

I shuffled over to the edge of the platform and waved so he could see me again, then put my finger to my lips in a really exaggerated way to try to shut him up. He squinted up at me for a moment then nodded vigorously and called loudly, 'Okay! I'll be quiet now.'

As I started up the next ladder, I thought about the last week and a half. What was it about Micah that had made him seem so wise and spiritual, when now he looked like an idiotic clown? I could have done with one of his mystical silences right now; as I pulled myself up into the narrow confines of the bell tower, I could hear him again.

'Lucy! Are you all right? Can you hear me?' I squeezed around the side of the mechanism and waved at him to get his attention, then made cutting motions against my throat to try to shut him up, shooing him away to the shady side of the street. If anyone came past and saw him staring up, they'd be bound to look too. After a moment, he seemed to get what I was on about and, when I looked again, he was strolling up and down under the trees in a really shifty way. If that was him trying to look nonchalant, I could only hope the local constabulary were busy somewhere else.

So finally, there I was, tugging away at the amazingly tight knot I'd managed to tie in my semi-inebriated state just two days earlier. I was so busy concentrating on trying to loosen the folds of material from round the hammer that I didn't pay any attention to the fluttering sounds from above me in the roof. It was only when I triumphantly pulled my cropped jeans free and found my purse that I looked up and saw the colony of bats, blinking anxiously at me in the darkness.

Chapter Twenty

Back on the ground again, I felt myself relax. That had been more of an ordeal than I'd been expecting. Not half as much, though, as it would have been trying to explain to the magistracy what my jeans were doing impairing the workings of a beloved local landmark. Mission accomplished.

I was, however, still stuck on the wrong side of the security fence and Micah was out of hissing range. He was visible, through the gaps in the metal bars, still pacing up and down and occasionally casting baleful glances up at the tower. If only he'd been psychic or magic enough to know I needed him. But even if he could help, he wouldn't be strong enough to pull me over so, finding some crates, I balanced them dangerously in the wheelbarrow I'd used the previous night, and bruising my thighs afresh, eased myself over, landing hard on the other side. Micah must have heard the scuffling sound because he came hurrying over.

I turned to face him and was touched by the expression of concern on his face. 'Don't worry, Micah. I did what I set out to do.' I glanced at my watch. It was very nearly three. Time to get going, but I pulled him into the shadows and held my finger up, waiting. In the quiet of the early morning, I could hear the whirring of clockwork and then, yes – three clear, loud, portentous bongs. I'd never been so pleased to hear them in all my life. Micah looked at my delighted face, realisation slowly dawning.

'All back to normal now!' I smiled triumphantly.

He rubbed his hands together enthusiastically. 'You know, I could have got up there much more easily. I'm rather good at that kind of thing.'

I smiled sceptically. I really couldn't imagine that. 'Well, it was ... er ... useful having you there to help get in to the place. I couldn't have managed that on my own. But they won't be renovating it any time soon. The place is like a bat motel.' I thought about what I had left to do and a wave of tiredness swept over me. I yawned and leaned back against the wall, then slid down on to the floor for a moment to get my breath back and work out what to do next.

Micah looked down at me for a moment, then joined me, crossing his long legs in their skinny jeans. Neither of us said anything for a while, but the darkness and the peace felt intimate.

'So what went wrong, Mr Psychic?' I asked him quietly. 'Was I a blip in your untarnished record of predictions, or was it the other way round? You just hit lucky with the fairground and the other stuff?'

He turned his head to me and I couldn't make out his expression. 'What do you mean?'

'I mean, are you a fake or not? You were spot on with some things.'

He looked forwards again. 'No, I'm not a fake. I just messed up with you and I still can't quite work out why.' He sighed. 'I'm usually so sure.'

I needed to know and put my hand on his arm. 'You're absolutely right about Tam's baby, aren't you? Everything's going to be all right, isn't it?'

He nodded fervently. 'Oh, yes, I'm one hundred per cent sure about that. Knowing things like that is one of the best parts of my job.'

I snorted. 'Oh, come on! No way is being a psychic some kind of job. You don't see an opening for those in the Sits Vac.' I laughed at the idea of it. 'Wanted: person who can see the future; but then presumably you know we want you so you'll have sent your CV anyway!'

I realised at that point that Micah wasn't laughing. Perhaps I'd offended him.

'The thing is, Lucy, I'm not exactly a psychic – or at least, not how you imagine. But I do know what's coming for people, though I admit I cocked up with you.'

I didn't understand. He wasn't really explaining anything.

'So you are ...?'

'I think I'm what you could call a celestial being.'

I rolled over on the ground laughing at this. Crikey! Was there no end to this man's self-belief? 'Oh, come off it!' I dug him in the ribs. 'You're taking the piss! Prove it!'

He raised his eyebrows. 'I'm not "taking the piss", as you so elegantly put it and, no, I'm not going to prove it. I don't need to. I got everything right, didn't I? Except you. And even when I met you, I knew there was something wrong. You didn't fit the profile I was given. I was looking for an older woman.' He paused and leaned his head against the wall. 'I'm going to be in such trouble,' he whispered.

I rubbed my eyes. Was tiredness making me hallucinate? 'You mean, you are an angel?'

'Well, not completely,' he muttered. 'But I will be, if I manage to finish this task properly.' He tapped his fingers on his legs and fidgeted. 'The thing is, I've slightly stepped outside my remit, to be honest. We're strictly told we mustn't intervene in things – it's one of the first rules – but I guess I'm a bit of a show-off and I couldn't resist.' He shook his head. 'They'll never promote me now. You've no idea how tempting it is when you can feel things so strongly. When you know the truth. I can't resist telling people. I suppose I just got a bit carried away, that's all.'

'So that evening at the theatre – you were just there "doing a turn"?'

He shrugged. 'Yes, I suppose so. I hadn't been able to find one of the people whose name I'd been given – your name actually. Lucy Streeter. I was sort of wandering about aimlessly and then I bumped into that woman and we got talking and she invited me to go down to the theatre for the fund-raiser. I find it difficult to let people down, and she was so friendly ...' He trailed off, a bit embarrassed at himself.

I held my head, trying to compute the information. Here I was sitting against a wall in the middle of the night surrounded by normal life, and taking in this mind-blowing revelation. Some bits didn't add up. 'So ... why does an angel need a flat to stay in?'

'We don't roost in trees, you know. We get sent with quite a list of people to ... you know, tell them it's time. "Bringing them home", we call it. And Lucy Streeter was the last in quite a long list. We're a bit short-staffed and I've had to cover quite a lot of the region by myself this week.' His tone was so matter-of-fact, but I could feel my mouth had dropped open as I listened. 'I'm due to be reassigned but I had to finish this first, which is why, when you turned up on the doorstep a couple of hours ago, it threw me a bit.'

'Understatement of the year!' We both sat in silence for a while, me thinking about what I'd just been told, and him, presumably thinking of how he was going to explain himself to the powers that be. I had to ask. 'So the gates?'

He looked confused. 'What gates?'

'The gates to heaven. Are they really pearly?'

'I don't understand.'

'Well, I sort of imagined they were like the type of gates you see on posh houses in the Thames Valley or Solihull – automatic and all ornate and gold.'

He pondered this for a moment then shook his head. 'No, it's not like that really.'

'And are there clouds, and people ... like you ... just in white with little harps? And halos? Do they exist?' He smiled at my imaginings. 'And come on tell me, what does He look like? Has he got a beard and all that?'

He smiled indulgently and shook his head patiently. 'No, Lucy, it's not like that. In fact, I can't tell you what it's like.'

I was disappointed. 'What? You mean, you're not allowed to?'

'Well, I've never been asked, to be honest, so if there's a policy I don't know about it. But what I mean is, it is *indescribable*. There are no words to do it justice. It's not like anything you will have experienced so I have nothing to compare it to.' He closed his eyes. 'It is so much more wonderful than you could ever imagine. People have tried to paint it too. Loads of them. But no one has even come close to getting it right. It gives us all a laugh actually, seeing them try.'

'What about William Blake? Michelangelo?'

He thought about that for a moment. 'Yeah, they made a fair stab at it but it's so much more.'

I pondered his description. 'Well, it sounds like something to look forward to. Can't wait to get there.' I put my hand to my mouth and laughed. 'Or am I being presumptuous? I mean, is there an alternative for the bad ones?'

'Put it this way, they don't have a good time of it. There are staff to make sure of that. But don't worry, Lucy, you'll be fine – so long as you don't go off the rails between now and—' He stopped and I realised what he'd almost said. Did I want to know?

'And when will that be?' I smiled uncertainly.

'Ah, you can't trick me twice! I'm not telling you that until the time is really right.'

I pushed his arm teasingly. 'I hope you've improved your accuracy rate by then – or they allocate someone else to the job!'

At that moment the clock tower rang the quarter-hour and I look at my watch hastily.

'Come on, my angel.' I pulled myself up and put my hand out for Micah. 'We've got more work to do, you and I.'

Chapter Twenty-One

I marched purposefully up the street with Micah puffing along behind me. I could hear the birds beginning to sing ominously in the park and even though the sun was nowhere near peering over the horizon, there was a light in the sky that warned of dawn. I glanced back at Micah trying to keep up and, even though I believed him, deranged as it may sound, he appeared faintly comical, this gangly angel in his skinny jeans, white T-shirt and baseball boots. Not what I'd envisaged at all, and certainly not the stuff of nativity plays and children's drawings

'Lucy, slow down!' he panted behind me. 'Where are we off to now?'

'I can't really tell you,' I called back over my shoulder. 'You're going to have to go with me on this one – I think I deserve it, don't you?'

He didn't answer – I'm not sure he had enough breath he was panting so hard. Odd. You'd imagine angels to be fitter somehow. We turned in to the road, and I checked Richard's car wasn't parked outside, then headed into the alley behind his house and tried the back gate. There were no street lights here and I could see very little in the dark. Thankfully for me, Richard has always been a little negligent in the security department, and with a hard shove from my shoulder, the gate opened to his tiny terraced back garden. In the murk I could make out the small table, four metal chairs, and a selection of pots and shrubs.

'Shut the gate behind you,' I whispered to Micah and, because I had turned my head to talk to him, I missed the brick edge of a flowerbed and tripped, landing on my knees on the brick path.

'Shit, shit, shit!'

'Ssssh!' Micah helped my up. 'Lucy, we're not going to break in, are we?'

I ignored him again and rubbed my leg frantically. I'd ripped the knee of my jeans and I could feel sticky blood on my fingers.

Letting my eyes get used to the dark now, I squinted up at the back of Richard's house. I had to hope he hadn't put the alarm on. He rarely did – his theory being that no one would care if it went off and he had nothing worth nicking anyway except an impressive back catalogue of yachting magazines. The French windows out to the garden were locked, of course, but the bathroom window above appeared to be slightly open at the top. The joy of these small terrace houses is that they often have an outhouse attached to the back with a flat roof and Richard's was no exception.

'Right – another leg-up please.'

Micah, obviously considering himself something of an expert in this department now, was standing, hands on hips, assessing the situation. 'No, I don't think we can get the lift on this one. Turn around, Lucy, and look the other way.'

'You're not—'

'Just turn around, will you?' he said, slightly more impatiently, so I did what I was told and a moment later I heard him call from above my head.

'How did you manage that?'

'I have my talents.' Tentatively he put his foot down on the felt of the flat roof, just to check he wasn't going to end up in the shed below, then he turned to me and put his hands out. 'Okay, up you come.'

My scaling technique was very inelegant and it hurt my knee

as I swung my leg up to the roof. As I joined Micah, a light went on in the house next door and we both froze and held our breath. Through the frosted glass we could see a figure go in to their bathroom and the smudged profile of someone having a pee. We both stood stock still until the light went off again. The window was stiff but between the two of us, we managed to shove it open. I was the first through and the scent of Richard – was it soap or aftershave? – hit me, making me realise how much I did, indeed, love this man.

'Right, follow me.' I led Micah out on to the dark landing, trying to remember where Richard's answering machine was. I knew what it looked like because he had the same one as me – I'd bought mine on his recommendation – but where the hell did he keep it? The sitting room? Everyone kept it in there or in the hall, didn't they? We slowly descended the stairs. The light from the street lamps poured through the fanlight above the front door and threw everything into shadow. His bike was propped up in the hallway – why on earth didn't he keep it in the garden? – but there was no table for telephones in the narrow passageway. The sitting room was lit up too from the street, but all I could make out were piles of books, a plate and glass, and a phone handset on the coffee table in front of a deep armchair – a tableau of where he had last sat watching TV. I could feel panic rising.

'What exactly are we looking for?' Micah made me jump coming up behind me in the silence. 'Tell me, then I might be able to help.'

'The answering machine,' I whispered back urgently as if he was a halfwit not to have known already.

'Is it in the kitchen?'

'No, I don't think so.'

'Is there a study? And whose house is this that we're standing in at four o'clock in the morning, if it's not too impertinent to ask?'

Richard's office! Of course. I headed back towards the stairs. I'd never actually been in to what was a converted back bedroom, but had seen through the doorway on trips to use the bathroom once or twice. Now I pushed open the door and turned on the desk lamp. A low light flooded the room and I quickly pulled down the blind at the window. This room was a part of Richard I didn't know and I felt strange and guilty to be trespassing in it. One wall was covered with bookshelves crammed to bursting with books of all sizes and, under the window, was a wide wicker chair piled high with boxes of glasses for the Deli. His chaotic desk was on the other wall, above it two large pictures, one the infamous *London Calling* album cover with Paul Simonon smashing his guitar on the stage. Next to it, in complete contrast, was a print by Klimt. The room was cosy and lived-in and I could imagine Richard sitting here doing the accounts or poring over boat catalogues. There was a noticeboard above the desk, too, with business cards and scraps of paper stuck in it, and I smiled when I saw he'd pinned up the shot of Sally, Karl and me taken in the harbour at Honfleur last summer. We'd sailed across the Channel in a pretty hair-raising trip and we all looked scruffy but tanned and happy – probably to have survived the crossing.

The desk was covered in papers and, on top, the handwritten receipt from the *Serenity*. My eyes widened at the price he'd paid for her. He'd have to sell his boat on the Hamble to cover this, surely? Either that or the muffin trade was doing better than I thought.

'Is that it?' Micah pointed to a narrow CD cabinet beside the desk.

I turned to where he was pointing, and there was the answering machine perched on top of a pile of CDs. And there was the message light.

Not flashing.

For a moment I didn't understand. On my machine at home, it flashes when there's a new message, and when it isn't, or you've listened to a message, it simply shows nought or the number of saved messages. And Richard's machine simply showed the figure '1'. Had it not picked up my message? Had I called the wrong number? I knew I hadn't because his recorded message had answered, his voice as deep and distracted as ever. I pressed play and heard my own voice start speaking. I pressed stop again as if I'd been burnt.

Then I buckled as the implications became clear. Richard must have heard the message sometime in the last four and a half hours. But how? He'd gone to the boat hours ago – Sally had said so. And he can't have been here when I called because he didn't pick up the phone. Could he have called in from somewhere to check his messages? What kind of bad luck was that! I must have moaned audibly.

'Look,' Micah sighed, 'I've scaled a wall, climbed through a window and am now standing in the house of someone I don't know – I think I deserve an explanation?'

I slumped down in to Richard's desk chair. 'Oh, God.'

'He might not be able to help,' Micah offered helpfully.

I put my head in my hands. 'It's so truly, truly awful that it's going to take a bloody miracle to put this one right.' I could have wept.

Micah crouched down beside me and rubbed my back tentatively as if I might bite. 'What have you done, Lucy?'

'It's Richard,' I mumbled through my hands.

'Who's Richard? I assume he is the house owner?'

I nodded. 'He's my friend. And then on Friday, cos ... cos you said that Friday was my last day and cos I was so stupid,' I remember I banged my hand on my grazed knee at this point

228

and winced because it hurt, 'so stupid as to believe you, I left a message on his machine.'

'What message?'

'A message saying I love him.'

There was a pause. 'Oh.'

'And he's down on the Hamble and I thought I could ... or at least I hoped I could wipe the message before he got home but he's obviously heard it or something because the light isn't flashing and I can't delete it because then he'll know I've been here and broken in – oh bloody, bloody hell, this is a total disaster.' I eventually drew breath.

Micah didn't say anything for a moment. 'Well,' he began eventually, 'I have no idea what being "down on the hamble" means – is that some sort of euphemism?'

'It's a river. He sails.'

'Oh, I see. Well, this Richard – is he married or something?'

'No. He has a girlfriend, though. Or he did at least. They change with the weather.'

'Does he love you?'

This time I snapped. Didn't he understand anything? 'No! Of course he doesn't. We're just friends and now I've spoiled everything.' I threw my hands up in despair. 'What the hell am I going to do, Micah? It's your fault I did this and I need you to work out what I'm going to do. He's too ... he's too important to me to lose.'

Micah leaned back on his heels and crossed his arms. 'So, if he's that important to you, Lucy, what's wrong with having told him how you feel?'

'Because it'll never be the same again!' I was almost shrieking now, rocking in despair. 'And I'll have to see him every day and he'll avoid me, all embarrassed. And then he'll get married one day, and I'll have to stand and watch him with another woman and he'll feel all apologetic and sorry for me!'

'Lucy, calm down.' He rubbed my arm gently. 'Sometimes you have to take risks. Sometimes you have to do and say things because they come from your heart and they need to be done or said.' I shrugged. It was nonsense of course. 'If Richard is your friend, and if he is a true friend, then it won't matter that you said those things.'

'I wish I could believe you, but I've blown it now. It'll be, "Poor Lucy, in love with Richard, you know, but he doesn't love *her*."'

Micah frowned. 'Would it help to know that what people think doesn't really matter in the end?'

I weighed this up for a split second. 'Nope, that doesn't help at all, actually! Right now, this could be a disaster of apocalyptic proportions.' I realised what I'd said and laughed and Micah smiled broadly.

'Trust me, Lucy. It's really not!'

'Come on.' I stood up. There was nothing I could do to salvage the situation so, feeling entirely defeated and completely desperate, I left the room. 'We'd better get out of here before I get found out and it's even more embarrassing, and I'm in the local papers for breaking into my friend's house. How freaky would that be? Besides, I need to find out if I can emigrate before Monday so I can curl up and die with shame under a stone somewhere. I don't suppose you have the power to turn back time?'

He shook his head and pursed his mouth. 'Don't even go there. That's really advanced stuff. I can't even get the basics right.'

Quietly we made our way back to the bathroom and clambered, without speaking, back through the window and, with great difficulty and very slowly, lowered ourselves on to the terrace.

Chapter Twenty-Two

Saturday and the sun is rising

Dragging my feet now, we made our way back down the road and, at the corner where we would part, I stopped. Ashamed and appalled with myself, I couldn't even raise my eyes.

'Thanks, Micah.'

'For what?' I could hear the smile in his voice.

'For coming and breaking in with me. It wasn't fair to make you do that.'

'Lucy.' He put his hands on the top of my arms. 'That's okay. Think about what I said, though. I might be right.'

'Your record of being right when it comes to me is not great, let's be honest.'

'No, but ... well, anyway.' At that he leaned down and kissed me on the cheek. 'Now, you need to get some sleep. You've done quite enough for one night.'

I sighed. 'Wish I could. I'm afraid that – thinking *I wouldn't be here*,' I said with emphasis, 'I did some artwork on my shop, and Fen's too, remember?'

'Oh.' He understood immediately. 'I forgot in all the excitement. We'll need another bucket then?'

I put my hand on his arm gratefully. 'No. You've been more than helpful. I'm sure I've got something at the shop. You go off and have a rest, or hang upside down, or whatever it is you people do!'

Micah looked disgustingly perky. 'Rest! We don't need to rest. Come on. I'll give you a hand. I'm getting quite good at this. Who knows? Paint removal might come in handy as a job if I get demoted!'

'Do they have a lot of graffiti in heaven then?'

'They might if the writing's on the wall,' he laughed, and nudged me in the ribs at his awful pun. He slipped his arm through mine and led me up the road, and with him beside me, I felt curiously safe and comforted, despite the deserted streets. The last few days had been so lonely and, even though I knew for sure that I would never be able to share it all with anyone ... normal ... Micah understood exactly what I'd been through and that was comforting.

As we walked, my mobile banged annoyingly against my leg. I don't even know why I'd put it in my pocket when I'd left the house so many hours ago now, but I pulled it out and turned it on. Three missed calls and a text message popped up. The calls were from Richard, of course, and they'd come in the last few hours. My heart leapt, but he'd left no messages. Which confirmed my worst suspicions – he'd heard my little outburst and wanted to check I hadn't taken leave of my senses.

The text was from Nat and sent about four hours ago:

Thought I'd come home after party 2nite. Hope ok. Won't wake you. It'll be very late. x

This time my heart lifted with joy. Nat was coming home. At last, something good was happening. I texted back:

Can't w8.

One down, one to go. Half an hour later, we were outside my shop. With fresh water from home, we'd done what we could at Fen's – and I wasn't too inclined to make a perfect job of it – but on mine the pink paint was drier and harder to shift and I cursed quietly as I scrubbed at it. Micah and I worked in silence, except for the odd expletive as he dripped water on my head attempting to wash off the words on the top line.

'Oi, that went down my ear.'

'Sorry.'

The pink of the dawn light was merging in with the pink paint, making it hard to see and I could hear the sounds of the town waking up. My heart began to pound with anxiety and I rubbed even more vigorously. Gradually the words I had daubed disappeared. I stepped back to look. I could only just make out the odd letter now but the sentiment was still too obvious: "Forced ou … bu …. ness … unscrup … landl … Saye …"

Standing on my toes, rubbing hard again, I barely registered a car pulling up behind me and I jumped guiltily when I heard someone clearing their throat.

'Oh – hello, Officer.'

'Morning, madam, sir. Are you the owners of this property?'

I dropped the cloth back in the bucket and dried my hands on my jeans. 'Well, not the owner. I rent it, yes. This is my shop.'

The young policeman seemed unsure of how to continue. 'And would you say it's usual for you to be – er – cleaning the windows at this hour?'

I followed his gaze over my shoulder. Clean they were not. Although the letters were no longer visible, the glass was streaked with pink smudges that virtually obscured everything inside. I cast about for an explanation and Micah and I exchanged blank glances. What possible excuse was I going to give this earnest boy with the sticking-out ears, who looked little more than a teenager? Then it came to me.

'Kids!'

'Sorry, madam?'

I crossed my fingers firmly behind my back. 'It's those kids! I was just ...' I was about to say at a party but I'd be breathalysed next if I wasn't careful. And he might ask for witnesses. 'Just walking ... I'm an insomniac, you know. And I saw the windows were covered in graffiti, so I went home to get some water to wash it off before any of my customers saw it.'

'I see.' He nodded slowly. 'And you didn't see anyone suspicious in the vicinity?'

'Oh, no.' I shook my head slowly, as if I was actually thinking about it. 'The street was quite deserted.'

His radio chirped static and we both stared at it for a moment. 'What kind of shop is it, madam?'

'A clothes shop,' I replied definitely. 'I design and sell women's fashions.' He couldn't conceal his disbelief and I felt him scrutinising my scruffy, paint-dripped jeans and T-shirt.

'And you were helping her, sir?' He asked Micah, politely but clearly deeply suspicious now.

'Of course,' Micah answered grandly. 'As any gentleman would.'

The officer moved away slightly and I could hear him talking into his radio, spelling things out in that weird way they have – Victor Romeo Bravo – that sort of thing. I couldn't really hear what he was saying, and I could feel Micah's unease beside me. I was about to reassure him and say everything would be fine, when the officer turned back to us, looking far less friendly.

'I'm afraid I'm going to have to ask you both to accompany me down to the police station.'

'You can't be serious!' I blurted, panicky now. 'This is my shop! You can check. Ask anyone.'

'Quite possibly, madam, but we have had reports of a person answering your description involved in similar incidents in other parts of town. We need to ask you a few questions. You do not have to say anything,' he went on, ominously, and my ears started to drum as he mentioned terrifying words like 'harm your defence' and 'something you may later rely on in court'.

Micah and I sat side by side like naughty children in the back of the patrol car – at least he hadn't cuffed us. It was entirely inappropriate but the thought of Nat as a small boy kept popping into my head. He would have given his right arm to have ridden in a patrol car and here I was fulfilling his dream. It might have been nerves but I couldn't stop a giggle bubbling up and had to turn it swiftly into a cough.

The car radio spluttered the whole time and as he drove, his sticking-out ears silhouetted against the windscreen, my captor informed the control room that we were on our way. The first problem arose as we arrived at the station and were asked by the portly, bald desk sergeant to empty our pockets and provide some form of ID. He had to ask us loudly over the noise of a drunk serenading the reception area with a rendition of 'Danny Boy'. I didn't recognise him at first but when he lurched up to the desk, it became horrifically clear that it was one of the tramps from the park.

'From glen to glen—' he slurred, then broke off abruptly when he saw me. 'Darling!' he grasped me in an unspeakably vile grasp. The stench of pee and Carling Black Label almost overwhelmed me.

'Back off, Billy,' the officer snapped. 'I don't know what's got into you lot this evening. Did one of you win the lottery? You're the fifth in tonight. Leave the lady alone.'

'Lady? Lady? She's no lady,' he gurgled. 'She's an angel. We've had such a party thanks to her and we drank to your health, luv. All night!' He threw is head back and laughed wheezily, exposing gapped teeth beneath a scrubby growth of beard and moustache.

The policemen looked at me with renewed suspicion and sensing that, along with everything else, I was in grave danger of being charged with aiding and abetting public drunkenness, I turned my back. I shrugged at the officers, and tried to divert them as Billy was escorted to the back of the station, the dulcet tones of 'I'll simply sleep in peace until you come' fading with him. So much for me trying to do some good for the community – fool that I was.

'ID? Right,' I said, patting my pockets futilely. 'That could be a problem. I must have left it at home in my other jeans.'

'Right then, name and address please, and date of birth.' His pen was poised over the form.

I gave him the details, mounting a charm offensive. My dad had always worked on the principle that the more polite you are with public figures, the better. It hadn't always worked for him, though – I remember one summer holiday when he'd waved magisterially at the customs officers who had promptly pulled us over the stripped the car. It didn't seem to be having much effect here either.

Then the officer turned to Micah.

'And what about you, sir?'

'Er ...'

Micah looked at me, his eyes pools of terror, and I looked back at him, suddenly realising how complicated this might become.

'I don't ... exactly ... have ...' he started cautiously, never taking his eyes of my face and willing me to help him out here.

'He's with me,' I blurted. 'We live together. He's my partner. My boyfriend.' I knew I didn't sound very convincing, so I grabbed Micah's cold hand in mine and stroked it as lovingly as I could. 'Aren't you, darling?'

At first Micah's expression was blank, as if he didn't really get where I was coming from on this, then realisation dawned.

'Oh, yes! Yes, I am ... er ... darling.' And he clasped me enthusiastically to him, grinning at the game we were playing and nodding violently at the officer, who was looking more and more sceptical.

'I see,' he said, his eyes moving between us. 'Take a seat over there, please. The custody officer will be with you shortly.

The word 'custody' made my heart leap. That was the sort of term they used in films before they threw someone in the cells, and with every passing minute, and there were many of them, I felt more and more anxious. We watched the comings and goings, our fears rising each time someone came through the door that lead to the back of the station. Micah and I barely spoke but I couldn't help thinking that, if we were charged with some heinous crime, then he'd be all right, flitting off into the clouds, and I'd be left to face a hefty fine.

It must have been seven o'clock before we were interviewed and, by then, my stomach was rumbling with a combination of anxiety and hunger. I looked back at Micah as I was lead away, trying to imagine how he would explain it all in his interview, but there was nothing I could do about that. I'd urged him out of the corner of my mouth, as we'd waited, not to say anything too weird and just stick to the facts that he was helping me out and knew nothing about why, and he'd simply nodded. Which wasn't very reassuring.

By the time I came out, about an hour later, I could have eaten my arm with hunger, but all I wanted to do was go home and climb under the duvet. I felt dirty and I don't just mean my clothes. The two interviewing officers had played bad cop, bad cop, asking me over and over again if I'd been in any other part of town. Lying through my teeth, and confident there were no CCTV cameras on Sayers' seedy street, I flatly denied it over and over again. Then they came on to why I had been washing my windows in the early hours of the morning, and what I'd been doing until then. It was fair enough – it even sounded unconvincing to me – but, dredging up some nonsense Tam had told me once about symptoms and herbal remedies for sleeplessness, I prattled on about the burden of insomnia, hoping that the tiresome level of detail would wear them down.

I must have bored them into submission in the end because, after I had signed my statement, they informed me that I wouldn't be charged 'on this occasion' (as if there would be others!) and released me into the waiting area. Alarmingly there was no sign of Micah and I sat on the edge of my seat for an agonising ten minutes, imagining the nonsense he would be telling his interviewers. Would he be able to hold back from telling them about the church tower? Was he even capable of lying and if so, would that put paid to his hopes of promotion?

Finally the door opened slowly and Micah emerged, his face irritatingly smug and upbeat. Behind came two officers, both young, almost too young to shave, and I can only describe their expressions as euphoric. They were smiling blissfully, like something from a painting by Raphael, and they wished him goodbye in the warmest tones.

'Don't ask,' he muttered out of the corner of his mouth as we collected our belongings. And I didn't because on my phone, handed back by the desk sergeant, were about six missed calls from Nat.

'Mum!' he gasped when he answered my call. 'Where the hell are you?'

'It's okay, darling. Just had a spot of trouble.' I laughed lightly to dispel the situation. 'All sorted now. Ha ha ha. Where are you?'

'I'm outside your shop. What in God's name has happened? The windows are all smeary and there's a bucket on the ground.

Are you closing down or something?' He sounded frantic and I tried to calm him.

'I'll explain later. Could you … would you mind coming to pick me up?'

'Where are you?'

I winced. 'At the police station, as a matter of fact.'

Luckily, I managed to persuade Micah to head back to his flat before Nat's little car came around the corner. Exhausted now, I slumped into the passenger seat but still couldn't resist a motherly reflex.

'You're not drunk, are you? I mean, you said there had been a party.'

He looked at me, with my paint-splattered clothes and hair, then at the front door of the police station, then back at me.

'I don't think that even warrants an answer, Mum.' He smiled, relief on his face, and I realised just how worried he must have been coming back to an empty flat I clearly hadn't been in all night. 'Are you going to tell me what's going on?'

I sighed. 'Can I jump in the shower first, sweetheart? After that, we'll make a cuppa and some bacon sarnies and I'll tell you all about it.' Then I shut my eyes as my son drove us home.

Chapter Twenty-Three

The jets of hot water cascaded over my aching muscles, and I washed my hair and my body two or three times to wipe away the paint and the vestiges of the last twelve hours. I was alive, I'd managed to escape a criminal conviction, and I was pretty sure I had enough on Sayers to discredit him. And now, Nat was making me breakfast. Except for the tricky matter of Richard, things were looking up. I felt a rush of love for my son as I towelled myself dry. Thank heavens I was here for him, alive, and everything was as before.

I slipped into some comfortable pyjama bottoms and a vest top – both too scruffy even for the charity shop – and wandered through to the sitting room, rubbing my hair dry with a hand towel. But there was no smell of bacon. Instead, Nat was standing in the centre of the room. The atmosphere was static with tension.

'Er. No cuppa?' I tried tentatively.

He held out his hand and in it was my letter. He must have just found it. On the sofa in front of him was strewn the envelope and the cash that I'd tucked in with the letter. In all my desperation to sort out my graffiti, retrieve my jeans and my dignity, I had completely forgotten about my letter to Nat. I suppose I'd thought I'd be home long before he arrived and have time to tear it into little pieces, put it in the bin and just carry on with life as before – no questions, no explanations needed.

'Oh.'

Yes, *oh*.' He ran his fingers through his hair. 'Christ, Mum. What's this all about? And why did you leave me a letter like this, on the mantelpiece of all places?'

I floundered for a reply to that.

'I mean, isn't this quite important – finally telling me who my dad is? And I come home to find it propped up like a fucking invitation or something! Have you gone mad?'

Well, if I wasn't mad, then I was stupid. That letter lying limply now, written in maudlin self-pity with the truth about his father and me and where he lived now, should have been thrown away as soon as I knew Micah's prediction was nonsense. Maybe it should never have been written.

Getting no reply from me, Nat lifted the letter up again. 'And you've put here: "I'm telling you this in case you ever need to know." What?' His eyes flashed at me. 'Has this Neil bloke got some terrible genetic problem or something?'

'No I—'

'And he sells cars. Christ, Mum. Couldn't you have done a bit better than that?' I had never seen Nat look so bitter. His face was twisted with anger.

'Don't be such a snob. You're as bad as Grandpa. There's nothing wrong with selling cars, Nat.'

'Yes, there is. Don't you know how that shatters all my dreams? I'd built up this man – my *dad* – to be great and mysterious and clever. And all he does is sell fucking second-hand cars in Leamington.'

'Nat, you never asked and don't swear.' I moved towards him but the sofa was still between us. 'If you'd asked, I'd have told you anything you wanted to know. All of it. But you never did and I didn't want to push it onto you.'

'I did ask, Mum, but you always brushed it away or acted so weird I knew you didn't want to talk about it. So why now,

Mum? Why have you decided *just now*,' his voice was sarcastic, 'is the right time for all these revelations?' He emphasised the last word heavily.

'Because ... Because I thought it was time. In case something ever happens to me and I haven't had time to tell you.'

'Great.' He folded the letter roughly and pushed it in to the back pocket of his jeans. 'Anything else you want to spring on me? You're getting married? You've joined a mad religious cult? You're acting weird, Mum.'

I waved my hand airily, trying to dismiss it all as trite but knowing this situation was slipping out of my control. 'Nothing, darling. Nothing for you to worry about.'

'That's what you always say. But I am worried. The hair, turning up at uni, throwing your cash around.' He waved at the notes strewn on the sofa. 'And this morning at the police station? What was this morning all about?'

'Look, it's complicated. It's to do with the shop and the landlord. I think I've found out he's a crook and ...' I tailed off because, as much as I could tell him about Fen and Sandy, I couldn't explain with any conviction why I'd defaced my own shopfront. And how could I account for the way I had been behaving? Not unless I told him the whole story and I just could not do that.

'Do you know,' he hurled at me then, like a parent confronting a teenager, 'do you have any idea how worried I was when I got home and you clearly hadn't been here all night?'

'I could have been with a friend,' I tried. 'I am an adult, you know! I might even have been with a boyfriend.'

'But you weren't,' he virtually shouted, 'because you answered my text then you weren't here. And your friends? I knew you weren't with them because I've rung them all. Tam was in a right state – you know what she's like – and Sally thinks you've gone quite mad. She tells me you've hardly been in the shop all week.' I put my hand up to my mouth, aghast at the ripples my behaviour had caused. 'They're as worried as I am. I even left a message for Granny and Grandpa on that mobile of theirs – if they can work out how to read it. And Richard! Richard is out of his mind with worry. He's called me from his boat about six times. He said you'd left some kind of weird message.' I felt the blood run from my face. 'And now this ...' He cast about for a word. 'This *revelation*! I thought we trusted each other, that we were close. Instead you put it all down in a letter. You can't even face me with the information. You keep your bloody cash. You can't buy me off, you know!'

With that he picked up his bag and, panic rising, I realised he was going to leave. Before I could answer him, he headed towards the door. 'I'm off.'

The front door slammed behind him, shattering the silence. In all of this mess, this was the lowest point. Micah, Sayers, Fen, Sandy, the shop and my future, even the stupid things I'd said to Richard, paled in comparison to Nat's reaction to finding out about his father like that. It didn't matter that for the first time ever I had told him, at the bottom of the letter, how he was the most important thing in my life and how I loved him in a way he would never imagine until he had children of his own. That meant nothing compared to his anger and pain.

My appetite disappeared with Nat and, devastated and confused, I mechanically made myself a cup of tea and slumped defeated onto the sofa. Everything he had said went through my mind. Looking at it from his point of view, I could understand entirely why he was so upset. His little world had changed in a moment and his mother, to blame for everything, had simply stood there open-mouthed without an explanation.

I toyed with my phone. I wanted to ring him so badly and beg him to come home, but my rational brain – or what was left of it – counselled me to let him calm down. The people I did need to contact, however, were Tam, Sally and Richard, but I couldn't face actually talking to him so, coward that I was, I simply texted to them all: 'Sorry to have worried you. I'm fine. Was with a friend so missed your calls.' It was feeble but I wasn't ready to explain more.

I must have fallen asleep where I sat, half-drunk cup of tea propped in my lap, because when I woke with a start, it was stone cold and there was an insistent banging on the front window. My heart pounded. Could it be Tam or Sally, responding to my text? I wasn't up to seeing either of them. I got up, feeling groggy, peeped around the side of the kitchen window to see who was there and was startled to see my dad's face looking back at me. Knocking on the window was a habit he and Mum had developed when Nat was little, to see if he was sleeping before they rang the bell on their regular, checking-up-on-the-errant-daughter visits. Dad had never come here on his own before though, so perhaps he worked out how to open Nat's text, and had come to see if I was under a bus. I could have done without seeing him, too, but now he'd spotted me, I had to let him in.

'Ah! You're here,' he announced as I opened the door, taking in my sleepy face and scruffy attire. He seemed ill-at-ease and hesitated before starting to talk. 'Only Nat sent us a message. I think you had him quite worried.'

I led the way in to the sitting room. 'Yes.' I muttered. 'Funny how the roles change, isn't it? I'm now getting a ticking-off from my son for being out late.' I omitted to mention my brush with the law. Not sure how my dad would have handled that.

He stood, awkwardly, in the middle of the room, where Nat had stood a few hours earlier – how long ago I wasn't sure. There was still money on the sofa and my dad eyed it without comment.

'Well,' he continued, 'I just thought I'd come and see that you're okay.'

'I'm fine,' I said, looking down at myself. 'As you can see. I was simply out with friends.'

'And I wanted to see this haircut your mother's sure I'll hate.'

'Right. And do you? Hate it, I mean?'

He inspected me then shrugged. 'Well, you know what they say.'

I did. It was a familiar old joke in our house from when I was growing up: 'What's the difference between a bad haircut and a good one?' The answer was: 'About two weeks', which I'd thought very witty at the time. It made me smile a little bit now even after everything I'd been through – and everything that had passed between me and Dad recently. Looking back, perhaps he was trying to lighten the atmosphere by reminding me of jokes we'd had when I was younger, but it just made me feel sad. I saw a look of hope flicker in his eyes when he saw my response. Nat's fury had sapped my energy completely and I couldn't be bothered to feel angry any more. Maybe thinking I was going to die had put everything else in perspective, changed my view on life and about what matters.

'Cup of tea, Dad?'

'If it's no trouble.'

So I busied myself in the kitchen and brought a tray through to where he sat, by the window, staring at the tiny garden. He was hunched over a little and, for the first time, I realised that he'd changed without my noticing into the old man he was. I poured his tea carefully and we chit-chatted about various things as we drank it and dunked Ginger Nuts. The roadworks at the roundabout, the weather – anything but what had happened the last time we saw each other or the cause of Nat's frantic message to them. As he drained his cup, I could see him bracing himself to speak and I tensed up in turn.

'Lucy, I didn't just come here to see your hairdo.' He smiled weakly, looking pleased with his little joke. 'It's about the other day and – well, I feel ... that is, your mother says ...' He stopped and sighed, then said abruptly, 'I'm sorry for the other day. You know – the things I said ...'

I had to stop him and I laid my hand on his arm. He looked down, surprised.

'Listen, Dad, let's not. Let's just ... not. I don't want you to apologise – or even to feel you have to. It's not like that. It shouldn't be.' I stopped, unsure of how to go on.

'The thing is,' Dad stepped in, 'your Mum said that, when you popped over yesterday, you mentioned that you thought ... that you *think*, that I'm waiting for you to make mistakes in some way. She was quite cross with me actually.' He smiled sheepishly. 'Called me a silly old fool, if you must know, and not for the first time!'

Suddenly he looked unsure of himself. Not the overbearing Dad of the past. Was this how I had seemed to Nat – no longer the infallible parent I'd always tried so hard to be?

I sighed. 'I *have* made so many mistakes, Dad, and it doesn't seem right for you to be apologising to me. If we start, we'll never stop and I don't want it to be like that between us. You, Mum, Chris and Nat,' – if he was still talking to me – 'you're all I've got and I don't want to keep looking back at things that have gone wrong in the past.'

'Lucy, my love, we all make mistakes. Wouldn't the world be dull if we didn't? But if I was too critical, it's only because I wanted you to be happy. The best for you. Isn't that what every parent wants?'

I thought about what Neil had told me about Dad warning him off, then had a vision of my son and the way he had looked at me before slamming out of the flat. 'Oh, it's all so complicated, isn't it? I've tried to do everything right for Nat but I don't think he likes me very much at the moment.'

Dad smiled ruefully now. 'I think every child dislikes their parents at some stage or other. Don't you? But that parent–child thing is a hard old link to break and all you can do is hope it comes good in the end. Before it's too late.' He looked at me searchingly and I realised he was asking for my forgiveness.

I couldn't trust myself to speak and simply rubbed his arm, feeling the loose old skin under my fingers.

Dad put out his hand too and cautiously ruffled my hair. 'Feels strange,' he said, embarrassed by this change in our relationship. 'You're different. But it's still you. Do you know, I may be an old buffer, but I rather like it. Makes you look very pretty. Carefree.'

I wish. He didn't stay long after that. I wondered if Mum would ask him what we'd said when he got home and I realised that their marriage was perhaps more balanced than I'd thought. I picked up my mobile again. Still no message from Nat. I wondered if he'd ever let me apologise for what I'd kept from him over the years.

Chapter Twenty-Four

Saturday afternoon

Restless and not knowing quite what to do with myself after Dad had departed, I left the flat and headed for the shop. One grim reality in all this was that I'd given away most of next month's rent to a bunch of winos, and hadn't taken a bean in the shop for days. One downside of being alive is that it's considerably more expensive than being dead, and I had to get sensible. My bubble of euphoria had well and truly burst now, and as I opened up and the peculiar smell of hot, stale air hit my nostrils, I felt dispirited.

The best I could think of was to re-group and get rid of some stock the old-fashioned way. Another bucket of warm soapy water and half an hour's elbow grease sorted out the window, and after that I set to with paint again, this time promoting my mid-season 'Sale', offering tempting but suicidally big discounts. If that didn't move some goods, nothing would. As I crossed out prices on labels with a red pen and wrote on new ones, I thought for the millionth time about my row with Nat. I hadn't heard a word, so I assumed that he must have gone back to Leicester by now. I imagined him sitting in his tiny room stewing with resentment. This was bigger than the problems he'd worried about over the years – girlfriends, exams, making the football team. Worries I'd always been able to dispel with some sound advice and a hug. This was seismic. Maybe his girlfriend would have explained things to him, helped him to understand. I wasn't crazy about her – what mother ever approves of the woman who takes away her boy? – but she seemed sensible enough. No, on reflection, it wasn't fair of me to expect someone else to do the explaining for me.

I had more stock in the shop than I'd thought, and my heart felt heavy with the urgency to move some of it. I even discounted some of the new autumn stock that had come on Friday. But the weather was hot and sunny – why would people be thinking of buying winter jersey, let alone heavily embroidered and frankly off-the-wall jackets in bright colours, when they were looking for shorts and T-shirt bargains? I felt weary with the stress of it all – perhaps the tension of the last few days had finally caught up with me – but I think it was more than that. I knew that making enough to cover the rent shortfall would be near impossible, but I was damned if I was going to let Sayers win. I'd sell a kidney first – though I wasn't quite sure how one goes about such things.

Carefully I took down Tam's coat from the window and covered it with one of the suit bags I'd had made and logoed for the most special items. In its place, I dressed the mannequin in an aqua-blue linen dress and wrapped a silk and velvet embroidered scarf around her headless neck. Then, just because I felt like it, I placed over her shoulders one of my more outrageous creations, a bolero jacket embroidered in a peacock feather design, which had been relegated to the storeroom cupboard for years. No one had ever bought it, so I'd take whatever I was offered for it now.

It was while I was marking down some trousers in the back that Tam arrived through the front door, left open to let in some fresh air.

'Where the hell have you been? And what the hell are you doing?' she screeched after reading the words on the window.

'"Giant Sale"? You can't bloody well do that, you ridiculous woman. It'll ruin you.'

I kissed her on the cheek. 'Which question would you like me to answer first?' I tried to smile to reassure her. 'Nat got fussed over nothing. I'm sorry he texted you – I was just out last night. That's all. And I'm having a sale because I need to shift some stock.'

She looked sceptical. 'Yeah, maybe, but you're not going to give it away! Fifty quid for that bolero? Have you lost your mind?'

'Probably, but I can't meet this month's rent and that's before the landlord hikes it as a result of the rent review. Anyway, he's planning to evict us all and redevelop the street.' I filled her in briefly about Sandy and Fen.

'Bastard!' She shook her head resolutely. 'You can't let him do that. We'll think of something. I'll lend you the money, for God's sake.' I loved her for her enthusiasm and support. And her naïveté.

'Tam, you're a darling but quite honestly I'm asking myself if it's all worth the effort. Let's be honest, who wants to buy stuff like I sell? These days, people buy their clothes from supermarkets where they can get jeans and a top for a tenner. All made in the Third World, of course.' My mood was becoming grimmer by the minute. 'No one's bothered by two-bit designers like me any more.'

'Oh Luce, this isn't like you,' Tam practically shrieked. 'What will you do? Let me pay you for my beautiful coat now.'

I took down the suit bag from the rail at the back and handed it to her. 'No, have it – as a baby gift from me.' Was I completely insane? I should have been charging her hundreds.

'Absolutely not. I shall pay you what it's worth.' She rubbed her hands together with glee. 'Can I take another peek?'

I unwrapped the coat and carefully, as if in reverence, she

ran her hands over it. 'It's a work of art, Luce. I can't wait to wear it.' She turned round to me. 'I see Nat was home for the weekend? I spotted him somewhere earlier. He's looking so handsome.'

'Oh, did you?' relief flooded through me. 'I was worried. He's mad at me and stormed off.'

'Nat, mad at you? I thought he didn't do mad?'

'So did I, but he's found out a bit more about his father and he's a little ... shall we say, disappointed.'

Tam frowned for a moment. 'Kids can be cruel, can't they? Maybe you ought to introduce him to his father if you can find him.'

'I have found him.'

'*What*?' she asked breathlessly and leaned back against the table, pushing out of the way the pile of post I'd dumped and ignored when I arrived. 'When? I mean, you never let on?'

'It was only last week. I thought it was about time I made contact.'

She folded her arms in front of her and surveyed me, a smile playing on her lips. 'Crikey, you had quite a week, didn't you? What with the hair and all. Is it the hormones? Have you hit the Change early or something? You seem to have transformed completely!'

Hormones? Yes, I suppose they might have contributed to my inexplicable behaviour. That and a death sentence recently commuted. Either way, it had done wonders for my view on life. For too long I'd been toeing the line so I wouldn't offend people, or because I thought I might look foolish, when in fact under this mousy exterior, I knew what I wanted all along.

'Look, gotta go. We're going out to dinner and I need to get some overpriced flowers or something to take.' She took out her cheque book and wrote me a cheque for more than I deserved, ignoring my protests, then picked up her bag. 'Take it, you need it, and it's Giles's money anyway! Can I possibly leave my beautiful coat here until later in the week? Just make sure you don't sell it on to someone for a fiver.' Her expression was pained and she dropped her shoulders. 'Oh, Luce, this is so stupid. What can we do?'

I gave her a warm hug. 'Nothing, Tam darling. I'll be fine. Lucy Streeter is a survivor.'

Tam thought for a moment. 'You may be a survivor – I know you are. I think you're brilliant. But sometimes things aren't always fine and you need some help. And what about the other shop owners in the street? You can't all sit back and let this happen.'

I snorted. 'We've tried, believe me. The Crew have been really solid on this.'

Tam looked puzzled. 'It's none of my business, but it doesn't sound like the So Solid Crew to me. Two of you have caved in to this landlord bully already, and it's made you all suspicious of each other. Don't they call it divide and rule? I know this "sale",' she waved her arm at the chaos as if she had a bad smell under her nose, 'is a short-term necessity but it's also a route to disaster. You'll go under and Sayers will have his way.'

I reeled. This wasn't any Tam I knew and loved. 'So, Mrs Assertive, what's your best advice?'

'Confront the man. Nail him if you can.'

'I've tried, but he's not easy. He's like the Wizard of Oz and you have to go through a whole raft of ordeals to get to him.'

'But it's Saturday. He'll be at home in the garden, enjoying the sunshine and the fruits of your labours.' She glanced at her watch. 'Look, I have to go cos I'm meeting Harriet, too.' She hugged me close. 'Don't take this lying down, my girl.'

I worked on for another hour. Quite a few curious passers-by came in and fingered the sale stock on the rails. I even sold two tops and a belt to a couple of ladies I'd never seen before. They muttered surprise at never having spotted the shop, and I'm sure they meant well, but both were carrying shopping bags from high-street chains. People are like vultures when they can sniff a bargain, aren't they? All the while, Tam's rousing battle cry, like Henry the Fifth's to his troops at Agincourt, ran through my brain and I could feel my dander rising and my resolve stiffening. Sayers ... where did he live, I wondered? Somewhere flash and tasteless, I bet. Reaching for the phone book, I looked up the name. There were only four Sayers in the area – that's if he was even listed. One was in a block that I knew to be sheltered housing, and that seemed unlikely. The other two were in the same street, around the corner from a hairdresser I used to go to, and that didn't sound right either for a man with as much to prove as Sayers. So, on a stupid whim, I shut up the shop early, rushed back to the flat to check if there were any messages from Nat, and grabbing a small Dictaphone I'd had for years in the back of a drawer, jumped into the car and headed for the fourth in Nelson Avenue.

There's a Nelson Avenue in every town in Britain. It's full of big-ass houses, overconfident and overblown, all architecturally distinct, facing the road and all built ridiculously close to each other. It's the type of road estate agents refer to as 'sought after', though not by me. Not to my taste ranch style, mock Tudor or mock Georgian with white-painted Doric columns on the porch. Then there's the thirties-style house with grey pebble-dash and small windows. And the gates – just as pearly as I imagined in my vision of heaven. But way flashier. The flashier the better – somewhere between Southfork and Versailles.

And sure enough, as I pulled up in front of 'Rivendel' (also known as number forty-eight), the gates were sublime. And blissfully open. Leaving my car on the verge, I headed in to the driveway, passing an immaculate front lawn oddly dotted with topiary in exotic planters. Austrian blinds festooned every window but there was no sign of life through them. I was encouraged, though, by two large Lexus (or is the plural Lexi?) parked in front of the double garage, a large SUV and a brace of Range Rovers parked alongside. Was Sayers having a do? I hadn't anticipated that. I wasn't even sure it was his house. Too late now. I'd come this far so, fiddling with the Dictaphone and hoping to goodness the ancient batteries still worked, I rang on the doorbell of the white double front door.

Nothing happened, not even footsteps in the distance, so I peered through the window either side. The predominant colours were white and gold, with sparkle provided by chandeliers and Venetian mirrors. Mrs Sayers clearly had a good interior designer and the décor would have done Barbie proud.

I waited. And waited. What now? Backing away from the house, I noticed a side gate. Would I be done for trespassing? And types like Sayers usually had a Dobermann or two to keep the riff-raff at bay. But by this point I didn't really care, so I lifted the latch and went though to the back garden.

By the time I got back to my car fifteen minutes later, at great speed, and with my heart pounding fit to burst my eardrums, I wasn't sure I believed what had just happened. And I was sure no one else would, so all I could hope was that the Dictaphone had done its job.

The large terrace at the back of the house, hidden behind an elaborate wrought-iron pergola and tubs tumbling with summer planting worthy of a gold at Chelsea, was full of people and chatter. I could make out several men in loud shirts and blonde women in white wrap-over dresses, big sunglasses and even bigger hair. I almost lost my nerve at this point and was about to turn tail when a woman called imperiously: 'Hello?'

Boldly I walked on to the terrace to be met by an audience of intrigued faces. The woman came towards me, glittery and gold with leathery over-tanned skin that made her look, in effect, like a handbag. 'Alan?' she called over to a man with his back to me – and it was the man himself. He turned, barbecue prongs in hand, a charred sausage impaled on the end, revealing an apron featuring a naked woman.

He clearly didn't recognise me at first and frowned, then his expression darkened. 'What the hell!'

'Is this a friend of yours?' the woman I presumed to be his wife asked, without taking her eyes off me. Perhaps she thought I was some fancy piece who'd come to claim paternity or something. My flesh crawled at the thought.

'No,' he answered shortly. 'She's a tenant.'

'She's called Lucy,' I said. I put out my hand and his nonplussed wife allowed me to shake her cool, bony one, her myriad rings and bracelets jangling. She looked me over, then she turned away, confident now I was no threat.

'What the hell are you doing here?' Sayers hissed under his breath. Then, when a couple of men joined us, glasses of beer in their hands and a red flush to suggest they weren't their first, he forced a laugh.

'Ms Streeter, isn't it? Come to pay your rent?' He guffawed at this. 'Bit of an unconventional way of doing business. Wouldn't the post do?'

I felt small as they towered over me, and I wished I'd put on my high heels, until I remembered they were at the tip.

I bristled. 'Unconventional? You'd know all about that, Mr Sayers.'

'Wooah!' one of his friends leered. 'Feisty one, Alan!'

Sayers held my gaze. 'Yes, she can be a bit of trouble this one.'

'You have no idea how much,' I replied, realising just how vulnerable I'd made myself and shaking a bit now with fear and anger. 'I'm not prepared to let things go, you see. Or to go along with your plans.'

Sayers raised his eyebrows. 'Oh, not this again,' he sighed. 'I've told you, your co-tenants—'

'Have caved in under your *persuasion*,' I finished, emphasising the last word heavily.

'Up to your old tricks,' the redder-faced of his companions butted in, stumbling a little and spilling his drink. 'Whoops! Where's this then, Al?'

'Paradise Street,' I replied before Sayers could. 'But not exactly Paradise any more, is it, Mr Sayers, since you've stopped fulfilling your landlordly duties?'

Red Face butted in again: 'Paradise Street? Is that another of your empire-building schemes? There's no stopping you, is there, you old dog! He's the property tycoon of the Midlands is Alan. Don't get in his way, love.' And he threw a beery arm round my shoulder. I was getting used to lunges from drunks. He whispered theatrically in my ear, 'He's nasty when crossed.'

'Shut the fuck up, Martin,' Sayers said quietly, with a terrifying intensity that made the man cower back like a dog that had been kicked. He stumbled away and the other man followed. The atmosphere had changed suddenly and I was frightened, here on a terrace on a benign, sunny afternoon, surrounded by people. But I couldn't go anywhere and I had to achieve what I'd planned to.

'You blackmailed Sandy and Barry, didn't you?' I asked quietly, though not so quietly that the Dictaphone wouldn't pick it up.

Sayers leaned in so close I could make out the open, sweaty pores on his nose. 'Drop this now or I'll make you fucking sorry.' His breath ran over my face.

I arched back. 'Did you tell them you would reveal stuff about what Barry owed the Revenue if they talked?'

He narrowed his eyes and they bore into me. 'I paid that stupid bitch more than enough and then she tried to get clever with me, and I don't like clever, Ms Streeter. No one gets past me because with information comes power. I know a lot about you. I know a lot about all of you. That little Paki, for example.'

'His name is Deepak,' I spat.

'Whatever. I could make things very tricky for him getting his "cousin" through immigration. And that bloody Irishman? I've enough to make sure he scuttles back to County Cork before you can say IRA.' A droplet of his saliva hit my lip and I flinched.

I had to get the actual words. 'So you admit you did black-mail Barry, then?'

'Blackmail? Intimidation? Call it what you like. I call it run-ning a business and I'm not going to let you get in the way. *Capice?*'

I think it was that last word that made me realise I'd had more than enough.

'Right, I'll leave you to your party then,' I said loudly, look-ing round the terrace. 'Thanks for your hospitality.' And as I turned, I plucked the sausage from the barbecue prong in his hand. 'Don't mind if I do.'

The Dictaphone had done its business, and back in the safety of my flat, my heart rate still not quite normal, I listened to our exchange again. The soundtrack was a bit muffled at times, but it was clear enough and, feeling like Columbo, I took out the cassette and stored it safely in my almost-empty knicker drawer.

It had been quite a day, and after a scratch meal of beans and a tin of tuna, made even harder to digest by my disquiet at not having heard yet from Nat, I fell into a deep and exhausted sleep.

Chapter Twenty-Five

Monday

Sunday was agony. I gave up trying to contact Nat, who was clearly ignoring me. I made excuses to myself that perhaps he'd lost his phone or run out of credit, but it was far more likely that he was still too angry to communicate. Time would heal, of course. It always does, but my greatest fear was that it would change our relationship for ever. What if he never trusted me again? What I wanted more than anything was the opportunity to sit him down and explain it all to him. I had really believed that glossing over everything, giving him the barest details, was for the best, but now I realised I owed him more than that. How would I feel not knowing anything about *my* father? For all the rows and disagreements we'd had over the years, at least my dad was still there in my life.

As I fidgeted around the flat and picked deadheads off the plants in the garden, it struck me that my dad too had been guilty of that great parenting crime: wanting to protect me from the big bad world. That wasn't such a terrible sin, was it? And if I could forgive my dad, I could only hope that Nat would forgive me.

The hours seemed to drag by, and thank God for Sunday shopping – though I don't suppose He approves of the idea at all. I managed to occupy myself in the centre of the day re-stocking the fridge and replacing the knickers and basics

I'd thrown out in the confident belief I wouldn't need them. As I reached the self-scan checkout and unloaded my trolley, I looked down at its contents and couldn't help but smile. My normal self-denying provisions had been replaced by Shreddies, chocolate and full-fat yogurts. No more pleasure deferral for me. If I was going to carry on living, the least I could do was enjoy it! Even the knickers were lacier than was strictly necessary, and though you might think that's a trivial detail, for Lucy Streeter it was a seismic shift.

The other issue – the one that wouldn't leave my head and that made the agony almost unbearable – was the thorny problem of Richard. Presumably once he'd had my text to say I was okay, he'd gone back to sea and I knew that phone coverage was ropey on the Channel anyway. But perhaps I was kidding myself again and he was too embarrassed to get in touch. I had all day to think about what I was going to say when I saw him again – I even practised some phrases out loud as I moved ornaments around the flat pointlessly – but it all sounded trite and stupid. Hopefully I'd be able to convince him I had been too drunk to know what I was saying and we could laugh it off.

But what if I'd lost my best friend? This is what kept coming into my mind as I sat in front of my computer, *Antiques Roadshow* on quietly in the background, while I drafted a document with all I'd discovered about Sayers. I'd texted everybody – Richard included, but not Fen, of course – with a businesslike round robin request for a Paradise Street Crew meeting with some urgency, and it occurred to me that I should drop in and invite Henry to join us. I could pay my drinking debt at the same time.

My sleep that night was fitful and I eventually gave up at about six and, after a cool shower and a bowl of wicked cereal, headed for the shop.

My 'Sale' sign seemed to have worked miracles and for a

Monday morning I had an unprecedented flow of customers through the door. Mainly ladies going on holiday and wanting something light and cool to wear, and even a couple of young girls looking for unusual prom dresses. They gushed, as only teenagers can, over the fabrics and the detail, declaring the designs 'lush' and 'awesome', and I even got a promise they'd tell their Facebook friends about me – after the prom, of course!

Stock was shifting and by eleven I was gasping for coffee – no surprises that I hadn't dared stop at the Deli as usual – and it was while I was stirring instant into a cup that a familiar voice called my name.

'Micah! What a surprise!'

He had a broad smile on his face as he looked around the shop and ran his fingers over one of my jackets. 'These are beautiful,' he breathed. 'Do you do them in my size?'

I snorted. 'Do you need clothes where you come from? Don't you get issued with them from a central depot like they do in the army?' I laughed.

He scratched his head, his face amused. 'Where *do* you get your ideas from? You really are in for a surprise when you get there. Which reminds me ...' His expression grew more serious. 'I've come to say goodbye because my work here is finished.' I must have looked bemused because he carried on. 'Lucy Streeter? I found the right one.'

'There are two of us round here?'

'Three actually. You're not as rare as you thought. But now there's only two.' He paused as the implications of what he was saying sunk in.

'Oh, I'm sorry. I see. Was she ... ill? Please say she was old and ready to go.'

He nodded gently. 'Yes, she was very elderly. Ninety-two, in fact, and she said she'd been waiting for me for ages. It was very peaceful.'

We didn't say anything for a moment, while I wondered what the protocol was for saying goodbye to an angel. 'It's been … interesting meeting you, Micah. A teensy bit stressful at times, but interesting none the less.'

He put his head to one side and appraised me. 'It's been interesting meeting you, too. I've learned a lot. And about the stress. I'm sorry about that. I'll be in for a good ticking-off, if that makes you feel any better. But was it all so bad? You've changed your hair and everything – are you glad you made those changes happen?'

I paused, thinking back about how much living I'd fitted in and how easy it was to alter the course of your life. All it took was a nudge.

'I'd rather not have had the sword of Damocles hanging over me but, yes, on the whole I'm happier where I am than where I was. Except for two things.'

'Oh?'

'Because I thought he'd be left alone if I … you know, died, I told my son about his father and he's none too pleased about finding out now. I think I screwed that one up royally.'

'How old is he?'

'Twenty-two.'

Micah shrugged. 'He's young. He'll get over it, and besides, your reasons were all couched in immense love and you can't go wrong with love.'

'Mmm, I'm not so sure.' I took a sip of my coffee then smiled ruefully. 'What about the Richard thing?'

'Have you seen him yet?'

'No, but it's only a matter of time in a town this size.'

Micah looked at me intently. 'I know my record on accuracy hasn't been too brilliant. But one thing I do know, you needed to tell him how you felt or how would life move on?'

'But it might move on in ways I don't like and that frightens me.'

He came towards me then and embraced me, careful not to spill scalding coffee all over me. In fact, I think he kissed my hair in a sort of benediction. 'Life is risky. Be brave, Lucy. You're good at bravery. You just didn't realise it.' Then he made for the door.

'Good luck, Micah,' I said through wet eyes. 'I'll miss you, but then again, I hope I don't see you again for a very long time!'

He smiled enigmatically. 'I might have been given a different patch by then,' and, I can't work out now if it was my tears or the sunlight coming in through the door, but one minute he was there and then he wasn't.

I was on my second cup of coffee and making good headway through a packet of Ginger Nuts, when what I so wanted and so feared finally happened. The phone rang and I only just got to it before the machine kicked in.

'Hello?'

'Mum.'

'Nat, darling.' I held my breath. At that moment, two more women came in through the door. 'Sorry, I'm closed,' I waved at them and they backed out confused as I shut the door firmly behind them.

'What was that?'

'Oh, just a couple of customers.'

'Right.'

'Are you back at uni? Want me to call you back?' I felt awkward as if I hardly knew him.

'Yes. No. No, it's fine. Yes, I'm back. I've got a module to complete by the end of the week – end-of-term pressures and all – so I had to get back.'

'Did you have a good trip? Was the traffic all right?' This was inane small talk, but I was so thrilled that he'd phoned I couldn't risk losing him.

'Mum, look, I'm sorry I didn't come back home yesterday.'

'That's okay. You were angry. It's understandable.'

I could hear him sigh at the end of the phone. 'Yes, I was angry but only because it was such a shock really. I think I'd buried all that stuff about fathers, and finding out this man was a reality – well, it was a bit unexpected.'

We were making progress. 'Yes, I'm sure it was and I was at fault really for not telling you stuff even if you didn't actually want to know. He's a nice man, your dad, you ought to meet him.'

'Mum, I have.'

My heart leapt with shock at the words. 'When? How?'

'Yesterday. I just turned up at the garage – well, you'd put the address in your letter and I just took a risk that it would be open on a Sunday morning. I'd walked round and round after I stormed out on you, just thinking it all through. I was quite livid actually – I even kicked over a bin in the park – but then I sort of ran out of anger and I thought I might as well face it.'

'Was he ... I mean, he must have been surprised?' My hands felt clammy, and I had to admit to a wave of jealousy and fear. Nat had been mine exclusively for so long and now the other 'half' of him had slipped into the jigsaw. Would he prefer Neil and want to be with him?

Nat laughed. 'Yes, you could say that! What was weird is that he had a photo on his desk of his ... other children, and the boy – he looks just like me, Mum! I've got a brother and sister.' He had no idea the impact these words had on me and my throat hurt with the effort of trying not to cry.

'And?' I managed after a moment.

'Well. I didn't stay long. But we're going to meet up in a

week or so, just him and me. I *think* he's pleased to have met me. He's quite cool, isn't he?'

'Cool or cool? Define cool.'

'Not in-your-face friendly, you know.'

I smiled. He certainly got the measure of Neil quickly.

'But quite cool for an oldie too.'

'Less of the old, young man,' I teased. 'I'm the same age as your father.'

'You don't mind, Mum, do you? Me going and stuff?'

'No, darling. I don't mind. You have every right to meet him, and I'm glad.' I hoped I sounded convincing as I felt the ties that had bound us through the years slowly loosen and Nat easing away from me. But perhaps, just perhaps, I could admit to a sense of relief. That I didn't have to shoulder all the responsibility any more. That I could share, and with that sharing would come some freedom for me.

'I went to see Granny and Grandpa, too,' Nat continued. 'And, Mum, I had no idea really.'

'About what?' Had my father been criticising me? Talking me down to Nat would have been unforgiveable.

'About the sacrifices you made for me.' He paused and I couldn't think of anything to say. 'Grandpa sat me down and told me about what happened when you were pregnant with me, and how independent you'd been and how much he admired you and your determination to get it all right. He even told me I had to look after you because you were precious.' He chuckled. 'I've never seen Grandpa like that really. He even likes your hair, for Christ's sake. He's usually such a grumpy old bugger.'

By now the tears were pouring down my face. 'Yes, isn't he just, the old sod,' I sniffed.

'Don't cry, Mum. It's all right. Listen, I've sort of got to go. Gemma's come in. I'll be home this weekend – promise I won't creep in late. Dan's having an end-of-term party on Saturday night so I'll text you when I'm on my way. Bye. Oh, and Mum, try to stay on the right side of the law!'

So, Micah had been right. It *was* okay. Nat had forgiven me – well, enough for us to build on – and that was the best thing I could hope for.

'Oh, and another thing.' I thought he'd put the phone down. 'That bit at the end of the letter. I love you, too.' Click, and this time he was gone.

Chapter Twenty-Six

It didn't really matter to me after that what kind of day I had at the shop. As it happens, quite a number of people came by and I took a few hundred quid. By four, things had quietened to nothing and I turned at last to the pile of post on the table. I hadn't opened a thing for days and most of it was circulars. There was a letter from Sayers' office, as expected, dated early last week and reminding me of the rent review, with some ominous wording about the market and 'values reflecting the prestige of the location'. Blah, blah. I wished now I'd had the courage to leave my graffiti for all to see. Nasty little shit.

In amongst the bills and windowed envelopes, though, was a handwritten one. The handwriting, in black ink, was looping and extrovert. It was addressed to the shop name – not to me – and must have been hand-delivered. There was no stamp.

Dear Lucy – I hope I've got that right.

Apologies for writing to you but I have called by a few times at your shop in the last week and it always seems to be shut. You may recall you met me at Martin's party the other night – I was the one in pink glasses? – I was admiring your beautiful dress but there were lots of people there, so you have probably forgotten. I didn't have a chance to explain that I live locally, but I am a film producer and am beginning work on Madame de Pompadour *– you may have read about it in the press. It's the latest film by Francis Gonzales, the film director.*

I could feel myself frowning at this point. What was she on about?

I am utterly enchanted by your work, especially the coat that you've had in your window. The detail is extraordinary and your friend, whom I met at that lovely delicatessen up the road, said that you had done similar pieces in different styles, and how you'd never had the chance to explore this side of your work. I wondered if you would be interested in submitting some designs for the film? No promises, of course, but I think you have a unique and very creative eye and this is something we want to bring to the production.

She'd signed off 'Muriel Featherstone-Grey', and her mobile phone number.

For a moment I thought this was some kind of joke – a wind-up – then I think, but I can't be sure, that I actually stamped up and down with glee. I kissed the letter and I think I may have made a strange squeaking sound because as I was hopping round the shop, a shadow fell across the floor as someone came in.

'Hello?'

Richard was standing in the doorway, his face, tanned from sunshine and sea air, unreadable.

I could feel myself blushing a deep, deep shade of red. I've always been prone to blushing – I could never lie at school because guilt was writ large on my face – but I remember thinking, keep dancing Lucy – that way you will distract him and he'll forget about the phone call.

'Is this normal behaviour?' He was leaning against the door jamb, half in and half out, one foot on the step and the other on the threshold.

I stopped, feeling faintly ridiculous. 'No, but then this isn't normal.' I waved the letter at him. 'It's from a woman who was at Martin's party the other night.' I looked at the signature again. 'Muriel Featherstone-Grey. Sounds terribly posh. Anyway, she has seen some of my stuff – well, not much really – but she is a film producer and she wants me to submit some designs for her film.' I was gabbling nervously. 'It's *Madame Pompadour*, so lots of silk and embroidery and huge skirts. It's probably nonsense or it's for some obscure American TV channel but, hey ...'

A smile spread across his face and his eyes crinkled in that way I'm so familiar with. 'I know there was someone looking for you – she came in a couple of times but we had no idea what for. Luce, that sounds fantastic. So I was right to bring this then?' From behind his back he produced a bottle of champagne and two glasses.

I stood stock still now. 'Are you telepathic or something?' Why had he bought champagne? Was it because ...? But his next sentence dispelled all that.

'Not exactly.' He pushed himself away from the doorway and came into the shop. His height seemed to dwarf everything around him. 'I was in the Deli and Tam dropped in a little while ago and said she was bothered about you. She mentioned the suicide sale and all that.' He indicated the window vaguely. 'So I thought a glass of fizz might bring you to your senses.'

'How decadent!' I was stalling for time. 'Booze in the afternoon and on a Monday too!'

'Who cares? Sometimes you just have to break the rules, and I thought you were up for a bit of subversion these days.' He put the long-stemmed glasses carefully on to the table and, expertly pushing out the cork, poured us both a glass. All I could do was stand there, the letter in my hand, and watch. I knew – we both knew – about the big, fat elephant in the corner, but I was frozen, unable to think of a way to escape.

He handed me a frothing glass, held his up and we chinked a toast.

'Here's to you.'

'It's a bit premature to be celebrating, isn't it?' I replied, taking a sip, nervously.

'Well, you never know. You could be heading off to Hollywood, leaving us all behind.'

I snorted. 'Yeah, right. Like I say, it'll probably come to nothing.'

'Maybe, Luce.' He leaned back against the table as Tam had done earlier. 'But it's what you should be doing, using your talents like that. It's a fantastic opportunity. So,' he held up his glass to me, 'let's celebrate that. And at least you wouldn't have to worry about the Sayers problem as you swan around the studio in that Californian sunshine.'

I smiled at the image and took another sip. 'I think we'll all be okay, actually. I've been doing a bit of sleuthing ...' And I filled him in on all that I'd discovered, making the visit to Nelson Avenue sound more of a gas than it really had been.

'Christ, Luce! You shouldn't have done that,' he spluttered on his drink. 'I can't believe it! What on earth possessed you to take such a risk?' His face was tight with concern.

'Because we *had* to do something or he'd have got away with it. He's too clever by half – too ruthless. And without a shred of scruples. And I *care*, Richard. I care about what happens to us – I mean everyone in the street, of course,' I added hurriedly. 'It's just that before, I was too chicken.'

'Before? Before what?'

'Before ... the last few days.'

He didn't pursue this and I was glad. 'You've been reckless but you've done well, Luce. We should have enough to nail him. I'll call a solicitor friend. The little we've got is enough to get him off our backs, I think, even if we can't have him put away.'

'But we have to be realistic, Richard. Sayers or no Sayers,

the rents will go up eventually. We've been pretty lucky so far. What will you do then? Will you and Sal be able to find the extra money every month – I mean, can you afford it?'

'I doubt it, but I'm not sure I'll carry on with the Deli, not now without Sally.'

'Without Sal? What do you mean?'

'Karl has finally asked her to move to Australia with him.'

I was delighted but I wasn't sure Richard would be. 'Are you okay about that?'

His expression was genuinely enthusiastic. 'I'm delighted for her. I like Karl and, besides, she can't sit around here serving lattes and waiting for him. He's hardly going to settle in Leamington and I can practically hear her body-clock ticking! No, I've been thinking for a while that I might diversify a bit.' He looked a bit sheepish.

'What? Sail away on the *Serenity* and never be heard of again?' I blurted without thinking.

'I was considering that but I'm not sure I could get the crew I want and, anyway, something that happened recently changed my mind.' He paused for a moment. 'But I have got a plan B. I've actually got a bit of money put aside. I've been looking to expand for a while. Doing something creative. I've seen some premises down by the park and I've got this idea for a gallery. Sounds a bit grand, I know – more of a place that would exhibit work, offer workshops and studio space, and it'll have a café, of course. That sort of thing. There're various grants I can apply for to help me get on my feet ' He trailed off.

'That sounds brilliant, Rich. The town needs somewhere like that. You dark horse, you.' I raised my own glass this time. 'Here's to you!'

'Trouble is, it really depends on someone else. A partner ... '

'A partner? Do you have someone in mind?'

He looked up at me now. 'Yes.'

'Who?'

'You.'

'Me?' I squeaked.

'Yes. You've got tremendous vision and flair, Lucy, and you ought to explore that more.' He looked around at the shop. 'It doesn't need you to run this place. You could get someone in while you do what you should be doing: designing.'

Explore – Muriel Featherstone-Grey had used that word in her letter. Had it been Richard who'd talked to her about me? I'd assumed she'd meant Sally.

'Hey,' he went on, 'perhaps you could use some of the workshop space to put your drawings together for that producer?'

I felt somehow deflated. All he wanted me for was as a business partner. 'It's a tempting idea, but I've no business sense.' I shrugged. 'I'd be no use to you. Look how this place has limped along.' I waved my arm out at the piles of sale stock, some still waiting to be hung out.

'I think you did this because you had to, Luce. Because of Nat and having to provide for him. But he's a big boy now, and maybe it's time for you, hey?' His voice sounded gentle and I dared not look at him.

'How was the boat?' I asked by way of diversion, my eyes glued to my feet. A shaft of sunlight coming in the doorway caught the end of my pumps, which were grubby with dust from the floor.

'Hard work. I had to do some essential maintenance and have some meetings with the harbour people. Then I'd promised some friends a day's sailing yesterday.'

The elephant was getting bigger and bigger. I could practically feel its breath. I didn't say a word and kept my eyes trained on the toe of my pumps.

'Thing is,' he carried on, 'I got held up with a supplier on Friday, so left late. But I'd been expecting a call about this gallery place and, on my way down in the car, I checked in on my messages on my machine at home.' I couldn't move. 'And the oddest thing happened.' I could hear a smile in his voice but I dared not look up. Was he laughing at me? Was he going to make me suffer cruelly for my stupid outburst? 'There was a message I hadn't been expecting.' He was stringing this out with glee. 'It was this woman telling me the most amazing things.'

I looked up, beetroot now.

'In fact, they were so amazing that I tried to call you straight away but you didn't answer. In fact, you didn't answer at all and I was frantic. I spent the next few hours ringing everyone I could think of trying to make sure you were okay. They all thought I was mad. Especially Nat.'

I squeezed my eyes shut in embarrassment and my toes were curled up inside my pumps.

'You sounded so ... different.' He went on, holding my gaze, his eyes warm and twinkling. 'But there you were saying things I've waited years to hear, Luce.'

I must have frowned with incomprehension; I have no recollection except my amazement at his words. He put down his glass and came and stood in front of me.

'When I kissed you the other night, my darling, you have to understand it was all I've ever wanted to do. You have no idea the self-control I had to exercise not to take you to bed right then and there. That whole evening we spent together, you in your knickers. Christ, I thought I'd explode with desire! But you seemed so changed, I thought you were pissed or something and you'd regret us making love, and I couldn't have borne that.' He put his hands on my arms and gently rubbed them, their warmth seeping through my skin. 'You'd seemed content for years with us being just friends and I thought that was better than nothing – the best I could hope for. The chance to go to the cinema with you, go down to the boat, have you around me. Then there you were,' he threw his head back and laughed with amazement, 'telling me that you loved me and that you always had.'

The excuses I'd planned pathetically evaporated, but I still didn't know what to say. Richard filled in the silence, placing his hand gently on my cheek. 'I've listened to the message again and again since then, just to be sure, Luce. Then you said something about going away. Is it the film thing? You know I'd never stop you, but I'm not sure how I'm going to deal with being without you.'

'That's all changed. The going bit, I mean,' I added quickly. 'I feel so stupid for saying that stuff. I mean, I hadn't really intended to say anything but then, well I can't explain really ...'

'God, Luce, I thought I'd died and gone to heaven! Didn't you mean it, everything you said?'

I couldn't see him through my tears. 'Oh yes, I meant it. But Rich, I don't understand. What about the girlfriends? And, well, you never showed the slightest interest in me.'

He laughed wryly. 'The girlfriends! No one was going to come close to you, so I surrounded myself with women who'd present no challenge whatsoever – except I misjudged Katrina. She nearly had me cornered.' His eyes twinkled again. 'Were you jealous? Please say you were, just a bit.'

'I couldn't possibly say.' I smiled back at him, my face aching with pleasure.

'Don't you remember how I practically proposed to you the other day in the park? You're the only woman I have ever met – except Sal, of course – who positively enjoys standing on the bow of a boat and getting soaked. What more could I ask for? You're my figurehead! My perfect woman!' He leaned down and kissed me gently then. Not a hungry kiss, just a gentle exploration because we'd been in one place together and were now moving experimentally into another. This was more than I could ever have hoped for. But what if ...? I pushed him gently away for a moment.

'You're my best friend, Richard. What if this spoils things between us?'

He rubbed his nose against mine, then kissed my cheek, my ear and my neck.

'Why should it? *I* know I've been in love with you since I first met you trying to clean that bloody canopy with a yard brush. The only difference is, now you know, too.'

I chuckled. 'Fair enough. That's a good enough explanation for me.' And I put my arms around him again and pulled him close.

Now

So that's my story.

My cup of tea has gone cold and I really ought to grab some sleep now before it's time to get up for another day, but I couldn't go back to bed until I'd told you everything.

That was all two months ago and it's been a time of fascinating changes. Fen has been officially blackballed by the Paradise Street Crew and we're boycotting his closing-down sale, taking great glee in buying anything we need from the huge DIY store that's a drive away. The shop is due to close any day now, but the odd time he has shown his face in the street, he's avoided looking anyone in the eye, as well he might, and he scuttles away like the rat he is. We confronted Sayers, the entire PSC descending on his office, and we played him back my taped conversation with him at the barbecue. His mouth opened and shut like a fish as he heard himself dig his own grave, so I don't think we'll bother going to arbitration over any rent increases. We had a celebratory piss-up afterwards and, amazingly, there's been a builder around all week mending gutters and replacing roof tiles.

In case you think me remiss, I did go in and pay Henry for the Scotch. He was surprised to see me again and even more surprised when I asked him to join the Crew. It makes me smile to see Henry's rough edges rubbing next to Martin's marble-smooth ones, but that's what makes our street worth saving.

I've even seen him walk past recently with a takeaway coffee from the Deli!

I've been round to see Mum and Dad maybe more often than ever. They can't disguise their glee that their daughter has finally managed a relationship with Richard and I even overheard Dad telling his sister, Joan, about the film designs and that 'I was finally using my talents'. A few weeks ago I'd have bristled at that, but now I can see that he's proud of me in his characteristic, understated way. I don't think I'll ever be brave enough to confess to the tattoo though.

Tam has had her first scan and all seems well. I made the right noises when she came to show me the pictures that only a mother could love, but my excitement for her grows with the baby. She's even asked me to design a Christening gown. Harriet's wedding went beautifully – the PSC squeezed into a pew. Tam's coat was the wow she hoped it would be – she very nearly eclipsed the bride – and has already resulted in some enquiries, including one from a London friend of Tam's who's something at Condé Nast. But how ridiculous is this? As a result of my first meeting with Muriel, I'm not sure I'll have the time to make anything else for a while. She brought with her the early sketches for the costumes and, with the help of a small advance, has asked me to come up with some proposals for the detail on the more ornate dresses and jackets being created by the head design team. I've been buried in the library for days going through books and have had a crayon in my hand ever since. I've probably been through a rainforest with the amount of sketches that I've rejected on the way. My confidence is growing all the time, though, as I play with colours and ideas at the table in the shop. The sale has been chugging along nicely with a rich seam of new customers who never knew I was here. Shame it took my fan base so long to arrive.

I work a lot at home, too, because I've got help in the shop and you won't believe who: Mrs No-Buy (she's actually called Gail). She came in again one day and we got chatting – turns out she had time on her hands after quitting a job in London because of the commute. She's a one-woman PR machine who seems to know everyone in the Midlands and the shop is buzzing, with Gail deciding for everyone else what they should buy.

So what have I learned through all this? That I should have done something about the rubbish on the corner years ago. It's always clean now and that's one achievement I'm proud of. That you shouldn't throw away your unpaid electricity bill (they cut me off), or go giving away your money to tramps. That too many hot chocolates with whipped cream makes getting into your jeans a challenge. That if you have your hair bleached blonde, it's a pain in the neck to keep having your roots done, and I may revert to mouse again any time soon.

But only my hair. Mouse I will not be. Never again. I don't for a second regret confronting Sayers or wrapping my jeans around the church bell. I'm sure, even if I'd been found out, I'd have been the Joan of Arc of Leamington Spa and they wouldn't have found a jury to send me down.

I haven't been back in that chat room – perhaps I will one day to let them know I'm still around and that not all predictions should be believed, but that internet stuff is all too wacky for me. I think I only went online out of a desperate need to share my fear with someone else. Oh, and on the wacky front, I saw Sylvie in town today. She crossed the road with Pascal in his ergonomically designed buggy so she wouldn't have to talk to me. I'm not expecting a Christmas card from her this year.

We won't be here anyway. Richard and I have decided to sail the *Serenity* in the Med. He's going to take it there before the weather gets bad. How lovely will that be? We'll need a holiday before the gallery project takes over our lives; Sal will run the Deli until they close up in the New Year and she and Karl tie the knot. So far, Nat seems quite happy at the prospect of being away from his mother and tradition for the first Christmas ever – I think he'll be with Gemma and, hopefully by then, he might even raise a glass with his father and his new family. I could be offended if I chose to be, but I also know he is delighted that Richard and I are finally an item. He told me I had been a blind fool. Any idiot could see Richard was mad about me. Is that any way for a boy to talk to his mother?

I'm not going to pretend that being with Richard wasn't all a bit weird at the beginning. The first time we made love – as fast as we could get back from the shop that day – I couldn't stop laughing, which put him off a bit.

'Hey, Luce,' he complained as he tried to undress me, 'this isn't supposed to be funny. I'm more used to applause.' But then he kissed my bare skin, and that was it. I was lost. We've found a whole new side of each other. I thought I knew him well, but now I know a Richard who sleeps naked, and pads around in boxer shorts making breakfast. I know how he cleans his teeth, frowns slightly when he reads the paper, kisses me with his eyes open and shudders with pleasure when I touch him.

I am still the same Lucy Streeter I always was, though I may look different, but I'm also not the same. And that's thanks to Micah. By getting it wrong, he got me into some awful messes and he turned my life upside down, but I like where I've landed. I think about him often and his strange existence; and I hope he knows things have worked out for me.

About a week after I saw him for the last time, I read about Lucy Streeter's death in the local paper. I couldn't resist taking some flowers to put on her grave. She must have been very much loved because there were bouquets everywhere. She was quite a girl, according to her obituary, and had driven ambulances in the war before becoming one of the first women to work in the council's planning office. I hoped she'd be proud of the work I'd done to stop Sayers in his destructive tracks.

I'm off back to bed now before the birds go into full dawn chorus. I hope I don't wake Richard when I slide in next to his warm body.

Or, on second thoughts, perhaps I do.

Acknowledgements

We have loved writing a book set in the area we live in, especially in such lovely towns as Leamington Spa and Warwick, but we have taken some shocking liberties with the geography of them, and we hope the local residents will forgive us – getting planning permission to change it to suit us would have taken too long! Special thanks to the following for all their help with plot, letting us use their experiences, and with checking facts. Rosalind Talbot, Victoria Jeffs, Tim Cox, Jeremy Wakeling, Marie Rendell, Bill Davis, PC Colburn at Stratford upon Avon Police Station, and the helpful people at The Whitechapel Bell Foundry who coped with our very odd questions. Any errors are entirely ours.

Thanks as always to Sara O'Keeffe and her delicate touch, all at Orion for their support, and to Mary Pachnos, our esteemed agent.